"The Black Sheep knitting series has it all: Friendship, knitting, murder, and the occasional recipe create the perfect pattern. Great fun."
—*New York Times* bestselling author Jayne Anne Krentz

Praise for *Knit, Purl, Die*

"The fast-paced plot will keep even non-knitters turning the pages."
—*Publishers Weekly*

"An engaging story full of tight knit friendships and a needling mystery."
—*Fresh Fiction*

Praise for *While My Pretty One Knits*

"The crafty first of a cozy new series. . . . The friendships among the likable knitters . . . help make Canadeo's crime yarn a charmer."
—*Publishers Weekly*

"Fans of Monica Ferris . . . will enjoy this engaging amateur sleuth as much for its salute to friendship as to Lucy's inquiry made one stitch at a time."
—*The Mystery Gazette*

A *Stitch Before Dying* is also available as an eBook

Meet the Black Sheep Knitters

Maggie Messina, owner of the Black Sheep Knitting Shop, is a retired high school art teacher who runs her little slice of knitters' paradise with the kind of vibrant energy that leaves her friends dazzled! From novice to pro, knitters come to Maggie as much for her up-to-the-minute offerings like organic wool as for her encouragement and friendship. And Maggie's got a deft touch when it comes to unraveling mysteries, too.

Lucy Binger left Boston when her marriage ended, and found herself shifting gears to run her graphic design business from the coastal cottage she and her sister inherited. After big-city living, she now finds contentment on a front porch in tiny Plum Harbor, knitting with her closest friends.

Dana Haeger is a psychologist with a busy local practice. A stylishly polished professional with a quick wit, she slips out to Maggie's shop whenever her schedule allows—after all, knitting is the best form of therapy!

Suzanne Cavanaugh is a typical working supermom—a Realtor with a million demands on her time, from coaching soccer to showing houses to attending the PTA. But she carves out a little "me" time with the Black Sheep Knitters.

Phoebe Meyers, a college student complete with magenta highlights and piercings, lives in the apartment above Maggie's shop. She's Maggie's indispensable helper (when she's not in class)—and part of the new generation of young knitters.

A Stitch
Before Dying

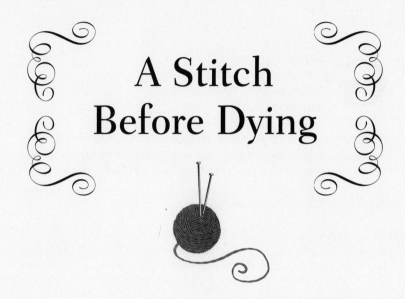

Anne Canadeo

G

Gallery Books

New York   London   Toronto   Sydney

Gallery Books
A Division of Simon & Schuster, Inc.
1230 Avenue of the Americas
New York, NY 10020

First Gallery Books trade paperback edition January 2011

GALLERY BOOKS and colophon are trademarks of Simon & Schuster, Inc.

For information about special discounts for bulk purchases, please contact
Simon & Schuster Special Sales at 1-866-506-1949
or business@simonandschuster.com.

The Simon & Schuster Speakers Bureau can bring authors to your live event. For
more information or to book an event contact the Simon & Schuster Speakers
Bureau at 1-866-248-3049 or visit our website at www.simonspeakers.com.

Manufactured in the United States of America

10 9 8 7 6 5 4 3 2 1

Library of Congress Cataloging-in-Publication Data is available.

ISBN 978-1-4391-9139-2
ISBN 978-1-4391-9141-5 (ebook)

With love and gratitude, to my dear parents,
Joanna and Louis Canadeo
(I think this one should have enough suspects for you).

The wise man does not fear death.

—BUDDHA

There are more things in heaven and earth, Horatio,
Than are dreamt of in your philosophy.

—WILLIAM SHAKESPEARE, *HAMLET,*
ACT I, SCENE V

Chapter One

*L*ucy was late, the very last to arrive. Everyone was waiting. She knew that for a fact when she spotted their cars, parked one after the next, in front of the Black Sheep Knitting Shop.

She quickly pulled over to the sidewalk and parked behind the rest, as if adding the final stitch to a neatly knit row.

At least she'd brought something good to eat, an apple crumble. They'd forgive her once they saw their dessert. It was that kind of crowd. The smell alone could earn her clemency.

The shop was closed for business at this hour, though all the lights inside were on, glowing warmly in the big bay window. Maggie had just changed the display from summer to fall—hand-knit items and skeins of yarn, dangling from birch branches, above a bed of cut-out paper leaves. Maggie, who was once a high school art teacher, had a sharp eye for color and design.

A dedicated knitter and excellent instructor, Maggie had opened the shop about three years ago. She'd been lucky to find the perfect spot, the first floor of a free-standing Victorian building in the middle of Plum Harbor's busy Main Street.

Set back from the street a fair space, the building had a peaked roof, a wraparound porch, and plenty of classic Victorian trim. Maggie had added flower boxes and a thick border of perennials along the brick path that led from the sidewalk and more flower beds in the front of the house. The shop looked very inviting, luring both knitters and nonknitters. And it didn't disappoint in the least once they went inside.

Lucy spotted her friends through the window, sitting in the rear room at the long farm table. They met once a week, rotating among their houses and Maggie's store, sharing knitting tips, good food, and gossip. The shop was their unofficial home base, the place they'd met several summers ago in one of Maggie's classes.

She hurried up the walk to the porch, her purse and knitting tote hooked over one shoulder, the baking dish balanced in both hands. Branches above swayed in a cool breeze and golden leaves drifted down, as if graceful ladies were shedding their finery at the end of a long evening.

The flowers Maggie had planted alongside the path—blue stasis, white flox, and dusty pink echinacea—flopped to one side, in one last burst of glory before the frosty nights set in.

Lucy smelled autumn in the air. The change of seasons made her sad. Maybe not sad, exactly, but keenly aware of time passing.

The shop door was unlocked and she walked inside.

"Lucy . . . there you are."

Maggie walked toward her with a smile, then reached for the pan. "Here, let me take that. It smells delicious."

"An apple crisp. With some extra stuff in the crumbs."

"And homemade, looks like. Okay, you're forgiven for being late. There's something I want to tell everyone. I've been waiting for you."

Lucy wondered what their fearless leader had hidden under her hand-crafted sleeve. Knowing Maggie, the surprise could be anything from some rare, exotic fiber to a demonstration of dying yarn with Jell-O.

Suzanne, Dana, and Phoebe sat at their usual places at the big table, their projects and tools spread out around them as they stitched away.

"There you are . . . everything all right?" Suzanne asked with concern. Suzanne had three children—twin boys who were eight years old and a twelve-year-old daughter—so she tended to mother anyone who even vaguely looked like they needed it.

"I was working and lost track of time." Not entirely accurate, but close enough for now.

Lucy had been stuck at her computer for many long hours today, working on a project with a tight deadline. She'd cut it close on her timing to jump in the shower and take care of her dog, before running out. Then a call from her boyfriend, Matt, had thrown her off completely.

There hadn't been an argument between them exactly. It was more like a nonargument, an emotional vacuum. The symptom of some bigger problem going on, she thought. Which was even more disconcerting in a way.

Her friends were always happy to offer relationship advice, even when she didn't want it. But she wasn't ready to talk about this yet. She didn't want to stroll in here and unload, like some emotional dump truck.

The center of the table held a platter of cheeses, olives,

and thin slices of French bread. There was also a bottle of sauvignon blanc and one of sparkling water on the sideboard, along with a pile of soup bowls, napkins, and silverware.

Lucy helped herself to a glass of wine and sat down between Suzanne and Dana. She took out her knitting project but didn't feel quite ready to jump in. She was working on long striped scarves for her nieces, in the colors of their soccer league, navy blue and yellow. Sophie and Regina, her sister's girls, had put in their order to her with an e-mail photo and were excited to see the real thing soon.

Lucy was almost done with the second scarf and planned to pack them up and send them by the weekend.

Dana's needles clicked away in her usual efficient style. The black mohair sweater dress she'd started last week was progressing nicely. The style was elegantly simple, without any complicated stitches, cables, or lace work. But there was definitely a lot of ground to cover.

With Dana's slim figure and blond hair, Lucy thought her friend would look great in the dress and all the hard work would definitely be worthwhile.

"How's it coming?" Lucy asked as she took a sip of wine.

"Slow but steady. I wanted to have it done for a conference I'm speaking at in October, but I'm not sure I'll make it."

A psychologist with a busy practice, Dana had an office only a few blocks down Main Street, which made the knitting shop convenient for breaks between patients, when she needed a little yarn-and-needle therapy of her own.

"Come on, Dana. You'll make that deadline easily. You knit like a plow horse." Suzanne's observation fell somewhere between a compliment and a complaint. Either way, Lucy knew it was true. "You just put the blinders on and plod along. Row after row. I'm the one with the attention span of a fruit fly."

Suzanne paused and held up the project she was working on, a chulo-style ski hat, a white background with a blue and purple snowflake design. "Okay, quiz time. Does this look familiar to anyone?"

"Alexis's ski hat?" Phoebe, the youngest member of their group, immediately nailed it. "You never finished that?"

Lucy had the same thought, but would have asked the question in a kinder tone.

Suzanne seemed unfazed by Phoebe's bluntness. "Nope . . . I actually lost it and never told Alexis. It just disappeared into thin air. I was moving some furniture around in the family room the other day and there it was, clinging to the back of the couch like a big spider. I must have been knitting one night in front of the TV and Kevin got a little . . . cuddly."

Phoebe winced. "Too much information. Maybe the hat crawled off in embarrassment."

The joke was a little mean, but Lucy couldn't help laughing. "I think the hat was just hibernating. Looks like it survived."

"I lost a few stitches here and there, but Maggie helped me clean it up." Suzanne held the hat up again for all to view. Several balls of colored wool dangled down like bouncy legs. Her friends claimed intarsia wasn't hard, but Lucy had yet to take on the challenge. "See, as good as new . . . almost."

Maggie emerged from the storeroom with a large pot of soup.

"Oh, that poor hat." Maggie shook her head. "If it could only talk. What it's been through . . . and it hasn't even been on anyone's head yet."

She carried the pot to the sideboard and set it down beside the pile of bowls. The storeroom had once been a kitchen and had all the necessary equipment intact, which came in handy, Lucy knew, since their passion for cooking and eating well was second only to their love of plying needles.

"Help yourself, ladies." Maggie began ladling soup into the deep, white bowls and then uncovered another basket of crusty French bread. "There's some salad, bread, and my homemade lentil soup with sausage . . . turkey sausage," she added, glancing at Dana, who was the most health conscious and didn't eat red meat.

"We all lose track of projects from time to time. It's like putting a book down and getting involved in another." Lucy stepped over and grabbed a bowl of soup and some bread and salad. "It doesn't mean you won't go back and finish at some point."

"But isn't it wonderful when you can totally focus and drift off to that happy, knitting place?" Maggie cleared the table to make room for the food, picking up a basket of wool and some pattern books. "Whatever you're working on just seems to knit itself. Know what I mean?"

They murmured in agreement, finding seats around the table again.

"Some psychologists call that 'R mode,' or right-brain thinking." Dana placed her bowl on the table and sat down. "When you're so engrossed in an activity you lose all sense of time and place."

"Exactly," Maggie nodded. "I call it knitting nirvana."

"With all due respect, Maggie, a person can get there without needles and yarn." Dana paused to grind some fresh pepper over her soup. "You can be writing, painting. Or doing something as mundane as washing dishes or mopping the floor."

"Follow your bliss, as they say," Maggie answered agreeably. "Mine always seems to involve yarn and needles. Never housework."

Suzanne stood at the sideboard, fixing a dish with salad and bread. "Forget that happy place. I just want to find a private place. Sometimes I just grab my knitting bag and lock myself in the bathroom."

"Wow . . . that's weird . . . and sort of sad?" Phoebe glanced around to see if the others agreed.

"What's my excuse?" Lucy asked her friends. "I don't have children, a husband, and five house pets. I haven't even finished the socks I started for Matt back in July."

And if our relationship continues its downhill slide, I might never. I'll just unravel the yarn and hide it away somewhere, Lucy thought with a silent sigh. An apt metaphor for a failed romance.

"We're all overscheduled. That's the problem. Double tasking. Trying to check off our never-ending to-do lists," Dana said.

"And rarely taking time for yourself." Maggie wasn't quite scolding them, but Lucy knew she wasn't speaking for herself, since she was a widow now and had no one left at home to fret over.

". . . and talking on the cell phone every second, on top of it," Dana added. "Even when I'm driving."

"That's the only time I have to catch up on calls," Suzanne said.

"Don't forget texting," Phoebe offered.

"Phoebe . . . you don't text while you drive . . . do

you?" The note of alarm in Maggie's voice caught everyone's attention.

"No way. That's stupid. I might read a few. Once in a while. When I'm totally stopped in traffic . . ."

"Please don't tell me that." Maggie sighed. "How about knitting? Are you mixing that with driving, too?"

Now Lucy wore a "caught in the act" expression and slowly raised her hand. "All right, you've got me. But only in really bad traffic. If I need to get the project done for a birthday present or something like that. I never give myself enough time."

"Who has enough time? Show me this person. I'd like to meet them." Suzanne picked up a piece of bread, stared at it and put it down again. "I'll tell you my philosophy—to me, time is like a pair of control top panty hose. You take it out of the package and it looks so squashed and tiny. And you say to yourself, 'No way am I going to get all this into *that*.' But somehow, you wiggle and squeeze and squirm. You yank it up and voila! You made it. Or mostly. It can get a little tight, but it works out most of the time." She sighed and picked the bread up again, this time, swiping on a taste of butter and taking a bite. "That's how my days go. Just squeezing in what I can."

"As if I didn't know it already, you're all stretched to the limit. Which makes my surprise an actual necessity," Maggie decided. "Not just an unexpected gift from the gods."

"The surprise. Finally . . . come on, Maggie," Phoebe coaxed, sounding more like a preschooler than a college student. "Give it up already."

Maggie sat back and took a breath. "I had a call this afternoon from an old friend, Nadine Gould. She's working at a beautiful inn up in the Berkshires. She asked if I was available next weekend to teach some knitting workshops there. It seems the hotel's new owner has gone a little . . . New Age. They're holding something called a 'Creative Spirit Weekend.' The teacher she had lined up for the workshops canceled and she's stuck. The inn also has a big spa," she added quickly. "There are fitness classes and all the treatments in the book," she added in an even more tantalizing tone. "Massages, facials, cellulite scrubs, mud baths, seaweed wraps . . . the works."

"That sounds great." Suzanne sighed with longing.

"It does, doesn't it? We were talking a few months ago about taking a trip together," Maggie reminded them. "You know I wouldn't enjoy myself for a minute without all of you along."

"Uh . . . yeah, you would. After a few guilty pangs," Phoebe countered.

"I'd soldier on, I suppose. Fortunately, I don't have to. They're paying me a pittance for the workshops, but throwing in free accommodations. I talked Nadine into giving me a guest cottage—two bedrooms, two baths, and a foldout couch in the sitting room. We can go up next Friday and come back Sunday night. Relaxation, enlightenment . . . knitting nirvana. What more could you ask for?"

"Sounds like that happy place," Lucy agreed. "But what about the shop?"

Lucy glanced at Phoebe and her other friends did, too. Phoebe's long hair was parted in the middle today, framing her face like dark curtains with magenta streaks. Phoebe stared at her soup bowl, suddenly looking glum and uncertain.

"Don't pout, Phoebe." Maggie leaned over and patted her hand. "I'll close up for the weekend. I wouldn't leave you here, like . . . Cinderella."

"Thanks, Maggie," she said sincerely. "I wouldn't do Cinderella real well. I really hate those singing mice."

"I love the singing mice," Lucy countered. "They're so cute."

"Well, singing mice or not, Suzanne got her wish." Dana put her reading glasses back on and took up her knitting again. "If you lock yourself in the bathroom at this place, I bet it has a sunken tub, Jacuzzi, and lots of scented candles. And no pesky kids knocking on the door."

"Sounds heavenly." Suzanne sighed, but didn't look excited by the invitation. "But it's such short notice. I have so much going on. The boys have soccer and lacrosse, Alexis is in the kick line at the homecoming game, and I have two open houses . . ."

Suzanne was a real estate agent for a broker in town, a full-time job she miraculously managed to squeeze in around the demands of family life. No wonder she didn't finish her knitting projects, Lucy thought. It was a wonder she made it out of the house once a week to their meetings. At least she fit the knitting group into her virtual panty hose.

Suzanne picked up her BlackBerry to check on more obligations, but Dana gently plucked it from her hand, then dangled it out of reach.

"Not so fast . . . we have to wean you off this thing. People can get addicted to high-tech toys, you know. Kevin can handle the kids," Dana said decisively. "It will be good for him to take over. Good for the kids to be alone with him, too. You know, Suzanne sometimes we take on such a big load because we think our families won't survive if we're not solving their every little problem. But they will, I promise."

"Dana's right. They can all live without you for a weekend. And they'll appreciate you more when you get home. Do you really believe that you're indispensable?" Maggie challenged her.

"No . . . it's not that," Suzanne insisted.

"Well, good. Because you're not. Your husband can handle the children and maybe your friends at the real estate office can take over the open houses."

"You'll be so mellow when you get home, you won't even mind that your own house is totally wasted," Phoebe added.

"Good point," Suzanne said wryly. "I guess I could find another agent to cover for me. Everyone's eager for leads right now."

Suzanne considered the suggestions, coming at her from all sides. She finally picked up her half-finished ski hat and waved it, a flag of surrender. "I give up. I'll try to work it out and get back you."

"I'm taking that as a yes," Maggie insisted.

Dana handed back the BlackBerry. "Here you go. But no laptops on the trip. I think we should have a rule."

"Okay." Suzanne nodded agreeably, but Lucy saw the twinkle in her eye.

"How about the rest of you. Are we all signed on?" Maggie looked at the others.

"I have patients on Saturday morning, but I'll move the appointments. Jack and Dylan are going to be in a father-son golf tournament on the Cape, so all I have to worry about is a cat sitter for Arabelle," Dana reported.

Try the Yellow Pages, under Animal Control, Lucy thought, but didn't dare advise.

Dana was very proud of her full-breed Maine Coon cat, but Arabelle was clearly crazy. In fact, Arabelle's feline social dysfunction was pretty obvious. To everyone but Dana.

Aside from Arabelle and Dylan, her high school–age son with Jack, Dana also had a stepson named Tyler, but he was in his first year of college and fairly independent now.

"Josh has a few gigs," Phoebe reported, "but I'm sticking with you guys. Don't tell him, but I could use a break from the Babies scene."

Phoebe's boyfriend, Josh, was on bass guitar and vocals for a group called Big Fat Crying Babies, who played something they called alternative smash rock, their own compositions mostly. They'd just cut their own indie CD, *Can't Stop Crying. Really*, and were making a name for themselves in the area. Phoebe was loyal to the cause, lugging equipment in and out of dance clubs and cheering loudly at all opportunities.

Suzanne turned to Lucy. "What about Matt? You guys have any plans?"

Lucy knew she meant no harm by the question, but it still hit the wrong button. She picked up her bowl and carried it to the sideboard.

"No big plans." She tried to keep her voice from sounding shaky, but didn't quite manage it. "He might have Dara with him next weekend," she added, mentioning Matt's seven-year-old daughter. "I'm not sure what's going on."

Well, that much was true. Should she tell them about her relationship troubles now? she wondered. Or save that tale of woe for the trip? Everyone seemed so excited about the spa. She didn't want to be the soggy afghan.

Next weekend at the spa would be the perfect opportunity to ask her friends for a dose of tea and sympathy. Green tea, most likely.

"I'll just have to figure out what to do with Tink," Lucy added. She hated leaving her dog, even for a weekend. If the spa permitted dogs, it was most likely only breeds that could fit into a designer handbag. Tink's tail couldn't even make that cut.

"Won't Matt watch her?" Suzanne said, voicing the logical choice.

"Sure . . . if he's around. I guess he would," Lucy murmured.

It was hard to ask your boyfriend to dogsit if you suspected he might be dating other people while you were out of town. Lucy considered the scenario with a secret sigh. Too bad there was no way for Tink to chaperone, or report back on what those big brown eyes had seen.

"So we're all set," replied Maggie. "Stay right here, I'll get my laptop. The inn has a great website."

While Maggie went off in search of her computer, the others cleared the table and took out their knitting again. Maggie soon returned and brought up the site. They gathered around Maggie to see the screen. The homepage showed a slide show of the building, inside and out. Lucy walked around the other end of the table and looked on over Dana's shoulder.

The rambling structure sat perched on the edge of a lake, a large Victorian with gingerbread trim, dark green shutters, turret rooms, and screened porches. The inn was pictured in all seasons, surrounded by lush gardens or covered with snow.

"What a beautiful building. It's a classic," Dana said.

"The inn was built in the late 1800s. A summer mansion for some wealthy family. I think it was turned into a hotel in the 1920s. Crystal Lake is very close to Lenox and Lee, near Tanglewood and all that," Maggie added, mentioning the world-famous performance center and school for classical music.

"I love that part of the Berkshires. Jack and I take the boys and their friends skiing and hiking around there," Dana said, meaning her son and stepson. "I've never heard of Crystal Lake, though."

"It's very small, only about two or three miles around. Perfect for a jog or fitness walk," Maggie noted. "The lake is closed to motorboats and jet skis."

"I like that idea," Dana said. "Sounds very quiet and private."

"Oh, they've thought of every last detail," Maggie promised. "'Enjoy complimentary afternoon tea beside the hearth or explore the lake on a canoe, paddle boat, or kayak.'"

"Anyone up for rowing?" Lucy asked. "Now that's good exercise."

"I like those boats with the pedals," Phoebe said.

"I'll try either, if I can sit on the other end and sightsee," Dana replied.

"Wait, there's more," Maggie cut in. " 'The inn is dedicated to rejuvenating the body and renewing the spirit in a breathtaking, natural setting. Our full-service spa offers the finest treatments, with techniques and ingredients gathered from around the globe. Seminars and activities—from hot yoga to tai chi—are guided by our staff of wellness professionals, professional artists, and mind-body experts to enhance your stay and enlighten your journey.'"

"I'd love to have my journey enlightened. I'm am so there," Phoebe said dramatically.

Suzanne leaned toward the computer screen to get a better look at the hotel. "Oh, look. It's Dr. Max. Is he giving a workshop, too?"

Lucy had never heard of Dr. Max, but Suzanne sounded as if she'd just spotted Brad and Angelina at the Stop & Shop.

"Yes, he'll be there." Maggie nodded. "Dr. Maxwell

Flemming owns the inn now. That's why the place has taken this new-age slant."

"Why didn't you say that in the first place? My schedule is clear for Dr. Max," Suzanne promised.

"Who's Dr. Max?" Lucy stared around at the others. She wasn't keen on keeping up with celebrity gossip, though she did scan the headlines on the magazine rack while waiting in the grocery checkout line.

"Where have you been, Lucy? Dr. Max has been on the talk show circuit for months. I just saw him last week on *Oprah*. He's a little holistic, but he makes a lot of sense."

Though Lucy worked at home, she only turned the TV on during the day in times of national emergency. She was pretty disciplined about getting into her office in the morning, but could easily waste hours answering e-mails and trolling the Internet, visiting her favorite knitting sites and blogs.

"Is Dr. Max holistic . . . or just holier than thou?" Dana asked before Lucy could answer. "He's the latest self-help guru to hit the bestseller lists, Lucy," Dana explained, flipping her knitting over to examine her stitches. "The pop psychology flavor of the month."

"I haven't read his book so I'm reserving judgment," Maggie said evenly. "But I understand from Nadine that Dr. Max has a compelling story. He had a very successful psychiatric practice for many years, somewhere around Boston. Cambridge or Newton. He was treating clients with the usual talk therapy and drugs for depression, that sort of thing. But one of his patients committed suicide and it changed everything. He lost his practice, his marriage, and professional reputation. He says he hit bottom, questioning his medical training and every long-held belief. Eventually he rose out of the ashes and decided he wanted to live his life a whole new way. Now he's on a mission to share his insights with the world."

"That's what I heard on the show. More or less," Suzanne chimed in. "Maybe I'll actually have time next weekend to read some of the book."

"I'd be interested to read it, too," Dana said, though her tone held a distinctly skeptical note.

"I'll bring a copy along," Maggie promised. "My friend Nadine gives both the book and the author a positive review. She works with him closely and has nothing but good things to say about him."

"I don't want to trash the guy sight unseen, but I'm pretty skeptical of pop psychologists with one-size-fits-all answers." Dana peered at the others over the edge of her reading glasses. "I can just imagine the workshops you were asked to do. Will I be knitting mittens for my inner child?"

"Your inner child needs mittens, too, Dana," Maggie gently returned. "It's not quite that bad. But the classes were planned by the workshop leader who canceled and it's definitely new territory for me." Maggie pushed the computer aside and stood up. "Here, let me show you what my friend asked me to do."

She walked over to the big cupboard near the table and carried back a basket that held a few balls of yarn and a set of needles with a few rows of knitting clinging to them. From the shape of what was done so far, Lucy had no idea what Maggie was working on. So far, it looked a lot like a misshapen, lumpy potholder.

There were some printed sheets in the basket, as well, and Maggie handed them around.

"Here's one technique I'm supposed to teach. 'Random knitting.' Ever heard of it?"

They all shook their heads. Lucy quickly scanned the sheet. She didn't read the instructions, but the photos of the randomly knit projects caught her eye. They were all amazingly artistic and unique—hats, sweaters, swirling coats, and a pair of mismatched but clearly related mittens.

"This technique is really just about the act of knitting and expressing yourself creatively," Maggie explained. "It's about throwing out all the rules and patterns. You just knit along, change colors when you feel like it, mixing purls and knits in any combination. Stitching rows that are different lengths, if you like. Have a vague idea about a hat or a sock? Well, just go for it. Why use someone else's idea of a sock? Let your intuition guide you and allow it to emerge from the stitchery." Maggie gazed at her friends. "Am I explaining it clearly?"

Lucy could tell by the expressions on her friends' faces that they shared her confusion. "But what's the point?"

"Self-expression. A pure product of your creative spirit, and individuality, of course," Maggie said with a sly smile.

"But what if nothing emerges? Do you just knit a glob of yarn and throw it away?" Dana asked. Lucy felt relieved to see she wasn't the only one who didn't get it.

"You can always use something like that for a pot holder . . . or a coaster," Lucy suggested, getting a laugh out of her friends. "In fact, it looks a lot like one of my first projects, a washcloth. Which did come out in sort of an abstract shape."

"You do want to eventually use these pieces for something useful. But this is a lot different from sloppy, beginner knitting," Maggie explained. She held the piece out and stared at it. "The intention and inner process is. I guess the end product doesn't really differ much, does it?" she had to admit.

"Anyway, when you're done, you often have an interesting woven bit, like this." Maggie showed them a piece she had finished, using the technique. Irregularly shaped, it was a few inches in circumference, a colorful mix of textures and stitches. Maggie had used a wide range of yarns, with no plan or pattern, but it all seemed to blend together, forming its own design. "Or it could be much larger."

"That's very pretty." Dana picked it up and looked it over. "You could sew this on a sweater or a handbag as an arty embellishment."

"Yes, you can do that, or put them all together and make a scarf or even a sweater or coat. Or if they're small enough, a piece of jewelry. When you felt these, they come out really interesting." Maggie showed them pictures of the randomly knit pieces that had been put together to form some attractive, one-of-a-kind creations. "Or a piece of fiber art," she added, showing them another photo.

"Is that all you're going to teach there, Random Knitting?" Suzanne asked.

"Not quite. I have to do some basic walk-in workshops and there's also something called 'Mindful Knitting' on the agenda. It sounds like a blending of meditation and knitting, which should be interesting. I'm not entirely clear about my role," Maggie admitted. "Nadine assigned a yoga instructor to help me so I guess it will turn out all right. They can't expect perfection, bringing me in at the last minute."

"You're a great teacher, Maggie. They're lucky to have you," Lucy assured her.

"We'll all sign up and make you look like the most popular instructor," Suzanne promised.

"Oh, you don't have to do that. You can always have a class with me here. There are going to be plenty of interesting speakers to choose from," Maggie replied quickly.

She had picked up her random knitting piece and Lucy watched her ply away, crazily mixing up stitches and pausing to snip and tie on a new type of yarn and even switch to a different size needle.

"That looks like fun. I'm going to start one right now." Lucy took out some number six needles and picked a small ball of nubbly orange yarn from the selection Maggie had prepared. "Guess I'll try this orange stuff."

"Just go with your gut," Maggie advised. "Anyone else want to jump in?"

"I'll stick with my dress. But I am definitely sitting in on the Mindful Knitting class," Dana promised. "That connection seems very clear to me. Knitting can be a lot like yoga. A calming activity that clears your mind and renews your energy."

"Spoken like a true yogi." Suzanne put aside the ski hat and rummaged around the basket of random yarn.

Dana, their resident yoga enthusiast, had been practicing for years. Several hours a week, at the Nirvana Yoga Center across town, she stretched and twisted her lean limbs into unbelievable and even painful-looking positions. Lucy found Dana's discipline impressive and thought the skill could come in handy sometime, say, if you were stuffed in the trunk of a car. Well, something more likely.

While yoga did not entice Lucy, the mindful knitting sounded interesting. She stitched away randomly, knitting a little, purling when she had the urge, ending a row when she felt like it, then starting another. She worked for a few minutes with the orange yarn, then picked out a fuzzy brown mohair and worked it in.

The women worked without talking for a few minutes, each concentrating on their project.

"Hey, Lucy, didn't I see you walk in here with a dessert-looking object?" Phoebe's brow was pinched, concentrating on her stitches. "I still have to finish a paper tonight. I wouldn't mind a little sugar rush."

Phoebe lived in the small apartment above the shop. When she wasn't working—or acting as unofficial stage manager for Josh's band—she took classes at a nearby college. It was hard to say what she was majoring in or when she'd be finished with her degree. You could call it a random college education, Lucy realized with a secret smile. But Phoebe didn't seem to be in any hurry and that was just fine for some people.

"That's right. Coffee and dessert. With all this spa talk, I nearly forgot." Maggie jumped up from her chair and headed back to the storeroom. "Why don't you serve the apple thing you made, Lucy? There are plates on the sideboard."

Maggie had put the coffee on earlier and quickly brought out the pot. Lucy dished out the apple crumble and everyone took a plate, spooning up the fruity confection before they even got back to the table.

"This is good," Dana said in a quiet, serious tone. "Taste's like maybe oatmeal and real butter in the crumbs?"

"You don't want to know," Lucy told her.

"I taste the oatmeal . . . but I don't want to know about the butter," Suzanne agreed. "The apples are delicious. Where did you get them?"

"At the orchard, near the beach. Matt and I took Dara apple picking last weekend." Lucy stopped herself from saying more.

"Did you have fun?" Dana asked.

"Yeah . . . we did." Lucy nodded. They'd been more relaxed

and had more fun on that outing than many lately. Probably because Dara was so cute, a great distraction, diffusing the subtle tension between them. But something was going on with Matt. She just wasn't sure what it was.

But she still didn't want to talk about it with her friends, Lucy decided. She'd save it for the trip. There would be plenty of time then.

"Enjoy your sugar and butter, ladies," Maggie advised between bites. "I have a feeling the cuisine at the inn won't involve any of the above."

"The price we have to pay for being pampered all weekend," Dana pointed out.

"It's going to be a challenge. But I'm up for it," Suzanne declared. She gazed around at the others, who all nodded solemnly.

Lucy was up for it, too. It was just the getaway she needed right now.

Chapter Two

eciding on which car to take to the Crystal Lake Inn required little debate. Only Suzanne's family-size SUV— aptly called a Sequoia—could comfortably seat all five of them, hold all the luggage—ample for a mere weekend, Lucy noticed—and Maggie's workshop supplies.

Negotiating the seating arrangement was another matter. Suzanne took the driver's seat, of course, which left the other four to sort out their preferences. Maggie claimed the front seat like a fifth grader on a field trip, scoping out the best spot on the bus. Though she didn't scream out, "I called it!" there was no question. She absolutely had to sit up front next to Suzanne.

"Or it won't be pretty, ladies. I get car sick very easily, I can't help it. I've been this way since I was a child."

"Assertive and fussy, you mean?" Dana asked sweetly.

Maggie glanced over her shoulder, but didn't dignify Dana's comment with a reply.

"Could be stomach acid," Suzanne diagnosed. "Have you tried chewing gum?"

"Gum doesn't help me." Maggie took the seat next to Suzanne and snapped on her seat belt.

Dana climbed in the back with a sigh. "Guess I'll have to settle for a window . . . and some sugar-free Mint Breeze. Anyone want a stick?" she asked, holding out a pack of gum.

"I'll have some of that." Phoebe reached into the car and grabbed a few pieces. "Don't worry, I'm going back to the cheap seats, where I can stretch out. Don't wake me up until we get there."

Clutching her big, funky, felted tote—which doubled as a knitting and overnight bag—Phoebe hopped into the car like a little goat and flung herself onto the bench seat at the very back of the vehicle. A cute little goat wearing purple lace stockings and an iPod, Lucy thought.

Lucy was the last to climb inside and sat across from Dana in the second row.

"Good, a window. I was hoping . . . but didn't want to seem so . . . persnickety." She leaned over the driver's seat and purposely dropped the last word into Maggie's ear.

"I am not fussy. It's just my inner ear. It's very sensitive to motion." Maggie sat up straight in her seat and pulled out her knitting.

"Doesn't knitting in a car disturb your inner ear?" Dana asked curiously.

"Knitting never bothers anything. In fact, it always helps. Remember that." Maggie seemed unfazed by Dana's goading.

Lucy had also brought her knitting and her iPod. Reading in a car made her dizzy, but she could knit without a problem. The ride from Plum Harbor to Crystal Lake would take a little over two hours. She'd grown up in Northampton, a large town just east of the Berkshires, so she knew the area fairly well.

The trip was pretty much a straight shot west from the Cape Ann coastline, and they'd timed their travel to avoid any rush-hour traffic.

"Everyone belted up? Off we go." Suzanne put the vehicle in gear and pulled out of the driveway.

They cruised through Suzanne's neighborhood, then down Main Street, en route to the highway. Maggie cast a longing glance at her knitting shop as they drove by. "I guess the shop will still be standing when we get back. I left a note on the door for any customers. I hope no one gets annoyed."

"They'll be back," Dana promised. "Annoyed or not."

Lucy felt the same. Maggie's clientele was unusually loyal. She was secretly casting a longing glance at the Schooner. She really needed another cup of coffee, but didn't want to ask Suzanne to stop. Everyone would pile out and go inside to visit with Edie Steiber, the diner owner and unofficial mayor of Plum Harbor. By the time Edie filled them in on the local gossip and got the lowdown on their plans, it would be lunch-time.

No, best not to stop in town at all. Not to visit with Edie. Or leave some last-minute dog instructions with Matt, she thought, as the SUV cruised past his veterinary office next.

Best to leave Plum Harbor—its connections and cares— far behind for a few days.

Despite Phoebe's promise to nap the entire way, she was still wide awake when they reached the highway.

"Road trip. Road trip," Phoebe suddenly sang out in a bright, excited tone. "Remember that old movie, *Thelma and Louise*? It's just like that . . . except with more characters."

Lucy glanced back her. Was that an *old* movie? Well, perhaps it seemed so to Phoebe. "I hope we all meet with a happier ending then poor Thelma and Louise. They drove off the rim of the Grand Canyon. Remember?"

"If only they had run off to a spa instead of running amok with a crime spree," Dana said, slipping on a pair of large sunglasses. "They could have had a happy landing . . . and a sequel."

"How true." Lucy had to agree. She also recalled that both women were running away from troubled relationships with men. As far as she knew, she was the only one in the car with that problem.

The week had gone by quickly and she'd never found a chance to ask Matt point blank what was up. He'd been away at a conference for most of the time, so they hadn't even gotten together midweek, as they usually did. She'd only seen him briefly when she'd dropped off Tink and all her supplies at his house this morning.

He'd been perfectly agreeable about dogsitting and given her a warm, affectionate hug good-bye and said all the right things when they parted. But still seemed distant and preoccupied somehow. Funny how men could do that.

This time apart would be sort of a test, she decided. Let him spend a weekend without me and we'll see if absence really makes the heart grow fonder.

Abstinence makes the heart grow fonder would actually make more sense, she decided, staring out the window until the passing view became a blur.

She gave herself a mental shake, determined not to brood about her romantic woes. She wanted to enjoy this minivacation. The time away from Plum Harbor was a chance to kick back with her best friends. Maybe one of those hokey-sounding classes at the inn might even lend her some inner peace and enlightenment.

As Lucy had expected, they arrived in the town of Lee

about two hours later. Maggie pulled out a second sheet of directions from her purse as they drove through the village and then followed a two-lane rural road up a mountainside.

"We stay on this road, Valley View, for about three miles," Maggie told Suzanne. "Then turn right at the third stop sign, onto Crystal Lake Lane. The inn is about three more miles from there. Says you can't miss it."

Suzanne was driving slower now, maneuvering the buslike vehicle very deftly on the tight turns and curving tree-lined road. One side was sheer rock, the other offering little shoulder and a steep drop down. Lucy peered out her window and quickly leaned back. Now the trip really did remind her of *Thelma and Louise*.

"There's another sign for the inn," Suzanne said happily as she pointed.

"Both hands on the wheel . . . please . . ." Maggie reached out and put Suzanne's hand back in place. "Let's get there in one piece. I had no idea this place was so secluded."

It *was* secluded, Lucy noticed. Luckily, they were driving up here in daylight; the ride would be treacherous and even a little scary after dark. She doubted this woodsy road had any lights.

"But it's so beautiful," Dana said with awe. "Look at the trees. We don't have any of these colors yet."

The area was famous for its fall foliage, a main tourist attraction, and Lucy could easily see why. The tall trees shadowing the road were a canopy of fall colors, a mix of golden hues, deep umber, and bright red.

Lucy stared out at the scene, wishing she'd brought a camera. "I'd love to make a sweater with all these colors."

"Nature makes the most creative combinations, that's for sure," Maggie agreed. "Is Phoebe still sleeping? It's a shame if she's missing this."

Lucy glanced back to check. Phoebe was still out like a light. She'd even slept through their break at a rest stop.

Lucy leaned back and gently shook her shoulder. "Phoebe . . . ? Wake up." When Phoebe didn't move, she gently plucked one side of her headphones out of her ear. "Wake up, sweetie pie. We want you to see the trees."

Phoebe finally roused herself and sat up, sleepily rubbing her eyes. Her long pony tail was pushed to one side, the magenta streak flat against her head like a neon pink stripe down the back of a punky skunk.

"Are we there yet?" she asked through a yawn.

"Yes, we are," Maggie announced. "Look. There it is."

Suzanne had made the last turn and the inn had come into view. At the very bottom of a long hill, the big white Victorian building stood on the edge of a crystal blue lake, surrounded by an amazing variety of trees—oak and Japanese maple. Copper beach and blue spruce and many more Lucy couldn't identify by name. The colors created an amazing display and she'd heard there were even hot air balloon rides for the most adventurous leaf peepers.

"It looks just like the pictures . . . which is rarely the case when you book a hotel on the Internet." Dana slipped off her glasses to get a better look.

"What a hunk of real estate," Suzanne oozed. "This lakefront property must be worth a fortune."

"I understand Dr. Flemming got a good deal from the former owners," Maggie said. "But he still sunk all his earnings from his bestseller into the purchase. Nadine says he wants to open more wellness centers and he's looking for investors."

"He'd better not look in this car." Suzanne laughed. "I couldn't afford to stay here for the weekend if we weren't getting the room for free."

"I can barely afford it, and they're paying me to come," Maggie countered.

Dana leaned forward to get a better view of the inn as they drew closer. "The man thinks big, you have to say that for him."

"He's an optimist. That's part of his philosophy. The world could use a little more of that," Maggie said.

Suzanne guided the Sequoia up a curved drive that led to the inn's entrance. A discreet sign posted nearby said TEMPORARY PARKING FOR CHECK-IN, and Suzanne steered into the first available spot.

Lucy was eager to stretch her legs. She got restless on long car rides and two or three hours was her limit. She jumped out and stretched, then followed her friends to the main entrance, which was covered by a high portico, and then through the heavy front doors, flanked by large wrought-iron urns brimming with autumn flowers.

It took her eyes a moment to adjust to the change from the bright sun outside to the lobby's muted light. She blinked and stared around at the understated opulence of the place, which was true to every adjective of the website's description—the woodwork and carved molding, paneled ceilings, wainscoting, polished floors, brass and crystal chandeliers.

Elegant love seats and settees were grouped around potted palms. A large hearth with a carved mantel was the main focus of the lobby to the left, the reservations desk to the right and another section for seating beyond that.

Just as they headed to the front desk, a dark-haired woman appeared in their path. Her face lit up when she caught sight of Maggie.

"Maggie, you made it. So good to see you!" She walked toward Maggie and hugged her.

"Nadine, you look wonderful," Maggie exclaimed.

Lucy guessed the woman Maggie so eagerly hugged back could only be Nadine Gould, Maggie's friend who worked here as the events manager and had invited Maggie to be a speaker.

"You brought your own fan club, I see." Nadine surveyed Maggie's friends with a smile.

"What could I do? They wouldn't stay away," Maggie insisted and quickly introduced everyone.

About Maggie's age, with smooth, reddish brown hair cut to her chin, Nadine gave Lucy the impression of someone who was efficient and businesslike. But she also announced her artistic side, with a multistrand beaded necklace and a plum-colored jacket sweater that both looked handcrafted.

A nice piece of work, Lucy thought, taking a closer look at the sweater. Maggie had mentioned that knitting had brought her and Nadine together and that her old friend was "very accomplished." Quite an accolade, coming from Maggie.

"What a beautiful place. Have you worked here long?" Suzanne asked.

"About a year or so. My sister Alice is the hotel manager. She hired me when Dr. Flemming took over. Wait until you see the spa and the cottage I've booked for you. You're going to love it," Nadine promised. "Have you had any lunch?"

"We only made a quick pit stop," Maggie told her. "We wanted to get up here right away."

"We'd better go in, then, and have a bite. They'll be clearing the buffet soon. You can register and get your room key later."

Nadine led the group to the dining room, walking alongside Maggie. The rest trailed behind like a flock of goslings,

Lucy thought, necks twisting in all directions at each step. There was so much to see.

Lucy leaned over and spoke privately to Dana. "I need to hit the restroom."

Dana nodded. "No problem. You know where to find us."

Lucy left the group and headed back toward the lobby. She noticed a discreet sign for the elevator and restrooms and followed the arrow.

There was another maze of couches, love seats, and potted palms on the other side of the front desk. She wandered into an alcove, thinking there might be an exit there, but quickly realized she'd walked into a private scene.

A man and a woman were engaged in a hushed but fierce argument. The woman, a thin blonde dressed in a dark business suit, stood with her fist clenched around a file folder. The man was much younger, in his midtwenties, Lucy guessed. He had thick brown hair and a day's growth of beard on his lean face. He wore jeans, work boots, and a navy blue sweatshirt with the inn's logo on the front in white. Obviously an employee of the hotel and not very high on the food chain. Down near his boots, Lucy noticed a gray metal toolbox.

The woman, of course, looked like a management type. The argument could have been a workplace conversation. But the emotional level seemed too intense . . . and their tone, too familiar.

"Are you crazy? You can't just take off the minute it's done." The blonde would have been shouting, except for her clenched jaw. "We need you here . . . you have to stay."

"Are you freaking kidding me? That wasn't the deal. You know it!" He was struggling not to yell. He leaned toward her, red-faced, his posture menacing.

"It certainly was. You don't remember? You must have been drunk. I'm not surprised." The woman sounded disgusted now. "Suit yourself," she challenged. "But you won't get paid."

His face fell in shock. "I knew you'd pull some crap like this. You make me sick. The both of you."

"You make me tired," she said, her tone suddenly flat. "Still acting out with your tantrums."

He gazed around, grabbed a vase off an end table, and threw it at the wall, where it crashed and broke into pieces.

The woman stifled a gasp and jumped back.

Lucy realized she must have, too.

The woman suddenly turned and stared at her. Her pale complexion turned beet red.

"I'm sorry . . . I was just looking for the restroom . . ." Lucy mumbled and took a few steps backward.

"Just outside and to your right. There's a sign on the wall." The woman's tone was shaky but polite. She spoke in an automatic voice, like a recorded message. Then she quickly crouched down and picked up the bits of broken pottery.

Her companion didn't help, just bent over and picked up his toolbox. He glanced at Lucy and sneered. Then he marched away, luckily in the opposite direction.

Lucy turned and quickly walked away, too. It was embarrassing to stumble into a private argument. It seemed like a rather grisly emotional exchange. Lucy didn't even speculate about its meaning.

After the ladies' room, the return trip to the dining room was much faster. As she paused at the entrance, looking for her friends, she was awed by her first view of Crystal Lake and the mountainside behind the inn, framed by a row of long windows.

She soon spotted her group and walked over to join them. She took an empty seat between Dana and Suzanne. Nadine was sitting next to Maggie, reviewing her teaching schedule.

"Did you get a chance to look over the session plans I sent?" Nadine asked.

"I did." Maggie nodded and snapped open her napkin. "I'm all set with the random knitting. We tried it together last week at the shop. It was fun. But I do have some questions about the mindful technique—"

Before Maggie could get into specifics, Nadine cut in. "Don't worry, I have someone lined up to help you with those workshops. Joy Kimmel, she's a yoga instructor here. We can figure that out later. Let me go over the final schedule with you first . . ."

While Nadine reviewed Maggie's teaching obligations for the weekend, the others decided to check out the buffet. Lucy knew that the inn served a strictly organic spa menu and no hard liquor, only organic wine and beer at dinner. While she didn't eat in an unhealthy way, she wasn't big on tofu lasagna or chickpea cakes and wondered what she'd find.

All the dishes looked surprisingly tasty and artfully displayed. Despite her wariness, it wasn't hard at all to fill up her plate.

"I'm not exactly sure what I'm eating," Suzanne said a few moments after they sat down, "but it has a tasty dressing and there's got to be week's worth of fiber in there."

Phoebe finally returned, looking pleased, though Lucy noticed she wasn't carrying back a dish of food. Only a large soda fountain-size glass filled with creamy purple liquid.

"Did you guys check out the smoothie bar? It's awesome. I know what I'm living on this weekend." Nadine and Maggie returned from the buffet, too, and took their places again. Nadine handed them each thick white folders with the inn's logo on the front and the words "Creative Spirit Weekend" just below.

"Here's the schedule of workshops and fitness classes. And the list of spa treatments. It's best to book ahead. We're expecting a big group this weekend with Dr. Max on the property."

"Really? Is he here yet?" Suzanne sat up and quickly searched the dining room. Nadine smiled at her.

"Don't worry. You'll see a lot of him," she promised. "He loves to mingle with the guests. Max is about connection. He's not some aloof, sage-on-a-mountaintop type."

Lucy was not surprised. From what she'd heard, the doctor's biggest selling point was his personality and he was looking for investors.

It didn't take an accounting degree to see that a healthy profit was needed to keep the chandeliers polished and pomegranate juice flowing in this place. No wonder he was a guru of the people.

"There's a special outing tonight. We only offer it once a month. A moon meditation retreat, up on the mountain." She leaned closer, speaking in a more confidential tone. "Dr. Max *might* lead the group. He's so busy right now, we can't promise. But if you're at all interested, you should sign up right away."

Lucy wasn't sure what a moon meditation on a mountaintop entailed, but she'd always loved camping and hadn't had a chance in ages to sleep out under the stars. She and Matt had talked about it, even about taking Dara for her first expedition. But somehow, it hadn't happened yet. The thought made her feel a little blue.

Nadine had launched into another description, drawing Lucy's attention again.

"The writing workshop is very popular, too—Finding Your True Voice. Students make these neat sock puppets and speak through them to write a personal narrative. It can hit on some deep issues and be very healing," she added in a more serious tone. "Some people say the session has helped them more than years of therapy."

Dana's eyes widened, but she didn't say a word. She inhaled deeply and took a final bite of a chickpea patty.

Lucy guessed Dana was holding back a "healing scream" just about now and hoped she didn't choke.

Dana pushed her plate aside and sipped her herbal tea. "So the benefits of all of these activities—meditating on the moon and all that—have been verified with scientific study?"

"Oh . . . absolutely," Nadine insisted. "And you know, dear, there are some deep, essential truths that just can't be measured in a laboratory."

Lucy could see Dana's eyes narrow as she readied herself for an intellectual battle. She hated to be called "dear" by anyone but her husband. And even Jack had to use the term judiciously. That totally burned her sesame butter.

"So many wonderful choices. So little time," Maggie cut in quickly. She gave Dana a quelling look. "We'll have to sort this all out back at our cottage. We'd better check in, ladies. I have a workshop to give this afternoon," she reminded them.

"We're setting up in the lobby, by the fireplace. It's a central location so folks can just drop in as they walk by if they like. You're all right with that, Maggie, aren't you?" Nadine asked.

Lucy knew for a fact that Maggie hated it when people wanted to just walk in and out of her workshops, as if she were demonstrating cookware at the mall.

But she smiled politely in answer. "I'm just going with the flow around here."

Lucy knew Maggie was just trying to fit in, but she sounded like she was speaking a foreign language.

Nadine stood up and patted Maggie's shoulder. "It's going to be a great weekend. I guarantee that you'll all have a lot of fun . . . and expand your comfort zone a little, too."

Clutching the pile of folders to her chest, Nadine trotted off to greet another group that had just walked in.

"'So many absurd theories, so little verifiable proof,'" Dana countered once Nadine had left the table. "So many gullible people, paying five hundred dollars a night for this . . . this . . ."

"Soy-based baloney?" Phoebe supplied.

"Now, now, Dana. Let's just pause and take a deep, cleansing breath," Maggie advised. "I know you don't buy into a lot of this stuff. But you don't have to take any classes or do anything you don't want to do. A walk around the lake, a dip in the whirlpool. There's the fitness room and the spa. There's plenty to do without offending your common sense," Maggie promised her.

Dana nodded, looking suddenly embarrassed and apologetic. "I'm sorry, Maggie. I sound like a spoiled brat. Of course there is, and I appreciate you bringing us here. It's absolutely gorgeous. It's just that, as a trained professional, this jargon gets under my skin."

"I understand completely. I think we're all in agreement there." Her voice dropped to a mere whisper, making them huddle closer. "If I start communicating with any of you via sock puppet, just toss some cold water in my face and drag me out of here. Agreed?"

* * *

They quickly checked in at the front desk, then set off for the cottage. Dana held a map of the grounds and Maggie had the key. "We just follow this path down along the water. I think I see a cottage past those trees."

"Good thing we didn't have to carry our bags down here. It's a bit of a hike," Suzanne noticed.

The cottage was very secluded, Lucy realized. You couldn't even see it if you were up at the inn and you couldn't hear a thing down here, either.

But the isolation was a good thing. The weekend would be peaceful and private in this setting.

"I already have my bag," Phoebe bragged, shifting her sack to one arm. Lucy admired her ability to pack so efficiently, though she would never want to trade wardrobes.

The sight of the cottage quickly lifted their mood. The small, white gingerbread house was built at the very edge of the lake and had a covered porch on two sides, one that hung over the water.

"Isn't this lovely? It looks like something out of a fairy tale." Maggie unlocked the door and led the way inside.

Though the cottage was antique looking outside, it was totally renovated within, the interior maintaining a warm, traditional feeling.

The first floor was an open floor plan with a vaulted ceiling. A wood-burning stove stood in the corner of the main room, which was decorated in earth tones, in a rustic style with touches of luxury. There were soft couches, covered in white linen and raw silk throw pillows, overstuffed chairs, and a rocker made of bent tree boughs. On a few end tables, Lucy spotted hand-thrown pottery and sculptures made of shells, stones, and other natural objects.

"There are plenty of lamps for reading . . . or knitting at night," Lucy noticed. "I doubt the hotel offers much nightlife, which is fine with me."

"I think they have a few lectures and activities planned. But nothing too wild. I don't see a TV, or even a radio," Maggie added.

"No, there aren't any," Suzanne replied. "We can watch the lake and the moon, instead of the nightly news. Much easier on the nerves."

All the furnishings seemed arranged for that purpose, turned to face the view of the lake and mountain through two sets of glass doors that opened to the wraparound porch.

The opposite side of the room held a compact but completely equipped kitchen, separated by a granite-topped island.

A spiral staircase made of dark wood wound up to the next floor. Dana went ahead to explore.

"There's a bedroom and bathroom back there," Dana told the others, walking past the galley kitchen and peering down a short hallway. "And a bed and bath upstairs. We'll have to figure sleeping arrangements at some point."

"I love this porch." Phoebe pulled open the door and stepped outside. "I can sleep out here tonight."

Maggie laughed. "It will be too cold for that, Phoebe. Though I bet it's pleasant in the summer."

"Let's not worry about bedroom choices now." Suzanne flopped on the soft sofa and put her feet up, then pulled a sheet out from her folder. "I'm going for some spa treatments. Look at this list. I might try the seaweed wrap . . . or the Dead Sea Mud Mask."

Dana sat next to Suzanne on the sofa and looked over her shoulder at the schedule. "Just a basic massage for me. I'll do a yoga class first. Or try tai chi."

"Go for it, ladies. I've got to hike back up to the inn for my first workshop." Maggie checked her watch, then opened her purse and quickly applied some lipstick. "Anybody tagging along?"

"I'll come," Lucy offered. She didn't feel like working out and wasn't quite ready to be wrapped in seaweed, like a piece of human sushi. Lucy maki roll, anyone?

Besides, Maggie had made this trip possible and she felt she owed her a little moral support.

"Wait . . . I'll come, too." Phoebe dashed inside from the deck. "I liked that random knitting you showed us last week. I might just knit like that all the time. I mean, who needs patterns? Patterns are so . . . confining. When I knit randomly, I really feel one with the yarn and the needles. It's knitting without borders. No gravity, no limits. It's like I've been totally liberated."

Phoebe ran off to find her knitting bag and Maggie turned to Lucy.

"We've been here less than two hours. The child sounds like she's brainwashed." Maggie gave Lucy a look.

"The pomegranate smoothie. It's gone to her head," Lucy whispered back.

"Let's hope that's all it is. I noticed that drink turned her tongue purple," said Maggie.

"She doesn't seem to mind. I think she said she liked that."

"Not surprising. Now her tongue matches the new butterfly tattoo on her shoulder," Maggie mused.

"I have a feeling there'll be more side effects from this place, before the weekend is over, more than Phoebe's purple tongue," Lucy predicted.

Maggie sighed and shouldered her knitting bag. "What can I say? On with the show."

Chapter Three

N adine Gould was efficient, Lucy had to grant her that. Maggie, Lucy, and Phoebe returned to the inn's main building a few minutes before the workshop was due to begin, expecting to scramble around, setting up for the class. Walking into the lobby they found a printed placard on a brass stand, advertising Maggie's workshop session:

RANDOM KNITTING WITH MAGGIE MESSINA

No knitting experience or equipment necessary.
Just bring nimble fingers and your creative energy.
Meet in the main lobby, adjacent to the hearth.

"Nice," Lucy said. "Very low-key."

"Yes, very inviting," Maggie agreed.

They quickly spotted the workshop location in front of the big hearth. A group of small couches and sitting chairs had been arranged around a low table that held Maggie's baskets of yarn and needles.

Many of the seats were filled, Lucy noticed. Nadine sat among the group and waved as the women approached.

"There she is. Our fearless fiber art leader. We have a nice group ready and waiting for you, Maggie," Nadine greeted her.

"Thank you all for coming." Maggie smiled and looked around at her students. "I'm Maggie Messina and we're going to try some random knitting this afternoon. Whether you're an expert or have never knitted a stitch, you should definitely enjoy this technique . . ."

While Maggie gave her introduction, Nadine slipped away. She had other activities to supervise, Lucy realized.

Maggie took a seat in an armchair and put her knitting bag on the table. "I find it's always nicer in a knitting circle if you know everyone's name and a little bit about them. Let's just go around and introduce ourselves. I'll start," she said. "You already know my name. Knitting's my game."

Lucy winced at the corny quip, which somehow drew a chuckle.

"I own a knitting shop called the Black Sheep in Plum Harbor," Maggie continued. "That's a town north of Boston, in the Cape Ann area. I give lessons there, create patterns, and sell all things that have to do with the art of knitting . . . well, I've already said enough. Who's next?"

Maggie looked to her left, at a woman who sat in a large wingback chair.

"Helen Lynch," the next guest announced herself in a deep, clear tone. "I live in New York, run a public relations firm, and knitting is just one of those things I've always wanted to try but have never had the time. So, here I am."

She smiled and adjusted her glasses—dark red designer frames. She was in her early fifties, Lucy would guess, but her salt-and-pepper hair and a few extra pounds made her look a bit older.

Her clothes and accessories were impressive. Tasteful diamond stud earrings paired with a silky steel gray yoga jacket and matching wide-legged pants. From her short, no-nonsense hairdo to her fancy fitness shoes, something about Helen said "time is money." Lucy didn't doubt she had never found the time to knit.

"Should we go next? Are you ready?" A senior in a light blue jogging suit leaned over and tentatively raised her hand. She sat beside a man her own age who wore an identical outfit. In fact, the couple looked a lot alike, the way older couples sometimes do, as if, with the passage of time and proximity, the border between them has blurred and their looks have merged.

Maggie nodded. "Yes, please. Go ahead."

"I'm Rita Schumacher and this is my husband, Walter. We're retired now but Walter used to be an engineer. We have three children and seven . . . no, six grandchildren."

Walter shook his head. "You don't have to tell them all that. The woman just wants to know if you can knit."

"Of course I knit. I've been knitting for years. I've never heard of this type, though. But I always like to learn something new. Keeps the switches clicking upstairs," She tapped her temple with one finger.

Walter took a breath. He seemed either bored or tired. Mabye a little of both. "I'm Walter Schumacher. My wife just talked enough for both of us. As usual. Nice to meet you."

Walter turned to the man next to him, who sat in an armchair at the other end of the coffee table. Lucy guessed he was in his early forties, bald on top and afflicted with an office pallor. His pale complexion contrasted sharply with a rim of dark hair, a neat beard, and glasses with heavy black frames. A bit of a snack food paunch was hidden by a baggy brown sweater. But he greeted the circle with an eager, friendly smile and a distinct spark of intellect in his dark eyes.

"Curtis Hill. I write for Commodore Travel Guides and I'm here doing some research for our annual edition about spas . . . I've never touched a knitting needle, but I have to try everything around here this weekend for my article," he added, making everyone chuckle.

"Commodore Travel Guides? I always use those books when I plan a trip. Very reliable." Maggie was impressed.

The woman seated closest to Lucy spoke next. It was hard to guess her age. Her looks were striking. She wore a white athletic outfit with dark blue trim. With long, shiny brown hair, blue eyes, and a lean build, she looked like a poster girl for the healthy, holistic lifestyle.

Then Lucy recognized her. She actually was a poster girl . . . or used to be. Her face and figure had been used to sell everything from diamond rings to diet dinners. She may have done some acting, too, or appeared on some cable show about clothes designers? Lucy wasn't sure. She couldn't quite recall her name. A definite almost-celebrity.

"Hi, I'm Shannon Piper. Yes . . . I used to be a model. Some of you might recognize me." She nodded and smiled, a brilliant smile that had not lost any wattage. "I left that scene long ago and I'm working on my inner beauty now. I live down in Westport, Connecticut, and I'm a stay at home mom with three children. I do know how to knit . . . a little," she added modestly.

She seemed nice, Lucy thought, for a former supermodel.

Everyone was looking at Lucy now and she realized her turn had come. "I'm Lucy Binger, a friend of Maggie's, and I'm visiting the inn for the weekend with our knitting group. I have my own small business as a graphic artist. But knitting is a big distraction from earning a living. So I just want to warn everyone if you've never tried it. It can be addictive."

The others in the circle laughed. Phoebe went next. "I'm Phoebe Meyers. I'm a college student and work part-time in Maggie's shop. I knit a lot, too. Lucy's right. Once you get into it, it's hard to stop."

"Thank you, everyone. It's great to meet you all," Maggie cut in. "Why don't we begin?"

Maggie talked a little more about random knitting, showing the group samples of finished pieces. Then she handed out supplies and worked with students who had never knit before. She asked Phoebe and Lucy if they would help, too.

Shannon and Rita seemed to be able knitters, swiftly casting on a row of stitches. While Rita was busily knitting, Lucy noticed, Walter sat and watched, holding an extra ball of yarn for her in his lap.

Curtis Hill was all thumbs, fumbling with his needles, tangling his fingers as he tried to cast on. He kept dropping his ball of yarn and it rolled under the table twice.

"I think I'm doing something wrong here . . ." he said nervously.

Before Lucy could answer, Phoebe walked over to help him.

Helen Lynch was the next to send up a distress signal. She peered down at her needles and shook her head. "I made a few starter stitches . . . but I can't get my needle in the loops again. This one won't fit. Is this the wrong size?"

She held her empty needle away, staring at the point.

Lucy could have predicted this problem. Helen looked pretty tightly wound herself and was bound to cast on stitches that could anchor the *Queen Mary*.

"Let me take a look." Lucy pulled up an empty chair, sat down, then took Helen's needles and yarn into her lap. "I think it's best if we just take these stitches out and start over," she said after a moment or two.

Helen looked upset by the suggestion, then waved her hands in surrender. "Whatever . . . no wonder I've never gotten too far with this stuff."

"Knitting feels a little awkward at first, but it isn't very hard once you get the hang of it. It can be very relaxing," Lucy promised.

"Good. God knows I need something besides pills. I've just been through a horrific divorce," she confided in a quieter voice. "A very toxic relationship. Max's book helped me figure that out . . ."

"Oh . . . that's too bad." Lucy wasn't sure what else to say. And people said that New Yorkers weren't friendly. She'd barely said two words to this woman and was getting her whole life story.

"Oh, I'm over it. Totally. But I needed to get away. Hit the reset button. I've been to all those beauty spas. They get a little boring. This place seems to have more going on."

Lucy pushed hard to get the stitches off the needle, thinking a little WD-40 could have helped. Lucy wasn't sure how Helen had made such tight line of little knots. She must have been a Girl Scout. Lucy tried to untangle the mess, then decided to just snip them off and start over. She found a small pair of scissors on the table and cut a fresh end.

"It's probably best to just start off fresh again. I'll cast on a few stitches to get you going." Lucy had cleared off the needles and tried to show Helen how it was done.

"Oh . . . you do that well. You make it look easy," Helen noted. "I like the classes here. You feel like you're doing something productive besides laying around, being kneaded like a piece of dough. I also want to check out that investors meeting on Sunday," she added. "Are you going?"

"Me?" Lucy quickly shook her head. "No, I'm not," she said simply.

"They haven't handed out any information yet. I keep asking," she said, sounding all business again and a bit annoyed. "But anything Max Flemming puts his name on is going to be hot. Did you read his book? It's terrific," she added sincerely. "He's got the magic. The man could sell Big Macs to vegans," she added with a sharp little laugh.

Lucy had to smile at that line. "Okay, here's how you start off. Just hold the strand of yarn like this, not too loose, but not to too tightly . . ."

"Look, there he is. Dr. Max." Helen sat up in her seat and pointed a manicured fingertip.

Lucy turned quickly. She was dying to get a look at this superstar. Everyone in the circle suddenly seemed aware that Dr. Max was walking across the lobby, coming toward them. They had all stopped knitting and waited silently, whispering to each other.

She noticed Curtis Hill slip an iPhone out of his shirt pocket and take a few discreet photos as Dr. Max approached, holding the phone low on his chest. For candid shots, Lucy guessed. Were there photos in Commodore Travel Guides? She couldn't remember. But maybe he just needed some for reference while he was writing.

Finally, Max stood right next to Maggie's chair and slowly

smiled. His gaze swept around the circle, making eye contact with each person in turn.

"Random knitting? Sounds very interesting. You know, some people believe that nothing in the universe is random. May I join you?"

Lucy stopped to think about the nugget of philosophy sprinkled into the greeting. Was life a series of random events or did we all have some special path? Some special destiny? She'd often wondered herself and now wondered if Dr. Max had the answer.

"Of course, have a seat," Maggie said easily. She made room for Max in the circle and he pulled over an empty chair. Lucy sensed a certain subdued excitement in the group, some murmurs and sighs.

He was taller than she'd expected. Lean and fit, with a youthful glow for his years, which she guessed had to be late fifties or early sixties. But a fit appearance seemed imperative for the proprietor of this place, an evangelist of wellness in mind, body, and soul.

His ample head of hair helped, Lucy thought. Some men were just lucky that way. Thick, white hair, combed back straight from a broad forehead gave the doctor a Lion King look. A wise, kindly lion, with large brown eyes peering out beneath shaggy brows.

Did Maggie feel shock and awe at her close proximity to the great one? If so, she hid it well.

Lucy glanced at Phoebe, who also seemed curious if not awestruck.

Maggie quickly explained the idea of random knitting to Dr. Max—knitting along intuitively, without counting stitches or consulting a pattern. "You can change the color and texture

of the yarn any time the mood strikes, or even change needles," Maggie added.

"Splendid." Max smiled widely, displaying his deep dim-
ples. "It's just a purely creative expression, knitting for knitting's sake?"

"Exactly." Maggie nodded. "You end up with a free-form
piece and can later put several together to make something
useful. Or use them for fiber art."

"I see . . ." Max looked over the samples, examining each
piece. "These are so beautiful and unique. Like autumn leaves
or seashells. The kind of objects you find only in nature."

Did Shannon Piper actually *sigh*? Lucy glanced over at her,
but the model didn't notice. She only had eyes for Dr. Max.

"That's just what I was thinking . . . but I didn't know
how to say it." Shannon met Max's gaze for a moment, then
seemed self-conscious and looked back at her knitting.

The supermodel was smitten, big time. She must have
some heavy father issues, Lucy thought. Dana would know
best about that. But there was no question. Shannon could
have been wearing a T-shirt with the slogan I ♥ DR. MAX! across
her chest.

"Do you know how to cast on?" Maggie asked him.

"It's been a long time since I've done any knitting, but I'll
give it a try." Max picked up a set of needles, then took some
time selecting yarn from the basket, finally picking out a small
ball of self-striping yarn in shades of blue. "This one is pretty,"
he said, pleased with his find.

"Blue is the color of optimism," Maggie pointed out.

"Yes, it is. The color of inspiration and serenity, too," Max
agreed eagerly.

Lucy frowned. She thought that purple was the color

of inspiration. But she didn't want to argue with a man who seemed an expert on the deeper meaning of the color spectrum.

"Colors have vibrations. Energy," Max went on to explain. "That's why we feel so good gazing at a blue sky, or staring out at that crystal clear lake. You don't have to do much more to feel refreshed at this place."

"Though there is more to do, if you want to," Rita Schumacher pointed out. "That's why we like it here. It's our second visit."

"I thought you two looked familiar," Max answered quickly. He leaned forward, his attention honed on the Schumachers "Have we met? I think I would have remembered."

"Oh, we saw you around, Doctor. But I don't think we got to mingle. I'm Rita Schumacher. This is my husband, Walter."

"Nice to meet you, Doctor." Walter nodded at Max, then coughed into his hand.

"It's wonderful to meet both of you. I love to see seniors here, exploring new ideas. Living with open minds and open hearts." Max's deep voice took on an vaguely spiritual tone.

"And don't forget an open wallet." Walter poked his wife with his elbow.

"Don't mind him." Rita shrugged off her partner. "He likes to joke around."

"Good for you. I like to joke around, too," Max said smoothly, ignoring the dig at the inn's high fees. "Laughter refreshes the spirit. I like to say it's Gatorade for the soul."

Phoebe turned to Lucy. *Gatorade for the soul?* she mouthed the words, rolling her eyes.

"He must mean the blue Gatorade," Lucy whispered back.

Luckily, Dr. Max didn't notice the exchange. His gaze was still fixed on the Schumachers. Lucy could practically feel the waves of love.

Max cast another gentle smile at the Schumachers and then looked back at Maggie.

"Now let's see . . . as I said, it's been a long time since I've done any knitting. I learned years ago, when I was traveling around a lot."

"Really? Where was that?" Maggie asked curiously.

"Those were my wandering years. I somehow ended up in the Himalayas. I came into a village on a mountaintop. A magnificent place. You felt as if you'd entered another world. Shangra-la, or something." His smile was wistful, remembering, his voice low and hypnotic. "I stayed there several weeks, a guest of the village elder. One of my first days, I was out walking in the morning and came upon a group of women, sitting cross-legged on the floor in a circle, knitting together at lightning speeds. They were using the yarn they'd spun and dyed themselves, gathered from the animals in their own pastures. No machines, everything by hand. They knit hats, gloves, scarves. Piles of hard work that was taken down the mountain to a market. I guess I never even noticed knitting before that day," he confessed. "But the solemn, purposeful way they sat and worked, on this isolated peak, up in the clouds, a stone's throw from heaven's door. . . . Well, there was something truly sacred in that moment." He paused while they all pictured the scene. "I sat near them and watched for a while. Then they beckoned me into the circle and taught me. Wordlessly," he added.

Max sat with his head slightly bowed and sighed, seeming lost in his memory. No one interrupted. "It was an amazing experience," he said finally. "I've seen knitting in a special light, ever since. That's why I wanted to include some knitting workshops in this weekend," he told Maggie. "Those women have the power to lift entire nations out of poverty with the humble tools of sticks and string. Their sheer persistence and nimble fingers."

"Yes, I know," Maggie said after a moment. "Knitting is just a pastime for most of us. But it can be a powerful force. In some parts of the world, the practice is critical to the economy and has done so much to improve the standard of living in remote areas. It does make me feel prouder of my own knitting, to remember that."

Max nodded, casting on a few stitches with the long tail method. "It must be the most popular, widely practiced handcraft in the world. With the deepest history," he continued. "I believe archaeologists have even found knitted socks in the tombs of the ancient Egyptians."

So that's where all my lost socks ended up, Lucy nearly said aloud. But Dr. Max looked serious and so did everyone else.

He had a quixotic personality. Smiling and laughing one minute, solemn the next. Intense on both sides of the emotional coin, part of what made him so interesting to listen to, Lucy thought. An important ingredient of his charisma.

"I'd be hard pressed to think of a region in the world that doesn't practice some type of knitting tradition," he mused aloud.

"We have the perfect person here to answer that question, a travel writer. What do you think, Curtis?" Maggie glanced at the other side of the circle.

The writer ducked his head and dropped his knitting again. He retrieved it quickly and sat up, red faced. Curtis was shyer than he'd first seemed, Lucy realized. Or maybe he was having an attack of celebrity jitters, too? She noticed that his iPhone had slipped under his knitting instructions now. She hoped he didn't leave it behind by accident.

"They don't let me out of the office much," Curtis said finally. "You'd be surprised. 'You don't have to go all the way to Tahiti to write about it.' my editor tells me. 'Just hop around on the Internet. It's cheaper and faster.'"

His reply drew a laugh, including Dr. Max, who had a big, deep laugh that was contagious.

Dr. Max had cast on a few more stitches and started to knit.

"That is ironic. Has the Internet made travel for travel writers obsolete now, too?" Max's observation drew another appreciative chuckle. "Well, as we were saying, you could even think of knitting as a universal language. What could be simpler—making knots with some sticks and string? It's a perfect practice to cultivate mindfulness and a peaceful heart. And a way to share your creative efforts with the world."

"A universal language. That's a strong concept. I like it." Helen Lynch paused just a moment to voice her approval, then returned to her handiwork, which so far consisted of poking one needle into the cast-on stitches, trying to work her way into her very tight loops. Lucy wondered if she should offer more help.

Nadine Gould suddenly appeared, alongside another woman. Lucy recognized Nadine's companion immediately. The same small, thin blonde who'd been arguing in the lobby alcove a little while ago.

The two women stood silently behind Max's chair, like female sentinels.

After a moment, Nadine stepped forward and touched Maggie's shoulder.

"Maggie, I don't believe you've met my sister, Alice Archer."

That made sense, Lucy thought. The women did look alike. But while Nadine had darker hair and an arty wardrobe, her sister Alice was the complete opposite, dressed for the corner office, in her conservatively cut suit, silk blouse, and pearl earrings.

Maggie put her knitting down and stood up, then shook hands with Alice. "Nice to meet you. Nadine has told me so much about you. We're grateful you could come on such short notice," Alice said politely.

While her words were gracious, her facial expression did not quite match the warm message. Her gaze darted around, watchful and even nervous. Well, she had a lot of responsibility as manager of the inn. It seemed obvious that Max was the talent while she ran the show.

"Thanks for inviting me. Would you like to try some random knitting?" Maggie offered her own seat, next to Max, and he finally looked up.

"Looks like fun. But I'm afraid I don't have time right now," she demurred.

"Having fun, Max?" Alice rested her hand lightly on Max's shoulder and finally drew his attention. The touch was brief, but the gesture spoke volumes.

"Yes, I am, Alice." Max looked out at the guests in the knitting circle. His smile was mischievous, like a boy who's been caught cutting class. "We're all having fun. That's what we're here for. On this earthly plane, I mean," he clarified.

"Some of us. No question about that," Alice replied. She was smiling on the surface, Lucy noticed, though the smile didn't quite reach her small blue eyes.

Max looked down at his random knitting again, but not before stealing a little eye contact with Shannon Piper.

Isn't Mommy a big meanie? She spoils all the fun, his secret glance seemed to say.

Alice leaned over, quickly whispered in Max's ear, then stepped back into sentry position again. He didn't turn his head, or acknowledge her in any way. He continued to knit, smiling pleasantly at the guests.

"Oh, here comes tea," Nadine announced brightly.

Two uniformed bellman rolled a silver tea service toward the hearth, along with a cart of miniature pastries and tiny sandwiches on a tiered serving dish. The delicacies would all be healthy, Lucy knew. But it did look delicious.

"Time for a break," Maggie announced. The guests put down their projects and wandered over to the tea cart.

Rita put her project in her knitting bag and strolled over to Maggie. "Thank you for the workshop, Maggie. It was very enjoyable. I'm sorry if my husband was a little cranky. He's not well and he tires easily," she added in a confidential tone. She shook her head. "We're going back to our room to rest now."

"That's all right. Thank you for taking part. Have a good evening," Maggie replied cordially.

Lucy watched the Schumachers shuffle off, hand in hand. But not before Rita meandered past the tea cart, where she wrapped some goodies in a paper napkin and stashed the packet in her knitting bag.

Curtis Hill stood up, fumbling with his schedule, iPhone, and knitting project. His knitting dropped on the floor again and he finally handed it over to Lucy. "Interesting, but I guess I'll just turn this stuff in."

"That's okay. I don't think random knitting is for every-body," Lucy said honestly. She set the needles and yarn down on the table, with Maggie's supplies.

When she looked, Curtis was taking more photos with his phone. Or was it a video? He seemed to be slowly scanning the room. "Amazing decor. It will be hard to do this place justice." He glanced over at Lucy and smiled.

Lucy couldn't have agreed more. "I like the way they've blended antiques with . . . Zen, I guess you'd have to say. That bonsai tree on the West Lake table, for example," she noted.

"Oh, yes . . . very interesting." Curtis swung his phone around. But he wasn't panning over to the bonsai tree, Lucy noticed. He was focusing on Dr. Max, who still stood talking to Maggie.

Dr. Max must have felt someone looking at him and suddenly turned. He looked surprised to find he was being photographed so candidly. Caught off guard.

Curtis smiled and put the camera phone away. "Just some shots of the lobby for my article. Thanks . . . I'll catch you later," he murmured and quickly walked away.

Lucy watched him for a moment, his head ducked down now like a turtle as he scurried across the lobby. People often said writers were odd ducks, a cliché that seemed unfair. But she'd worked with a lot of them and most of the time, the cliché held true.

"Excellent workshop," Lucy heard Dr. Max congratulate Maggie as he folded up his project, yarn and all, and stuck it in his jacket pocket. "I'm going to keep my project and work on it more when I have a chance. I'll catch up with your later in the weekend, okay? I'll show you my progress," he promised.

"Please do. Thanks for joining in. Your visit made it extra-special for the guests."

Max offered a charming smile. "You're very kind."

"Enjoy your tea, ladies," Alice said brightly. She touched Max's arm, guiding him away from the group. "Max has to get ready for the retreat tonight. He needs some rest. "He'd go twenty-four/seven if we didn't keep an eye on him. We have to watch that his chi doesn't get depleted," she added in serious tone.

Max and Alice headed off, with Nadine trotting close behind.

By "we" Alice had meant herself, Lucy translated. And by "chi" . . . well, Lucy knew that was a new age term for the life force. But it was more likely Alice meant Max had an easily tempted life force. This was a busy place, and ninety-nine percent of the guests were attractive women dressed in spandex. The good doctor was only human.

A "chi" problem could definitely tire a guy out and do some serious damage to Dr. Max's credibility. And when he was just getting some momentum, too. Moving into the big leagues. Alice seemed to be the self-appointed sentry at that gate, too.

Max acted like a naughty boy who had to be reined in, but like most men, he probably enjoyed the mothering, Lucy thought. He rebelled a bit, but that was part of the dance.

"Every pot has a lid," Maggie always said. "Even the bent one."

"That went pretty well, I thought." Maggie gathered up some stray balls of yarn and put them back in the basket.

"Yes, it did," Lucy agreed. "Do you think any of them will come back after tea?"

"I'm not sure. I think a few people might be going on that 'moonlight meditation' trip," Maggie replied.

"I wonder what time it starts."

"Are you thinking of going?" Maggie sounded surprised.

"I wasn't at first, but it might be interesting." Lucy had left her schedule at the cottage, but it wasn't hard to find a copy. The spa was littered with them. She looked down at the coffee table and found one among Maggie's handouts.

"Let's see . . . here it is. Meet in the lobby at five o'clock.

Wear warm clothing and shoes suitable for hiking," she read aloud. "Transport will be provided for those who prefer not to hike. Please see the front desk."

"That covers the dress code. But what do you actually do up there?" Maggie asked as she searched the couch cushions for stray needles.

"I'm not sure. I have to find the description . . ." As Lucy turned the sheet, looking for the event description, she saw Phoebe coming back from the tea cart, alongside Dana.

Dana was dressed in her yoga clothes and looked like she'd just had a fitness class. Her expression looked cheerful and relaxed, her hairline damp and upswept hairstyle just a little askew.

"Hi, guys. How was the workshop?"

"It went well. But we had a surprise guest star. Dr. Max. He sort of upstaged me," Maggie admitted. "But everyone was riveted. I'm not even sure they really knew what we were supposed to be doing."

"Of course they did. You explained it very well," Lucy corrected her. "But Dr. Max did steal the show."

"Wow . . . must be your lucky day, Maggie. I'll bet the rest of the instructors are green with envy when they hear Dr. Max crashed your session," Dana said.

"Oh, I have a feeling he likes to spread the joy." Maggie's tone was a bit sarcastic.

"The guy's just brimming with bonhomie," Lucy agreed.

"Brimming with what?" Phoebe looked up and squinted at Lucy. She'd just sat down to enjoy a plate full of tiny sandwiches, miniature pastries, and a cup of tea.

"Bonhomie . . . it means friendliness, amiability," Maggie explained.

"Oh . . . I thought you said . . . never mind." Phoebe lost interest in the conversation and returned to her snack.

"Gee, sorry I missed it. I would have loved to have seen him in action, up close and personal." Dana had also taken a cup of tea from the cart and a plate filled with fruit and one lonely-looking, nut-covered cookie. She sat down on a love seat and took a sip from her china cup.

"He's leading the retreat on the mountain tonight. We can probably still sign up. Want to try it?" Lucy sat down next to Dana and gave her a look.

Dana looked surprised, but considered the idea.

"Wait . . . I'll read the description." Lucy had finally found the event description on the back of the schedule and began to read it aloud.

"'Moonlight meditation retreat . . . the tides know it. The winds know it. Your intuitive self knows it—the majesty and power of the moon. Experience the mystical beauty and force of Sister Moon as . . .'"

"Sister Moon?" Phoebe sat back and blinked. "Whose sister is she? My sister?"

"The Earth, silly," Maggie said. "I *think* they mean the Earth," she added, sounding a bit less certain of her interpretation.

"Who cares. Go on, Lucy. This is getting good," Dana prompted

"Let's see . . . where was I? Oh, right. 'Sister Moon, an iconic symbol in art, myth, and worship for all times. Cleanse and recharge the spirit as you tap into the transformative energy of this mystical cosmic body.

"'Participants will hike to a safe, secluded campsite on Mount Wheaton. We will join in chants and drumming rituals around the campfire and a guided meditation. Campers will retire to their solo huts for the night and share morning refreshment, at daybreak before hiking back to the inn. A truly unforgettable experience. Sleeping bags and boxed meals are provided. Sign up at the front desk.'"

Lucy took a deep breath and looked up at her friends. "Well, I'm game. Can't say that I've ever willingly plugged into any cosmic energy. Though I have gotten silverware stuck in the toaster by accident a few times."

"I hope it feels better than that. I was thinking it might put a little curl in my hair," Dana said.

"Does that mean you'll go with me?" Lucy smiled at her.

"I guess so. If I can bring my knitting and a flashlight."

"I know you've always envied my curls, Dana. But I thought you were offended by all this metaphysical nonsense," Maggie said.

"I was a little cranky after the car ride. Low blood sugar, maybe. I lost my perspective. But some of my patients take this stuff seriously. I think I should learn more about it. It's the perfect opportunity. Besides, I might even get a paper or article out of this trip, if I take some notes."

"I see. So you're on a covert mission. Is that it?" Maggie sat down in an armchair with a basket in her lap and sifted through the balls of yarn, winding up loose ends.

"Not quite. I have no problems with the meditation. The practice has undeniable benefits. I meditate myself at times. As for the rest . . . let's just say, I reserve the right to a healthy skepticism. If I get a cosmic power surge, I'll let you know."

"Oh, I expect you both to come back tomorrow morning, positively glowing. Like little fireflies," Maggie predicted.

"Why don't you come, too? We should all go." Lucy hadn't been camping in years and was excited about the idea.

"I'm staying at the cottage, thank you very much." Phoebe selected another miniature sandwich from her plate and picked off a bit of garnish from the top. "My folks dragged us to some buggy lake every summer. That was more than enough camping for me. Why sleep out in the woods when you have a perfectly nice bed in a real building?"

"I thought you wanted to sleep out on the porch?" Maggie reminded her in a teasing tone.

"You know I was just joking about that," Phoebe replied. "It would still be a heck of lot better than camping."

Lucy laughed at her reaction. "I love sleeping outside. Even a hut will be fun. That's the main reason I'm going. There are no wild animals around here, Phoebe. Well, nothing too ferocious," Lucy amended, thinking of the brazen racoons and a ubiquitous skunk or two. "It could get chilly, though."

"I think we only have enough warm clothing for two crazy people to sleep out tonight," Maggie said decidedly. "We'll have to pool our things together just to outfit both of you."

"We will represent the group bravely," Dana promised.

"I'm sure you'll do us proud," Maggie replied. "But if anything happens, please don't ask us to come pick you up in the middle of the night."

Chapter Four

*D*id you remember that little folding umbrella . . . and the extra socks?"

Suzanne, Maggie, and Phoebe had walked over to the inn with Lucy and Dana and waited with them for the retreat to start.

Dana laughed. "For goodness' sake, Suzanne. I feel like you're sending me off to summer camp."

"Did you bring your knitting? That's more important," Maggie cut in. "It might get boring up there. I mean, after the moon-gazing thing."

Lucy patted her back pack. "I brought my random knitting piece from this afternoon. I hardly got it started. Do you think the huts have lights?"

"We can manage with flashlights, don't worry." Dana suddenly looked across the lobby. Something had caught her attention. "Oh, look . . . I think Nadine is rounding everyone up."

Lucy followed her gaze and saw Maggie's friend Nadine, standing in the midst of a large group of guests with her clipboard. Lucy was sure they were the retreat group. Everyone was dressed in windbreakers and fleece vests and a few had hats and gloves. Luckily the knitting group had brought along so many of their own creations. Lucy and Dana were both dressed in borrowed layers, sweaters made by their friends. Lucy also had Phoebe's poncho stashed in her backpack.

Dana picked up her canvas tote. "We'd better get over there and check in. I bet this trip has a standby list."

Lucy grabbed her small pack. "I guess this is it, guys. If anything happens to me, Phoebe . . . you take care of Tink, okay?"

Phoebe had a special relationship with Lucy's dog. They seemed to speak a secret language.

"Lucy . . . don't even say that." Phoebe seemed genuinely shocked. "But you know I would."

"Now, now. Let's not get silly. You two run along." Maggie shooed them off. "Play nice with the other children and don't wake us up too early when you come in tomorrow morning."

Dana and Lucy walked over to join the group and stood at the outer edge of the circle. Nadine was front and center, calling names off a clipboard.

Lucy looked around for familiar faces and saw a few guests who had been at Maggie's workshop—Shannon Piper, Helen Lynch, and Curtis Hill. As for the Schumachers, she wasn't surprised that they had skipped the excursion. They were well past the age for camping on mountaintops. Just as well, since Rita's inane chatter would have pretty much ruined the cosmic mood.

Nadine, who was giving out flashlights to the group, was not dressed for the trip herself, Lucy noticed. The sleeping bags and other supplies were already up at the campsite, she told everyone as she strolled among the group.

Curtis Hill stepped over and smiled, greeting them in his shy, awkward way. He was wearing a tan utility jacket and a black baseball cap.

"Headed up the mountain tonight, ladies?"

"Yes, we are. Do you know how far the campsite is?" Lucy asked him.

"I'm not sure. I think the hike takes about an hour. We should make it before sunset."

"That's good. I don't want to be walking around the woods in the dark," Dana told him.

"Oh, I think it will get interesting enough up there, once the sun goes down, without getting lost in the woods," Curtis replied with a little laugh.

Then he suddenly seemed to remember himself and forced a placid expression. He didn't seem that serious about the outing, Lucy noticed. He seemed to share her own attitude, and Dana's, curious about it, but not a true believer. The thought made Lucy feel more comfortable around him. He was one of their kind, a curious skeptic.

"Where's Dr. Max? Don't tell me he's a no-show," Dana said quietly.

"Oh, I hope he doesn't bail out on us. What would be the point?" Curtis asked, looking around.

"Maybe he's still resting his chi?" Lucy offered.

"His what?" Dana gave her a look.

"Oh, that's right. You weren't there . . . forget it."

Before Lucy could even start to explain, Dr. Max appeared, entering through a set of French doors that opened to a stone terrace behind the inn. Lucy heard a hush fall upon the group, then a flurry of excited whispers.

"Here he comes. Making his entrance. Our fears were

needless, ladies," Curtis quietly quipped, making Lucy and Dana smile.

Alice Archer slipped in behind him. Still dressed in her navy suit and heels, she was obviously not joining the hike.

Max, on the other hand, looked like a page from an L.L.Bean catalog in a khaki green military-style vest, heavy-gauge sweater, and tan cargo pants with serious-looking hiking boots laced up over the cuffs.

His hair was pulled back in a short ponytail, tied with a leather lace, a style which Lucy thought looked ridiculous on men over twenty years of age . . . with the sole exception of Willie Nelson.

Max wasn't carrying a pack, only a long, exotic-looking drum, which appeared to be made from a hollowed-out section of a slim tree trunk. Two drumsticks were stuck in weaving around the drum skin and a thick leather strap was slung over his shoulder.

"Good evening, friends. I'm here to guide all who have answered the challenge tonight. The call of the shimmering moon. Or rather, those who have allowed your instincts, your very primal core, to answer the call and follow me. Up that mountain and into the night and through the wilderness of your own soul."

He paused and slowly looked around the group, meeting each searching gaze with steady, dark eyes and a calm, self-possessed expression.

"If there's anyone here who would prefer to remain at the inn, please, honor where you are now. There's no shame in expressing authentic feeling," he reminded them.

Lucy liked that line. She made a note to remember it.

He paused again, waiting. When no one signaled they

were chickening out, he nodded. "All right. Let's begin our journey, from this threshold, through the long night and into the dawn. I will guide you safely," he promised.

The herd of campers began to move, following Dr. Max out of the hotel from the door where he'd entered.

"So, that wasn't just marketing copy," Lucy whispered to Dana. "He takes this very seriously. Is he really going to beat a drum and chant in the moonlight?"

"So are we," Dana reminded her. "Isn't that part of the program?"

Lucy picked up her pack. "Okay. Let's make a deal. What happens on that mountain, stays on that mountain."

Dana nodded in agreement. "Don't worry, pal. I hear you."

"I hope they're okay up there." Suzanne glanced at Maggie, seated across the table in the hotel dining room. Their waitress had cleared away the dinner dishes and was now serving dessert. She set a cup of organic ginger tea at Suzanne's place and one at Maggie's. "Maybe we should send a short text, just to see how it's going?"

"Don't worry, those women are troopers. I'm sure they're fine. Besides, we don't want to interrupt any mystical moments. I really didn't feel like camping tonight. But I'll be interested to hear what goes on."

"Yeah, I'll wait for the video on that one," Phoebe said. "The beds in the cottage look comfortable and too good to pass up."

"The mattresses are primo," Suzanne promised. "Some sort of super-body-supporting foam. I took a nap after my spa treatment and thought I was sleeping on a cloud. Being pummeled, polished, and pampered all day was exhausting," she added.

Maggie took a spoonful of her dessert, a cup of Greek yogurt with chopped almonds and berries drizzled with honey. "That's a good sign. It means that you're relaxing."

"Any more relaxed, and I'll fall into my mango sorbet." Suzanne took another bite of her dessert and yawned. "Guess I'll just head back to the cottage."

"I'll go back with you." Phoebe checked her big pink Hello Kitty wristwatch. "I have to check in with Josh. He should be setting up the equipment just about now."

"I'm sure he misses you. And notices now how much you help him," Suzanne told her.

"Being a total guy, I think not. But he can't help that. It's the Y chromosome problem," Phoebe countered with a shrug.

"Same with Kevin. I've spoken to him about three times today," Suzanne admitted.

"Is anything wrong?" Maggie asked quickly.

"Nope, they're doing just fine without me." Suzanne seemed surprised and even a little disappointed, Maggie noticed.

"Don't worry, Suzanne. I'm sure some crisis will erupt before the weekend's over and they'll be frantic for your advice." Phoebe patted her hand.

Maggie nearly laughed. Then she noticed that Suzanne did look as if she hoped that would come to pass.

"Nothing too awful, of course," Suzanne said.

"What time is it anyway?" Maggie glanced at her watch, thinking it was easy to lose total track of time around here. Life was so laid-back. It was already past eight o'clock, she noticed.

"Oh dear, I almost forgot. I'm supposed to sit out in the lobby for a while tonight and do a knitting session. Good thing I have my bag with me."

"Go ahead. I'll take care of the check," Suzanne offered. "We can settle up later."

"Thanks. I think I'm already late. I hope no one is waiting." Maggie jumped up from the table and grabbed her things— her purse, knitting bag, and woolen wrap stole. Suzanne and Phoebe watched her go.

"Good luck. We'll leave a light in the window for you," Suzanne promised. "A scented candle, probably."

"Sounds about right. I won't be too late. See you later,"

Maggie wandered out to the lobby, looking for her station. She found a sign posting the evening schedule and paused to read it through.

There were a few other activities noted for Friday evening, in addition to the retreat and her drop-in knitting session. A workshop about reiki, summoning the healing energy in your hands and another called Write It, See It, Have It about achieving your goals through journal writing and visualization.

Maggie thought there might be an element of truth to the theory of positive thinking, particularly visualizing goals and positive outcomes. Many professional athletes trained that way, she'd heard. Though the most successful people she knew fit the words "hard work" into the formula somewhere. As in, "The harder I work, the luckier I get."

She couldn't sit in on any of these topics tonight, however tempting they sounded. She had her own little bailiwick to cover, and she noticed that Nadine had once again stationed her in front of the hearth, where she'd held the Random Knitting workshop in the afternoon.

Maggie hustled over to her spot. Someone—Nadine probably—had already set out the basket of supplies on the low table and arranged the couches and chairs in a circle. So far, there were no guests waiting to learn knitting basics. Maggie was half-relieved and half-disappointed.

She settled in a big armchair and took out her own project, a coat sweater that she was working on for her daughter, Julie, who went to college in Vermont and had just left for the start of her second year. Julie had been home most of the summer, and Maggie missed having her around. Knitting something for her helped Maggie feel a little closer to her only child. A little sense of connection every day.

Ever since her husband, Bill, had died several years back, the house had grown considerably quieter. Once Julie went off to school, it had gotten downright solitary. But her daughter's company had livened things up during the summer, and it had been hard for Maggie to settle back into her soup-for-one routine again.

An adjustment, Maggie reminded herself. That's what life seemed to be, a series of small adjustments. Just like knitting through a long pattern, like the coat sweater. Change was the only thing certain in life, despite all our careful plans and designs.

Maggie paused and looked around the lobby, wondering if she'd have any students tonight. The lobby looked empty. So many had gone on the retreat. She wondered what Lucy and Dana were doing up on the mountain right now and felt sure they would return with tales to tell.

Lucy kept reminding herself to breath deeply and focus on the image of the nearly full moon in her mind's eye. But her right foot seemed to be going numb and she squirmed on the low bench, the left side of her bottom getting sore from sitting in one position too long on the hard wooden plank.

You would think that there's enough padding down there to sit here all night without noticing, she thought.

She'd tried meditating before and knew it wasn't easy. But tonight her thoughts seemed to be jumping around like drops of water hitting a hot skillet.

She took another deep, supposedly calming breath, trying again to settle down. The cool night air carried the scent of pine and the big bonfire Max had made. There was also a hint of the smoldering bunches of sage he'd waved around the circle at the start of the session.

As it turned out, Max had more exotic equipment on hand than the wooden drum. There were bunches of sage incense and a large fan, made of swan feathers, he told them. There were also some tiny brass bells on a shaker stick. And this was all just part of the warm-up act.

"Ever notice that so many religious services include incense burning? We find it in churches, temples, and holy sites," he told the group. "Ever since man began to worship, perhaps as far back as the Stone Age, incense burning has been used to cleanse negative energy from the atmosphere. Incense burning has a very powerful effect. The smoke produced creates its own energy, a new morphogenic field . . ."

Lucy had no idea what a morphogenic field was. It had to be a good thing, though, right?

"The sage smudge ceremony cleanses the area of negative energies," he'd explained as he lit up the fist-size bunches of dried sage leaves. "Like spraying air freshener when you've cooked fish for dinner," he added, trying for a laugh.

Max let the sage bunches flare up for a moment, then snuffed the flames out so that the embers still burned and gave off a thick plume of sharp, sweet-smelling smoke. He first twirled the smoke around himself, starting as his feet and working his way up. He mumbled and chanted to himself.

It sounded like a prayer, but none that Lucy had ever heard. Something about being a "clear and perfect channel."

Then he put some ash on his fingers and rubbed it on his forehead, throat, chest, and even his feet. He swept the smoking wand of sage around the circle with one hand, fanning it with the long white feathers in the other, so that the retreat group, about fifteen total, Lucy gauged, were soon immersed in the cloud of sage smoke.

Lucy had stolen a quick peek at Dana, who was covering her mouth with her hand and softly coughing. "I think Dr. Max was an exterminator in a past life," she whispered.

"I think so . . . and maybe I was a roach, with a spiritually curious nature," Dana whispered back.

Max stood in the center of the circle again, silhouetted by the fire. He threw his head back and spoke to the starry sky in a deep, sonorous tone. "Spirit guides, please bless and purify this space. Please bless and support our efforts here tonight and unite our inner light with the pure light of universal love . . ."

Lucy thought that had to be the end of the show, but it was only the curtain closer on act one. He put the sage wands aside and took up the drum. As she had imagined, there was some dancing around the circle, in a vaguely Native American step. He shook the small, tinkling brass bells over everyone's head, again trying to clear those pesky negative energies.

Then there was some more chanting and even a howl or two.

Finally, they were ready to begin the guided meditation on the moon, which was now about halfway through its ascent in the night sky.

The instructions were simple, nothing Lucy had not heard before—relax the body, take deep slow breaths, clear the mind of random thoughts, and focus on a single image. The glowing moon, of course and all it symbolized.

"Purity, cleansing light, creative powers. The very mystery of life and the portal to the spirit," Max told them.

Lucy tried hard to follow the instructions, but this was a lot to think about at once, especially if you were supposed to have a clear, tranquil mind and not really be thinking at all.

The instructions seemed contradictory, but she didn't have the nerve to raise her hand and ask that question.

She sat there, trying hard to stop thinking about a million and one things going on in her life that didn't have anything to do with the moon. Her problems with Matt. The deadline on her current project and the invoices the company had not paid on yet and the bills she had to pay. And she really needed to use the Porta-Potty and hoped it wasn't too far away, in some spooky spot of the woods. And how long did they have to sit here like this anyway?

Was that an animal scurrying through the brush right behind them? Animals would be afraid of the campfire . . . wouldn't they?

"Relax . . . breathe . . . if your thoughts wander, return to the moon's powerful image. Let the moon's glow neutral- ize and dissolve all worries and negativity. Let yourself go deeper . . . and deeper," Max's hypnotizing voice urged them.

But instead of following Max's instructions, Lucy opened her eyes just a bit, peeking out at the rest of the group. It was hard to see clearly in the flickering firelight. The big bonfire had started out an impressive height but had burned down almost to the ground.

Max stood with his back toward her side of the circle, strolling around the fire as he spoke in low, solemn tones. From the corner of her eyes, she noticed a movement. Curtis Hill sat close by, in a perfect meditation posture, his head tipped back and eyes closed. Except for his iPhone, which was balanced on one knee. He was taking more photos, she realized. Or maybe even another video?

She turned for a better look, and somehow, he noticed. He slowly covered the phone with his hand and slipped it back up to his jacket pocket, all without moving any other muscle.

Max had turned to the far side of the circle and was coming around the bend again. Lucy closed her eyes and took a deep breath, trying hard to relax again, which she knew was not the right idea at all.

She wondered what she doing up here. And she suddenly wondered what Curtis Hill was doing, too.

Chapter Five

Sitting alone at her workshop station in the lobby, Maggie made some good progress with the coat sweater. She paused to look over her work and noticed a woman strolling through the groupings of love seats and potted palms, headed in her direction.

Was she coming to knit? Maggie hoped so. She was starting to feel she'd wasted her time here tonight and was just about to pack it in and join her friends back at the cottage.

"Are you Maggie Messina?" the woman greeted her with a shy smile as she came closer.

"Yes . . . I am." Maggie put her knitting down and turned to greet the tall, zaftig blonde.

"I'm Joy Kimmel. The yoga instructor. We're working together tomorrow on the Mindful Knitting workshop. Nadine thought we should meet and talk a little."

"Oh, yes . . . nice to meet you, Joy. Nadine told me the same. I'm glad you found me," Maggie said honestly.

Joy held out her hand and Maggie shook it, admiring the

row of bangles that briefly jingled. Joy smoothed her flowing, Indian-patterned skirt and took a seat.

Her smile was infectious. Maggie automatically smiled back. It felt good to see a real live hippie again, awakening memories of her own younger days. So many of those styles had come back, the kids calling it boho chic or something like that. Maggie had a feeling that the embroidered peasant shirts and long skirts had never left Joy Kimmel's closet.

Joy had a very full figure, large on top and wide hipped. The style gave her a real earth mother look, as if she had not so much grown older in the same clothing but simply . . . inflated?

"I'm excited to work with you on the workshop. I don't know much about knitting, though," Joy confessed.

"I know next to nothing about meditation. So I guess we're even," Maggie replied with a smile.

"What are you making?" Joy looked closer at Maggie's project.

"A coat sweater for my daughter. She's in college, but still e-mails in her orders," Maggie joked. "I'm supposed to be holding a 'drop by and try it' session tonight, knitting for beginners. But so far," Maggie added, peering around the lobby, "no one's dropped by."

"I'd like to try. It will help tomorrow if I've done a little knitting, don't you think?"

"Yes, it will," Maggie replied. She'd been wary about teaching with a stranger, but Joy's positive attitude was a pleasant surprise.

Maggie pulled out a few sets of needles. A big basket of yarn was on the low table. "I guess a simple project to start would be best. How about a bag for a yoga mat? I found an easy pattern last week online."

"I could use one of those. What should I do?"

Joy sat up straight, readying herself to knit. She folded one leg under her skirt and centered her body on the sofa. She was surprising supple for a large woman. But that was a benefit of all the yoga, Maggie thought. She was sexy too, in her way, her charms the antithesis of anorexic model types.

Her long, straight hair was parted in the middle, framing a moon-shaped face and clear blue eyes. She had smooth, clear skin and bravely wore no makeup, or none that Maggie could see. A few crow's-feet and laugh lines showed, but she was very youthful looking for her age, which Maggie guessed to be somewhere in her early fifties.

Maggie pulled out the patterns from a folder she'd prepared and Joy chose one she liked. Maggie set her up with large needles and yarn. Joy picked a thick, nubbly multicolored yarn that would give the bag a fiber art look.

Maggie showed her the basics—casting on, knit and purl stitches, and how to decipher the pattern.

"Don't worry about it being perfect," Maggie advised. "This pattern is practically foolproof and some imperfections and unevenness in the stitching will make the bag more interesting looking."

"Just like real life," Joy replied in a wistful tone, working her needles in a focused but unhurried way.

"Yes, knitting does imitate life, I've often noticed that." The two women laughed at Maggie's favorite knitting motto.

Joy had an easy, relaxed manner. Back in the days of peace, love, and music, some would have even called it "cosmic." Maggie wondered if it was her genuine personality. Or just another nostalgic accessory, like the hoop earrings and jangling bracelets.

"Do you teach here all the time?" Maggie asked to start off the conversation. "Or are you just a guest speaker for the weekend?"

"Pretty much full-time. I came on the staff when Max took over. We go way back." Joy glanced at her. "I'm his ex-wife. I guess you didn't know that."

The comment took Maggie by surprise. "No . . . I didn't. Is there some reason I should have?"

"I guess you haven't read his book." Joy swept her hair to one side with her hand. "I'm in there. In all my glory," she said with a laugh. "It could have been worse. He paints a pretty fair picture, all things considered."

Maggie didn't know what to say. "It sounds as if you two have a very amicable relationship."

"We do. We both believe there's nothing to be gained from bitterness and conflict. Putting out those feelings hurts you more than it hurts the intended target. It hurts the entire world, like emotional pollution. It's been scientifically proven." Joy sounded so sure of that fact, Maggie didn't bother to question her. "I don't see how people can ever expect world peace if they don't weed their own little row of the garden," Joy added.

Maggie couldn't argue with that, though she thought the issue was a bit more complicated.

"Max gets most of the credit. Not me," Joy added. "I didn't treat him very well when we were together. I was the typical, spoiled doctor's wife. Not that I looked much different than I do now. But inside." Joy tapped the spot between her breasts where her heart would be. "That's what really counts. My expectations and values. I was stuck on the material plane . . . and I didn't even realize it."

Joy's voice held a definite "Can you believe that?" tone.

"It can happen," Maggie said drily.

Joy had reached the end of a row and held out her knitting for Maggie to see. "Very nice," Maggie told her. She wasn't overpraising, either, the way she did with most beginners. Joy's stitches were very even and had just the right amount of tension. She was taking to the craft quickly.

"When Max hit his low point, I dumped him. I was so disappointed in the way our lives had turned out. But he forgave me. That's the greatest gift a person can give. Don't you think?"

"I do," Maggie agreed. Along with some good jewelry, she nearly added.

But that quip would have been too snide and Joy seemed so sincere.

"You can read about it in the book. If you want to." Joy shrugged. "Now that he's done so well, people assume I feel shortchanged, or want him back. But I don't look at things that way. That's been his path and I have my own." She nodded to herself. "He's been very generous, offering me this job at the spa, for instance. He didn't have to do that."

"Of course not." Though Maggie was sure that Joy's salary as a yoga teacher was quite modest, while her ex-husband was now a multimillionaire. But Joy seemed content and thankful for her lot, seeing her glass more than half-full.

"That's the way Max is. Forgiving. Inclusive. All about connection. He answers negativity with love. He reaches out to heal the riffs and the wounds. Not just with me. Look at the way he's helped Alice Archer and her son, Brian."

"Alice Archer? She's known Max a long time, too?"

Once again, Maggie couldn't hide her surprise. But that

made sense, she thought. There seemed to be some deeper connection between Max and the hotel manager, more than a business relationship.

Joy stopped knitting again and smiled at Maggie from under her veil of fair silky hair.

"Alice's late husband, Edward Archer, was Max's partner way back when. Max's best friend, too. We were a cozy little foursome for a while, typical suburban couples, enjoying our upper-middle-class life. Until it all crashed and burned. It seemed like a disaster at the time. But I see it now as a great opportunity. A chance to start over for everyone," Joy insisted, looking up at Maggie again. "I've learned so much from that experience and grown immensely. And Max . . . well, he's the real success story. Max has taken care of all of us. He wouldn't be happy otherwise."

It seemed to Maggie from the very little she'd observed so far that the caretaking worked both ways in the connection between Max and Alice. Alice seemed to be toting her fair share of the load around here, too.

"How old is Alice's son?" Maggie asked curiously. "Is he in the book, as well?"

"Max mentions him once or twice, I think. Brian was only ten or eleven when Edward died. He's in his early twenties now. He started college, but that didn't work out," she added, leaving Maggie to guess why not. "He works at the inn, doing maintenance mostly. Brian is very handy. He can fix anything," Joy said brightly.

Maggie felt certain that working as a handyman in a hotel, even at this fancy inn, was not what the Archers had envisioned for their son, no matter how handy he was.

"Well, you can read the book. I'm sorry to go on about the

past. There's no point. We only have this moment. That's what meditation teaches you. Be here now. The future hasn't happened yet and the past is gone, like water moving down the river. No sense dwelling. It's a waste of precious time."

Maggie, who had known her share of sorrow, didn't believe in wallowing in tide pools of memory, either. She tried to enjoy life as it came, aware and thankful for the small, everyday pleasures. But she also believed in reflection, in a self-examined life. Wasn't that practice also a viable path?

It had been said that those who cannot remember the past are doomed to repeat it. But it was getting too late for a philosophical debate.

"Alice seems to take her job very seriously," Maggie commented after a moment. "Nadine tells me she has a lot of responsibility here."

"She does. But her caretaking can be smothering." Joy had come to the end of another row. "She doesn't understand the flow of relationships. The energy. Everything is so cut and dry to her. She talks a good game, but . . . I'm sorry to say this. I don't mean it as a criticism. Just an observation."

Maggie looked up, wondering what slanderous criticism was about to come down on poor Alice Archer now.

"Poor Alice. She doesn't quite get it." Joy sighed again, the sound indicating either sympathy or frustration, Maggie wasn't quite sure. "Max has never been very organized or a numbers sort of person. That's her strong suit, though. She's very left brained. She ran the practice when Edward was alive. It's only logical that Max would ask her to help him run this place now."

"Yes, that makes sense," Maggie agreed, though she did wonder why Max would rely so much on a woman who had no experience in hotel operations. Running a medical office was one thing, but this inn and spa were quite another. There seemed to be some other reason, beyond Alice's left-brained tendencies.

"She's a great help to him. No one would deny that. But Alice's help comes at a high price," Joy added. "She smothers him. He isn't used to that. You can't possess another person. Or force them to love you by controlling them. That's probably the fastest way to make someone fall out of love, don't you think?"

"Well, it might be," Maggie tentatively agreed, though the terms "commitment" and "fidelity" had to fit into the picture somewhere, Maggie reflected. Weren't they just talking about Alice's role in Max's business? How had they gotten on to this subject?

Joy continued on, in her rambling way, before Maggie could ask any questions.

"If your horse runs off and doesn't return, maybe he's not your horse, right?" Joy looked up from her knitting and smiled.

"Sounds familiar. Is that the moral to a folk tale?"

"Good guess. It's in the *I Ching*. The Book of Changes," Joy replied. She paused to check her slow, even stitches.

"I've heard of that. It's some Chinese fortune-telling thing, isn't it? You toss up coins, see how they land?"

Joy looked mildly amused by her answer. "That's part of it. It's really a book of philosophy, a system for understanding the laws that govern the universe. The balance of opposite forces and the laws of change. Ever-constant change," she noted. "I'm giving an *I Ching* workshop on Sunday. You should come, if you're free."

"Oh, it's sounds a little complicated for me. I don't even

check my horoscope in the newspaper," Maggie replied honestly.

Maggie didn't feel comfortable on the topic of consulting oracles or, for that matter, gossiping about all the people who ran the hotel. Even if Max Flemming *had* hung out his dirty laundry for all the world to read.

Joy seemed to sense Maggie's dismay or perhaps just noticed that she was suddenly quiet.

"I'm sorry I got into all this past history. I'm not usually like that. It's hard to talk about Max or his book without giving the whole picture, especially since I'm part of the story."

"I understand," Maggie said evenly. She was beginning to see that despite her laid-back, hippie-girl manner, Joy enjoyed her status as Max's ex-wife. The celebrity factor had rubbed off on her and not in a very flattering way. More like bits of shredded tissue in the clothes dryer.

"The point about Max—and his story—is very simple, really. Love is healing. Love is the key. The most important thing you can do in your life is to love and connect with other people. It's so . . . simple, but profound." Joy sighed and Maggie nodded in answer.

No arguing with that insight. But hadn't a few other people hit on that philosophy before Max Flemming got there?

"Max and I still love each other. On a certain plane. Some people don't get it. They feel so threatened," she added and Maggie had a good idea who she was talking about. "But we're just trying to get it right this time and finish our soul business."

Maggie guessed that Joy was talking about past lives and reincarnation now. Golly, the woman did jump around the cosmic grocery store, tossing everything into her cart, didn't she? Maggie didn't want to get into that conversation, either.

"Just read his book," Joy urged her. "It's terrific. It's trans-forming. Honestly. They sell it in the hotel gift shop," she added. "They also sell his CD set there."

He had a CD set, too? Maggie could only imagine what that was like. She didn't want to ask Joy, either. The woman had the potential of transforming into a walking infomercial.

"I do have a copy of the book and I brought it along," Maggie assured Joy. "I haven't had a chance to start it yet. But I intend to."

Especially after this introduction, Maggie silently added.

The two women parted a short time later. Joy thanked Maggie profusely for the knitting lesson. She seemed very proud and excited about her progress on the bag and promised to continue until it was completed. Maggie also promised to try some meditation on her own, and to tell Joy how she did.

After Joy's long session of disclosures, Maggie felt she really did need to clear her mind before returning to the cottage.

Toting her purse and knitting bag, she stepped outside to the stone terrace that fronted the lake. The area near the inn was illuminated with outdoor spotlights and Maggie noticed that the path to the cottage was lit, too.

It was a clear night and, as they'd all expected, the temperature had dropped. She cuddled into her thick, warm wrap and pulled it up higher and around her neck.

If the nip in the mountain air was not enough of a reminder that fall was here, the glowing moon—what some people would call a harvest moon—confirmed the season's change.

The sight was mesmerizing, Maggie thought. Certainly worthy of contemplation, even if she hadn't hiked to a mountaintop. She strolled along the lakeshore for a few moments, then sat on a bench and stared up at the black, star-studded sky, wondering what Dana and Lucy were doing right now. Were they getting a dose of the sort of cosmic conversation she's just had with Joy?

She wondered if the guests were free to come down if they felt uncomfortable or unhappy. They had to be, she reasoned. The inn seemed determined to keep their clientele happy.

Though it would be hard to find your way down in the dark. Very hard on foot and even difficult in a golf cart. It would really have to be an emergency, she reasoned. She wasn't sure why her mind had gone off on that tangent. Just silly anxiety.

Better to take a page from Joy's book and "be here now."

In this supernaturally beautiful setting, the lake was as still as a mirror with the moon and starlit sky above. Even the air seemed different up here, fresh and pure, the scent of the woods and lake mixing all together. Maggie took a few, deep calming breaths.

But just as she closed her eyes, she heard the sound of rustling leaves nearby. The sound of something moving through the woods. An animal probably . . . but it would have to be a big one to make such a racket, she reasoned. She glanced at the path that led to the cottage, but didn't see anyone there.

Suddenly Maggie caught sight of a thin beam of light darting around the treetops on the path that led away from the lake and up the mountain. The light disappeared so quickly, she wondered if she had imagined it. But she could still hear the rustle of leaves and cracking branches. She sat very still, watching the mountain, and saw the light once more for a single instant and the outline of a figure moving along in the night.

Then the light went out again and all she could see were the shadows of tall trees and brush on the dark mountainside.

Who would be walking in the woods at this hour? It was after 11:00, she noticed, checking her watch. She'd spent much longer in the lobby with Joy than she'd intended.

Maybe there's a security guard who patrols the grounds, Maggie thought. Or maybe a staff member is bringing Dr. Max some forgotten necessity?

It was a beautiful night. Some adventurous visitor might have decided to go out for a stroll. There were no rules against roaming the grounds after dark, not that Maggie had noticed. The guests at this place did seem blessed with more than the average quotient of adventurous spirit.

Case in point, she was sitting here right now, gazing at the moon and she wasn't even a true believer.

The mood was infectious, Maggie decided. The philosophies and optimistic mind-set here did push some buttons and tapped into the spiritual hunger that dwelled dormant within most people.

The promises of self-improvement and enlightenment were seductive. A quick fix to all of life's problems. If you could accept the wild theories and assumptions without questioning too much.

And if you were willing to listen faithfully to Dr. Max's CD set, available in the hotel gift shop—or online, for three easy payments, she guessed. Maggie smiled to herself and looked up at the glowing moon again. Its mysterious face seemed to be laughing silently along with her.

"Dana . . . are you awake? It's me." Lucy whispered against the door of Dana's hut. She could see a faint strip of light at the bottom of the frame and hoped Dana wasn't asleep yet.

Dana quickly came to the door and opened it. "Hey . . . are you okay?"

"I couldn't sleep. I think that sage smoke gave me a head-ache."

"I can't sleep, either. Come on in," Dana whispered back, quickly ushering Lucy into her hut. "Why don't we bunk together. I don't give an organic fig about Max's rules," she added. "Did you bring your sleeping bag?"

"I was hoping you'd say that. I left it right outside. Let me grab it before someone notices."

Max had made it clear at the end of the meditation session that everyone was to go directly to their hut and remain in seclusion and contemplative silence until daybreak. Lucy wondered if the vow of silence included snoring, which she'd heard of lot of on the way to Dana's hut.

The huts were scattered on both sides of the campfire area, in a random pattern, but all were about fifteen to twenty feet apart. The retreat group had chosen their huts while it was still light outside, before their boxed meal was served.

Lucy and Dana had picked neighboring shelters. But owing to Max's solemn instructions and the darkness, when the group had finally split up and headed for their separate quarters, Lucy had to make a conscious effort to remember which hut Dana had disappeared into after the meditation. She'd even been worried that she'd knocked on the wrong door. The structures were as identical as cheap Florida condos.

Although the huts had a rustic look, they appeared to be fairly new and tightly constructed. Each had a door in front and a small, glass-framed window on one side. The space inside was very narrow, just about double the width of the cot that sat pushed up against one wall. A small space heater stood next to the wall opposite the door. Lucy couldn't imagine coming up here in the heart of winter, but perhaps people did brave the elements for Dr. Max.

Once Lucy came back in, Dana had to sit on the cot to make room for her.

"This hut reminds me of a room I rented on my first trip to Paris. I think the hut is actually bigger," Dana added, looking around. "You didn't ask anyone back for coffee if you didn't really, really like them."

"Well, I'm glad you like me." Lucy tossed the sleeping bag on the floor and sat down. "I can't understand it. I usually have the best sleep of my life on a camping trip."

"This isn't exactly an average camping trip." Dana sat back against the wall, cross-legged on the cot, which was covered by her sleeping bag. "All that chanting and howling was starting to creep me out a little."

"Me, too," Lucy admitted. "I mean, it would have even seemed strange in broad daylight, but when someone is dancing around a bonfire in the middle of the dark woods . . . with ashes smeared all over his face."

"It was a little bizarre," Dana finished for her.

"Were you able to meditate?" Lucy looked up at her. "I didn't get very far."

"Neither did I. I do it all the time in yoga class. I think all the drama undermines the actual point of coming up here. Unless the theatrics are the real point?" she added. "But it looked like a lot of people around that circle were really swept up in the show—the incense and feathers . . . and the little tinkling bells on the stick."

"I liked the bells. They would make a nice mobile, on the porch or something." She'd also noticed that some in the audience were actually mesmerized. Shannon Piper and Helen Lynch, in particular, who were both sitting nearby.

"My mind was wandering too much to get anything out of it," Lucy added. "I was thinking about Matt a lot, I guess," she admitted with a sigh.

Dana gave her a sympathetic look. "Want to talk about it?"

Lucy met her glance, then looked away. "I don't want to bore you with more drama."

"Never, Lucy . . . don't be silly," Dana scolded her. She patted one end of the cot. "Come on up, there's room. Tell me all about it. The doctor is in for you," she joked in a friendly tone.

Lucy stood up and settled on the opposite end of the cot. Dana was a good listener and always gave such sound, sane advice. She practically felt relieved before saying a word.

They were staying up like middle graders at a sleepover party—talking about boys, of course—Lucy realized. They'd both feel pretty beat tomorrow. But at least there would be some upside to this zany campout.

Chapter Six

Something was wrong. An emergency. Lucy heard a siren. Off in the distance. Coming closer . . .

She tossed around in her sleeping bag, like a big fish caught in a net, fighting her way free of the clinging fabric. The air in the hut had become very close during the night and sleeping on the musty floor had made Lucy's head even stuffier.

She sat up and listened, trying to get a good breath.

Yes, there was a siren in the woods somewhere, coming up the mountain toward the campsite.

She stumbled up to her knees and shook Dana's shoulder. Her friend was still sound asleep on the cot.

"Dana . . . get up. Something's going on."

Dana groaned and rolled to her side, facing the wall.

By the time they'd finally shut the flashlight and gone to sleep it was after 2:00 a.m. Lucy glanced at her watch. It was half past six; four hours of sleep wasn't much. No wonder Dana didn't want to wake up.

Lucy stood up and peered through the small, smudged window. Pale, cool light illuminated the scene outdoors. She saw a few people milling around the campfire area and then noticed that some wore police uniforms. She saw two police cars parked near the edge of the woods, too.

She recognized Max, talking to two officers. He wore a hooded sweatshirt this morning, his long white hair hanging loose and uncombed around his stubble-covered face. Even from the distance, he looked haggard and older.

Suddenly, an ambulance rolled out of an opening in the woods, a narrow road snaking up the mountain that Lucy had noticed last night. Part of the road ran parallel to the footpath the hikers had taken. At one point, she'd seen some hotel employees fly by in a golf cart, loaded with sleeping bags and the boxed meals. At the time, she'd felt relieved to know there was a faster way and up and down the mountain then traveling by foot.

Dana rolled over and covered her eyes with her hand. "What's that sound? Is there a fire?" she asked, suddenly sitting up right.

"No, it's not a fire." Lucy felt sure of that. She didn't smell or see smoke. Doors would have been pounded on by now and everyone cleared out of the area.

She sat down again and rooted around for her shoes. "The police are here and an ambulance just pulled up. Let's go out and see what happened."

Dana nodded and sat up. She pushed aside her sleeping bag and Lucy handed up her sneakers.

Max had told the group that he was going to wake everyone before sunrise for another meditation session. But the sun was already up, Lucy realized.

Something else was up, too. Whatever it was, it wasn't good.

Lucy and Dana stumbled out of the hut. Other guests were coming out, too, groggy and bleary eyed, buttoning and zipping up the rumpled clothes they'd slept in.

Two more cars, identical dark blue sedans, had followed the ambulance and parked on the campsite. More officers unloaded. These wore street clothes with dark windbreakers on top that said STATE POLICE on the back. They talked for a few moments in a cluster, then fanned out around the site.

Lucy saw Dr. Max standing at the hut directly across the campsite from Dana's. He was talking to an officer who took notes. She saw the EMS crew go into the hut, but no one had come out yet.

"Someone must be hurt . . . or maybe they got sick during the night?" Lucy squinted, trying to get a better look at the action.

"Maybe," Dana said slowly. "But why would all these police be here for that? If someone was sick or hurt, wouldn't they just be taken to the hospital?" Dana glanced at her with a grave expression. "Come on. Let's ask somebody."

Lucy followed, digging her hands in the pockets of her sweater. The morning air was damp and chilly, nickel gray fragments of sky visible through the treetops. The entire scene was eerie and unsettling, as if she were stuck in a bad dream and couldn't wake herself up.

They walked over toward the center of the action, where Max still stood talking to one uniformed officer and one in a state police windbreaker in front of the hut directly across the campsite from Dana's.

Another officer approached and stood in their path. "Stay back, please. We need to keep this area clear."

"What's going on? What's happened?" Dana asked.

"Everyone will be briefed soon, ma'am. If you could just return to your hut, Detective Dykstra will speak to the group in a few minutes."

Dana and Lucy looked at each other. No way were they going to wait back in that phone booth–size shack. They stepped back a few feet, settling next to a tree, and continued to watch the action. The other guests, also pushed back like sheep by the uniformed border collies, stood by quietly, too. Watching and wondering.

"Look, the EMS guys are coming out," Dana said quietly.

Lucy had noticed that, too. She watched them walk back to their ambulance and then they just stood there, talking to each other.

The plainclothes police officers began to close off an area around the hut where Dr. Max had stood talking to police officers a few minutes ago. Using yellow tape, they enclosed a space a few yards around the wooden structure.

Another officer in a state police windbreaker and plastic gloves walked into the hut, while one outside carried a camera and walked behind the structure. Others were walking slowly around the area, starting at the hut and working their way to the yellow tape, staring at the ground. They also wore plastic gloves and carried small clear bags.

Not a very good sign, either.

She'd been at a crime scene once, when a friend of theirs had drowned in her pool. Gloria Sterling's death had seemed like an accident at first, but the police needed to investigate thoroughly, since she'd died alone. The plastic gloves and the orange tape had come out that night, too. And with good reason, it had turned out.

"This doesn't look good," Lucy said. "I'm getting a bad feeling."

"Me, too. I guess the sage smoke and tinkling bells last night didn't chase away *all* the negative energy," Dana answered quietly.

Lucy saw Helen Lynch standing just outside her door. She waved and walked over. "I think someone died. What else could it be?"

A blunt, bottom-line assessment. But the woman had a point. If the person in the hut was sick, the EMS crew wouldn't waste a minute taking them off the mountain. But if there was nothing to be done . . . well . . .

The thought was sad and stunning.

"Who do you think was in there?" Helen went on, glancing around nervously.

She pushed her glasses up a bit higher on her thin nose. Her salt-and-pepper hair was combed flat against her head this morning and covered by a black baseball cap. She looked even more birdlike than yesterday. And vaguely predatory.

"Let's see . . . there's Shannon and those two guys from Vermont, Paul and his partner, Chris . . ." Helen glanced around, naming every one she recognized. Lucy didn't know nearly as many of the names, but she did recognize most of the faces from mingling at dinner and sitting around the campfire last night.

Lucy suddenly turned to Dana. "I don't see Curtis Hill," she said quietly. She swallowed hard, looking around for the writer.

"Curtis . . . who?" Dana had not been at the knitting workshop and didn't remember him.

"The travel writer, you mean?" Helen cut in quickly. She

looked around, too. "You're right, he's not out here." She quickly counted the guests. "There were fifteen of us on the trip. I remember because I asked Nadine last night. I just counted fourteen. He's not in the crowd."

Lucy looked around again. She still didn't see him. "I don't remember which hut he went into last night. It might have been one of those near the campfire."

"I think it was," Helen said quickly.

Dana glanced at her but didn't say anything at first. "I think we need to hear what the police say. For all we know, Curtis Hill could still be in his hut. Or he could be back at the inn, drinking green tea and eating a whole-grain scone."

Lucy hoped so. She liked him. He'd shown them a clever but unassuming manner in the Random Knitting workshop. He'd struck up a conversation with her last night while the group sat around the fire, eating wrap sandwiches and edamame crisps out of little boxes Max had handed out.

He'd been curious to know what had brought Lucy and her friends to the inn for the Creative Spirit Weekend and what they thought of it so far and what they thought of Dr. Max. He'd seemed interested in their responses and genuinely friendly.

She did wonder now why he'd been taking his photos in such a surreptitious manner—down at the inn after the knitting workshop and then last night, in the meditation circle. But they were probably needed for his research and he wanted candid shots.

She hoped Curtis Hill was down at the inn right now, writing up his notes, sipping some tea, or even organic fair-trade coffee. She wished that she was doing that, too, and wondered now why she'd ever decided to go on this pointless expedition.

Lucy saw Shannon Piper standing alone in front of a hut a short distance away. She didn't look very much like a super-model this morning, or rather, she looked like one who'd been through a very rough night. She was pale with dark circles under her large eyes, her hair pulled back in a tight pony-tail. Bare of makeup, her features seemed washed-out and somewhat ordinary. She wore an oversize hooded sweater and hugged her arms around her thin body, either for warmth, or merely from nerves.

Lucy tried to catch her gaze, but she didn't notice. She bit down on her lower lip, her eyes fixed on the little knot of uni-forms still gathered around Dr. Max.

Finally, the officer that had first spoken to them ap-proached the group. "Gather 'round, everybody. We have some information."

The group of guests drew together, glancing at one an-other.

Everyone looked anxious, Lucy thought. She guessed that most had figured out by now what had happened, but it was different when someone told them point blank. She already knew that, too.

The plainclothes officer who had been talking mainly to Max, approached them. "I'm Detective Jim Dykstra with the Berkshire County Police Department. As you may have already heard, one of the a hotel guests, Mr. Curtis Hill, was found unconscious this morning in his hut. Attempts to resus-citate him were unsuccessful."

He waited a moment before saying more. Lucy heard a collective gasp rise from the group, as if they were all on a roller-coaster ride together and their car had taken a sudden dip.

It was just the coaster called life and the dip was the un-expected but inevitable, stomach-dropping confrontation with mortality. You could race along for long stretches without fac-ing it, Lucy knew, but sooner or later, you hit it. You just had to.

Detective Dykstra looked as if he was used to delivering this type of bleak message and hardly noticed their reaction.

He was not a tall man, but had a certain alpha dog pres-ence, Lucy thought. He wore a leather jacket over a pale blue sports shirt and khaki pants. He was bald on top with a fringe of gray hair, closely cut to his head, and a large mustache that hid most of his mouth. His gaze was steady, unblinking. He looked dutiful but not deeply concerned by the situation and spoke in an official and dispassionate tone.

"Due to the circumstances of Mr. Hill's death, we need to detain everyone at this site until we've completed interviews." He paused again and Lucy heard the predictable moans and groans from the group and some even shouted complaints.

"I realize these surroundings are not the most comfortable and we will do everything we can to get through this quickly and get you all back down to the hotel as soon as possible."

"What about some coffee and something to eat?" someone shouted.

Was someone really worried about getting their coffee? That seemed so cold-blooded, considering poor Curtis Hill was lying dead in that hut right now, Lucy thought.

"Can we use the Porta-Potty?" another asked.

"I can't hang around here all day. I have to get on the road by nine. I have an important appointment . . ."

The questions and objections went on a while. Detec-tive Dykstra finally raised his hands slowly in a signal to quiet down.

"Once again, I'm sorry for your inconvenience," he shouted over the hubbub. "A man has lost his life and we need to investigate the circumstances thoroughly and follow all necessary procedure. We're making arrangements to get some food up here and make you as comfortable as possible. Now, if everyone could just be patient, an officer will come by soon to take your statement."

Detective Dykstra was finished and started to walk away, to go about his business. Some pushier guests approached, but he quickly deflected them, sending them off to deal with uniformed officers, who had little or no authority, Lucy guessed.

Helen Lynch had wandered away, Lucy noticed, and she now spotted her talking to Shannon Piper. Shannon huddled into her doorway and Helen seemed to be inching up on her, like a small, pesky bird badgering a larger, long-legged one on the seashore.

Lucy turned to Dana. "Wow . . . so it was Curtis. Poor guy. I can hardly believe it."

"It is sad. I wondered how he died," Dana replied.

"The detective said he'd been found unconscious. He could have had a heart attack or a lot things." Lucy speculated.

"He may have had a heart condition or something," Dana agreed. "I think the police need to investigate due to the odd circumstances. It doesn't mean they've found anything suspicious or actually suspect foul play."

"Maybe not," Lucy agreed. "But they do seem to be going about their business in a pretty intense way. I mean, if there was nothing suspicious about the way he died." She looked at Dana. "This is all sort of creepy, don't you think? I'm glad you're up here with me, Dana," she admitted. "I'd feel really spooked up here alone."

"Me, too," Dana admitted. "Should we call the cottage?" She glanced at her watch. "It's barely seven. I don't want to wake them up with bad news."

Lucy would have liked to hear the familiar voices of her friends right now. To make contact with the world down at the inn, which seemed a safe haven compared to the mountain-top, but she didn't want to disturb the others, either.

"We might be waking them up. They may not have heard yet," Lucy agreed.

"Let's wait," Dana suggested. "We can always call later."

"How long do you think this will take? There are a lot of people here. I don't see too many police officers." Lucy looked around. There were lots of officers wandering about, but she only saw two talking to guests, asking questions and writing on slim pads.

Dana sighed. "Let's just say I'm glad I came prepared."

Lucy met her gaze. "Me, too. Let's find a quiet spot and get to work. You know what Maggie always says . . ."

"When the going gets tough—" Dana quoted.

"The tough get knitting," Lucy finished for her.

"Exactly," Dana nodded.

Maggie was an early riser. She never needed a wake-up call and rarely slept in, even if she wanted to. She'd always been that way. Her husband, Bill, used to tease her about it, claiming he'd married a human alarm clock. Among my other talents, she'd remind him.

Maggie enjoyed being up when the world was silent and calm. In the little cottage balanced above the lake, the start of the day was absolutely awesome in a tranquil, quiet way. While Maggie made coffee, she watched the lake through the big glass doors.

The water was as still as glass, a deep greenish-gray color reflecting the low gray clouds. The change from yesterday's fair skies made the lake look more interesting, even a bit mysterious.

A bird rose from a bank of straw-colored rushes, its swift, strong wings making a whispering sound that echoed to the opposite shore. The steady lap of the water on the pilings under the porch sounded like a familiar heartbeat.

It was so peaceful here. Who needed overpriced, fussy beauty treatments? Or lectures on color vibrations and cleansing your chakras? A few minutes of serenity surrounded by this natural beauty was enough to nourish the mind and soul.

Maggie had just poured a mug of coffee and grabbed her knitting bag, preparing to sit out on the porch, when she heard footsteps crunching on the gravel path that led to the cottage. She went over to the glass doors, expecting to see the wayward mountaineers returning home after their retreat. The sight of two uniformed police officers made her step back in alarm.

She put the coffee down and went out to meet them. "Is there something wrong?" Maggie still had her nightgown and bathrobe on, but had flung her heavy stole over her shoulders.

"There's been an accident on the mountain, ma'am. All the guests are being asked to come up to the inn," one of the policeman replied.

He looked very young, Maggie thought. Like a teenager, dressed up for a costume party.

"An accident? What type of accident?" Maggie felt a sharp

jolt of concern. "Do you know who was hurt? Was it a man or a woman?"

"The deceased was male," the younger officer answered.

Maggie pressed her hand to her chest. "You mean someone died up there?"

The younger officer looked at the older one. He suddenly seemed to be over his head.

The other officer, who looked more experienced, was taking a pad out of his back pocket. "A guest died during the night. We're investigating the circumstances right now. That's why we need everyone up at the inn for interviews. Can I have your name, please?"

Maggie took a quick breath. She could hardly believe what was happening. "Maggie Messina."

"Is there anyone else in there with you, Ms. Messina?"

"Yes . . . two other women. My friends. Suzanne Cavanaugh and Phoebe Meyers. They're still sleeping." Maggie felt her mouth grow dry as she watched him write down the names. "There are also two more women with us. But they went on the retreat last night. They're okay, aren't they? I mean, that man who died . . . was he the only one who was hurt?"

"All the other guests up there are fine. A little tense, though, from being kept on the mountain. As soon as we collect their statements, they'll be transported down." He closed his pad and stuck it in his back pocket. "Please wake up your friends and tell them what's going on. We need to wait here until you head up to the inn."

"You need to wait for us?" Maggie didn't get that part.

"Yes, ma'am. The property is secured right now. No one is allowed to come in or go out."

"I see." She nodded. "We'll be right out then."

Maggie headed inside, wondering what in the world had happened. It sounded like a serious investigation had started. She wondered what sort of accident the poor deceased guest had met with last night.

She wasn't really sure why the police had to wait for them to go up. Were they afraid she'd make a fast getaway? It would be hard to leave the grounds unnoticed, Maggie realized. A mad dash through the woods? Then what? The only way out in that direction was over the mountain.

As for a car chase, there was only one road in and out. If she were desperate enough, she might just strip down and dive in the water. A jackknife, right off the porch, and an Olympic-style swim for the opposite shore. The lake was so small, the police could probably reach the other side on foot as fast as anyone could swim it.

As Maggie considered the challenge of escaping the grounds undetected, she suddenly realized something. If she couldn't come up with an escape route, neither could anyone else.

So if there had been foul play on the mountaintop, the guilty party was most likely still on the premises.

No wonder the police were so vigilant. There could be a violent criminal roaming around the woods or even back in the hotel by now. The realization was chilling.

Maggie entered the cottage, wondering which of her friends she should wake up first. Neither of them would be very happy to be rushed out of bed . . . or even believe the reason why.

A short time later, Maggie, Suzanne, and Phoebe walked into the inn through the lakeside entrance of the lobby. A police officer standing at the door took down their names and told them to wait in the lobby to be called for an interview.

The lobby was filled with guests. Most of them looked confused, disturbed, and downright fearful, which was the way she felt, too.

"Well, what now?" Suzanne looked around at the confusing scene.

Before Maggie could answer, Nadine swept by. She was dressed in her usual arty style, an unstructured brick-colored blazer over black pants and a batik-print scarf slung around her neck. Strands of exotic beads and matching earrings completed the look. But under her business as usual outfit, she looked unnerved and exhausted and puffy-eyed from being roused out of bed at such an early hour.

"Hello, ladies. Awful news, isn't it?

"Absolutely. Terrible news," Maggie replied.

"We're all shocked and saddened," Nadine agreed. "The police need to interview everyone who was on the property last night. I'm trying to help, since I know the guest list the best. I suggest that you relax and have some coffee. I'll come and find you. This could take a while."

Nadine moved on to comfort and inform another group of guests.

"I guess a little coffee wouldn't be the worst thing while we're waiting," Suzanne said.

"I'll just wait here," Phoebe said stubbornly. "I couldn't eat a bite, knowing that some poor person died last night."

Phoebe had been the most upset to hear the news, Maggie noticed. Under the goth-girl outfits, piercing, and streaked hair, she was a very sensitive person.

"It will probably be a long time before they call us. What

else can we do?" Maggie glanced at Phoebe and lightly touched her shoulder. "We can at least get some coffee. I'm dying for a cup." She headed toward the dining room and her friends quickly followed.

There were many guests in the dining room, as well. Maggie noticed that a buffet had been set up and people were helping themselves. But she was with Phoebe. The horrific news had her stomach churning with nerves.

"I wonder how Dana and Lucy are doing." Suzanne said as they settled at a table. "I tried calling both of them, but Dana just sent back a short text. She says they're okay and should be back soon."

"I wonder what time the ordeal started up there. Probably very early. It was just a quarter past seven when the police came to our cottage," Maggie noted.

"I wonder who it was. There were only a few men on the trip. I guess if it was Dr. Max, someone would have said by now, right?"

"I think that news would have gotten around quickly. Even if the police didn't want anyone to know. I asked an officer who it was, but he said he didn't know the man's name," Suzanne answered.

"There's Nadine again. Let's see if we can squeeze out a little more information. I bet she knows the whole story." Maggie waved to her friend. Nadine was now working her way around the dining room, but quickly came over, her ever-present clipboard clutched under one arm like a life preserver.

"How's it going?" Maggie asked her.

"Terrible. It just gets worse and worse . . . you have no idea," Nadine dropped into an empty chair next to Maggie. "Who could ever imagine such a thing?" She stared around the group, looking pale under the streaks of face powder and blush that had been hastily applied.

"What actually happened?" Maggie asked. "We don't know much. Only that someone, a man, died on the mountain. We don't even know who it was."

Nadine took a deep breath and squared her shoulders. "It was the writer for Commodore Travel Guides, Curtis Hill. Max found him this morning. He called an ambulance right away and tried CPR. But Hill was gone. There wasn't anything they could do for him."

"Oh dear, that's awful. He seemed like a nice guy. Very clever. He came to the Random Knitting workshop yesterday," Maggie reminded her.

"I remember seeing him there," Nadine said sadly. "The police just told Alice that the medical examiner has completed his job and they're finally taking the body off the mountain," she said quietly. "I don't think the man's family has been contacted yet. One of the detectives asked to examine his room. I guess he'll look for contact information in there," Nadine added. "Alice had to unlock the door for him."

"I'm not sure how the police track down family members in this situation," Maggie said. "Maybe they use his license or cell phone?"

"Probably. It's unlikely they'd call his office on a Saturday," Nadine replied quickly.

"So he must have had a heart attack or something like that?" Suzanne asked.

Nadine glanced at her, then bit her lower lip. "You'll hear anyway. No sense trying to hide it." She sighed. "The police say that right now, it looks like he died from breathing in gas from the little space heater in the hut. Carbon monoxide. It's odorless, so there's no warning. They have to wait for blood tests and such to confirm it, but that's what they think happened from what they've seen so far. They asked Alice a lot questions about when it was serviced last, or if it had needed any repairs recently. They said they found that a pipe outside the hut in back wasn't attached properly."

Suzanne gasped and covered her mouth. "Oh my . . . that's terrible."

"It is awful. And so needless," Maggie added sadly.

Maggie's thoughts raced with the implications for the hotel. There would be some horrendous publicity and maybe even a lawsuit.

"I feel even worse about Mr. Hill after hearing that. But I have to admit, I'm relived that neither of our friends chose that hut to sleep in," she added quietly.

"Yes . . . well . . ." Nadine didn't say anything more. Maggie and her friends waited for what seemed like a long moment.

"The police don't seem to think it was a problem with the heating unit," Nadine admitted finally. "They said that someone had rigged the mechanism that way on purpose. Someone who knew what they were doing."

Maggie's eyes widened with shock. "Mr. Hill was killed intentionally?"

"What's up with that?" Phoebe cut in. "I mean, the guy was a just writer. Did he give someone a bad review in one of his travel guides?"

"Oh, I hope not. How crazy would a person have to be?" Nadine shook her head. "The police have no idea why it happened. But they seem certain it wasn't an accident. That's why they're taking so long to interview everyone and won't let any of the guests or staff off the grounds right now," she added.

"So we're all stuck here until they figure out who did it?" Suzanne's big brown eyes nearly popped out of her head.

"And that implies that the police suspect the murderer is still on the grounds." Maggie tried hard not to sound alarmed, but she heard a distinct note of panic in her tone. She'd had the thought at other times this morning, but now it seemed even more likely.

"Yikes!" Phoebe reacted in a hushed squeal.

"Oh dear . . . I guess you can see why we don't want all this information to get out to the guests. We don't want the hotel in a complete state of panic," Nadine answered quietly. "I don't believe the lockdown will last very long. The detective in charge said that they need to get everyone's statement and contact information. After that, they'll probably say most people are allowed to go. They can quickly weed out people who are totally unlikely to be connected to the crime."

Nadine paused and looked around. Then leaned closer to speak in an even more intimate tone. "The thing is, most of the guests paid in advance for this weekend and Alice doesn't want everyone demanding their money back. We've been trying to figure out how to persuade everyone to stay."

"I'll stay," Maggie replied quickly. "I mean, you hired me for a job and I'll do it. I'm not running out on you," she promised her friend.

"Thank you, Maggie. I was hoping you'd say that. Alice and Max are very upset, but there's nothing they can do. They told to me stick to the program and try to keep everyone amused and distracted."

The business as usual attitude did seem disrespectful to Curtis Hill, but Maggie could understand why the management was struggling to stay on course. Who needed an inn full of angry, frightened, bored guests?

"What can I do to help?" Maggie asked her friend.

"Oh, Maggie. You're a dear." Nadine reached over and quickly gripped Maggie's hand. "Just hold your knitting workshop, as scheduled. Just try to keep them amused and distracted." Nadine sighed again, repeating the instructions she'd been given by Alice and Max. "Quite a few have signed up for that session. I'll try to round them up for you," she offered.

Seems the police had gotten a head start on that, Maggie silently added. If her class was sparse, she couldn't take it personally, Maggie decided.

"There's Alice. I'd better run." Nadine jumped up from her seat, clutching her clipboard in a trembling hand. "Please don't let her know I told you all that stuff about Hill . . . you know, what the police figure out?" she whispered to the women.

"I won't tell. Don't worry," Maggie whispered back.

After Nadine left the table, Maggie said, "Listen, guys, you can leave if you want, after you give your statements. You don't have to stay here on my account. I'll take a bus back tomorrow night."

"Are you crazy? I'm not leaving you alone with a murderer on the loose," Suzanne replied quickly. "Nobody is," she added, giving Phoebe a look.

"Hey, same here. No questions asked," Phoebe assured them. "I'm sure Dana and Lucy would say the same. Who's going to get bored, with a cold-blooded killer roaming around?" Phoebe asked quietly.

Maggie sighed. She hoped Nadine hadn't heard that. Didn't the woman look frazzled enough? How could she be expected to keep all these guests content under these circumstances?

As usual, Phoebe had a good point. The police seemed to

believe whoever murdered Hill was still on the grounds. The thought elicited another wave of goose bumps. She glanced around the dining room, at a sea of ordinary faces, wondering who it could possibly be.

She suddenly noticed Alice Archer, weaving her way through the crowd, and now approaching their table. Dressed in a gray suit today, with a pink silk blouse underneath, she had a white wicker basket over her arm and flashed a thin but pleasant smile.

She'd stop at a table to chat and hand out little slips of paper from the basket. What in the world? Was she trying to distract everyone with some sort of raffle?

"Good morning, ladies," she greeted them. "I want to apologize personally for any inconvenience during your stay. As you've probably heard by now, there was a very unfortunate accident at the retreat. We all feel just devastated by the news." She cast her gaze down for a moment in a solemn expression, then lifted her head, once again bright eyed. "But I do want everyone to know that the weekend schedule will continue as planned. We also want you to take full advantage of the spa and all the relaxing and rejuvenating treatments. I have some coupons here," she announced, sounding downright chipper.

"Who'd like a massage today? A peppermint mud bath . . . or maybe a fandango wrap?" she added in an enticing tone.

The last choice sounded like some kind of Spanish sandwich, Maggie thought. But . . . interesting.

"I'll try the fandango," she replied on impulse.

"Wise choice. You'll love it. It draws out all the toxins," Alice promised, handing her a coupon. "Anyone else?" She waved the coupons like live bait over a porpoise tank.

"The peppermint mud bath sounds cool," Phoebe said. "Is the mud, like, flavored or something?"

Alice blinked, her smile stretching even tighter. "The mud is from the Mediterranean, dear. It's purified and mineral rich. After you soak, you're sprayed off with peppermint waters."

"That sounds like fun," Phoebe said happily. Alice blinked again but didn't reply.

"How about a cellulite melt?" Suzanne asked.

Very crafty, Maggie nearly said out loud. Suzanne had tried several treatments yesterday and already knew her preferences.

"Let's see . . . I don't have a coupon for that one handy, but I can make one up for you." Alice whipped out a pen and quickly scribbled Suzanne's choice on a slip of paper, then signed the bottom. "Here you go. Enjoy."

Before the group had even thanked Alice for their coupons, she had swept off to another table, sprinkling her spa freebies around the dining room like a shower of rose petals.

Suzanne waved her coupon. "Finally, my ticket to thin thighs. This one costs a bundle. That woman must be desperate," she added quietly.

"Who wouldn't be under the circumstances?" Maggie sympathized. "The inn has this special weekend going on and that big investors meeting tomorrow," she recalled. "I wonder if they'll cancel that now."

"Gee, you're right. I almost forgot," Suzanne said.

"We forgot about Lucy and Dana. We should have scored a few coupons for them, too," Phoebe reminded her friends and Maggie felt bad that she hadn't thought of that in time.

"Don't worry," she told Phoebe, "I think we'll be seeing

Alice again. We're in for the duration. The Mediterranean might run out of mud before this ordeal is over."

As if on cue, Maggie spotted the two missing Black Sheep, Dana and Lucy, walking into the dining room. Dana saw her first and waved as they stopped to pick up some coffee. Maggie waved back and even stood up. She suddenly felt so happy and relieved to see them alive and well.

"Look . . . here they come. Finally. Thank heaven," she murmured. Maggie took a steadying breath, suddenly feeling a great wave of unexpected emotion. Tears welled up and she blinked them back. She couldn't take her eyes off her two friends as they walked toward the table.

Even though she knew they weren't harmed last night, it was a different thing to see them face-to-face. Thank goodness they were safe . . . and hadn't chosen to sleep in the wrong hut.

Chapter Seven

"Well, we made it." Lucy strolled up to the table and gratefully dropped into a chair. "It was quite an experience."

"Indeed it was," Dana added in a tired voice as she dropped into the place beside Lucy.

Maggie leaned over and gave each of them a hug. "Oh, for goodness' sake . . . we were so worried about you when we heard."

"Why didn't you call us?" Suzanne scolded them. "We had no idea what happened. We were woken up by the police—"

"No one would even tell us who died," Phoebe added.

But before Lucy and Dana could answer their questions, Suzanne and Phoebe jumped up and hugged the campers, too.

"Group hug, group hug," Phoebe called out in the middle of the quiet dining room.

After one last heartfelt squeeze, they all stepped back and took their seats again. "You guys must have been, like, totally freaked when you heard what happened," Phoebe said.

"We were a little freaked," Lucy admitted. Not a word she

usually used, but it seemed to capture the feeling perfectly. "We thought about calling the cottage but it was so early. We didn't want to wake you up with such bad news. And there was nothing you could really do about it."

"We barely knew what was going on for a while, either," Dana added. "The police weren't very forthcoming with information."

"Start right from the beginning, when you stepped out that door and started up the mountain," Maggie urged them. "We want to hear the whole story."

"Then we'll tell you what we just heard from Maggie's friend, Nadine. It's the *total* inside scoop," Suzanne added in a confidential tone.

"What did your hear? Something about Curtis Hill?" Lucy asked eagerly.

Before Suzanne could reply, Dana added, "Hey, we were stuck up on that mountain, sitting on a wooden plank for the past three hours. I think we earned the right to hear the juicy gossip first."

Maggie glanced around and then leaned closer to Dana and Lucy. "The police don't want everyone to know, but Nadine says that they've already figured out Curtis Hill didn't die from a sudden heart attack, or even by accident. Someone tampered with the heating unit at the back of his hut and he was asphyxiated by the gas. Carbon monoxide poisoning."

Lucy and Dana both gasped. "How awful . . . that makes it even worse," Lucy said. "Who would do such a thing? He seemed like such a nice guy."

"It takes a certain kind of twisted mentality to think of something like that," Dana added sadly. "Why would anyone want to kill Hill? Revenge for a bad review in a Commodore Travel Guide? That seems preposterous."

"That's just what we said when we heard," Suzanne told her.

"Maybe it was a random murder. The horrible person who rigged the heater just wanted to kill anybody." Lucy shuddered at the thought. "That means it could have been either of us," she said, glancing at Dana.

"Don't even think about it." Dana reached over and gave her arm a comforting squeeze. "I just have a feeling this wasn't random. It's too . . . mechanical and premeditated. Too complicated," she added.

Lucy felt the same way. "There had to be something else. Something no one knows yet about Curtis."

Curtis had seemed friendly enough. But she thought again about the writer's secretive manner, taking photos with his iPhone when he thought no one was aware. Even the way he struck up a conversation with her and Dana last night at the campfire, asking so many questions, suddenly seemed suspect.

She'd told the police what she had observed and wanted to tell her friends, but Dana spoke first.

"I guess the police will figure out the whole story soon," Dana said, practically reading Lucy's mind. "That bombshell makes last night seem pretty tame. But we'll tell you what happened up there anyway . . ."

Then Dana and Lucy took turns filling their friends in on their strange night up on the mountain, including Dr. Max's dance around the campfire, the smoking sage and drum, the tinkling bells and chanting.

"Wow, the doctor puts on quite a performance, doesn't he?" Maggie said finally.

"It was intense." Lucy nibbled on a bite of cranberry, flax seed, and carrot muffin. She'd hadn't felt the least bit hungry on the mountaintop but now had a little appetite. "When we finally got around to the meditation, I was too distracted to get much out of it."

"Me, too," Dana admitted. "I don't like meditating in a group. There's something odd about that. I kept opening my eyes, to see what was going on. I couldn't help it."

"Me, too," Lucy admitted. She and Dana had already discussed this on the mountain. They'd had plenty of time to chat and knit while waiting to give their statements.

"See anything interesting?" Maggie asked.

"No much. Curtis Hill was sitting near me and I did notice that he had his iPhone out, balanced on his knee, while Dr. Max was on the other side of the campfire circle. He was taking photos or maybe even a video. But he sat with his eyes closed, as if he were meditating."

"Well, that would be logical. If Max made such a serious production out of the meditation session, maybe Hill thought he wouldn't permit him to have his phone out. Too much of a distraction."

"But why take photos or video in the first place? The light was very poor. Lucy would know more about this, of course, since she works with illustrated text all the time. But I doubt he could get any decent shots up there last night," Dana told the others. "And he's just writing some sort of description or review of the inn. I don't think that smoky campfire scene, with Max dancing around like a loon, was suitable for graphics in a travel guide."

"I thought of that, too. The conditions were poor," Lucy said. "But maybe he just wanted photos or video for reference when he wrote the article? I also saw him taking pictures down in the lobby, after Maggie's workshop."

"Pictures of what? Of me?" Maggie asked with surprise.

"Of the 'amazing decor,' he said. But I think he was really shooting Dr. Max, some candid video."

"Interesting," Dana said quietly. "Did you tell the police all that?"

"Yes, I did. They took it all down. I couldn't tell if they thought it was important or not."

"What else did you see up there?" Suzanne asked with interest. "This is getting good. How about you, Dana?"

"I didn't see too much. Most of the people there were very earnest, trying to glean some take-away lesson from the meditation, though I'm not sure they really knew what that was supposed to be." She glanced around at her friends, then leaned closer. "I did notice Dr. Max giving a few of the campers special attention. Shannon Piper and Helen Lynch, mainly."

Lucy and Dana had already talked about this, too, up on the mountain. Lucy had noticed the favoritism, though it was nothing that obvious. Dr. Max seemed very intent on circulating around the campfire during the meal, spreading his charm in a thick, even layer, like a swipe of organic peanut butter.

"Special attention? What do you mean by that, exactly?" Maggie asked, her interest piqued.

"Oh, you know. Just the way they look at each other; their body language when they talk," Dana replied. "Shannon found a spider or something in her hut when we first got there and Max had to run over and rescue her." Dana almost laughed at the story.

"Did he kill it?" Suzanne asked curiously.

"Actually, he scooped it up in a tin cup and tossed it in the woods. Dr. Max isn't into killing bugs, you know. Bad karma," Lucy told the others.

"Shannon told us this is her second time at the spa, so she's met Dr. Max before." Dana picked up a ceramic container of honey and poured a bit into her tea.

"It sounds as if you think something's going on between those two," Suzanne said in a gossipy tone.

Dana sipped her tea, her blue eyes peered at Suzanne over the edge of her mug. "I really can't say for sure. Shannon is sweet and sincere and exhibits all the signs of a guru groupie. She looks at Dr. Max as if he walks on Vitamin Water. Maybe it's just a crush."

"And she's a supermodel so it's a supersized crush," Maggie murmured in agreement. "He might just be courting her as an investor. We can't jump to any conclusions."

"Helen Lynch is considering investing. She told me yesterday," Lucy told the others. "He was giving her a little extra face time, too, I noticed."

"He's a busy bee, floating from flower to flower," Phoebe offered in a poetic tone.

"That's how you gather the honey . . . and the money," Suzanne reminded them.

"That might be his method, but I'm sure Alice doesn't approve. She keeps a close eye on him." Maggie glanced over her shoulder to make sure the hotel manager had not returned with her coupon basket.

"I'm surprised she let him go up there alone. Unsupervised for the evening. Even if she had to work to do down here, she could have gone up later."

"Come to think of it, I saw someone walking the woods last night. It must have been around eleven or even later," Maggie mused. "I didn't think too much of it at the time. But now . . ."

"You'd better tell the police," Suzanne cut in. "That could be important, too."

"Yes, it might be," Lucy agreed. "We've already given our statements. Have you guys been interviewed yet?"

"No, we haven't." Maggie took a sip of coffee and looked up to see Nadine coming across the dining room alongside the baby-faced police officer who had escorted them from the cottage.

She put down her cup and sat up straight. "But it looks like our names just jumped to the top of the list."

As Maggie had expected, the young officer had come to call her, Suzanne, and Phoebe to their interview. While they marched off toward the lobby, Dana and Lucy headed to the cottage to shower and change.

"Don't forgot, I'm leading the Mindful Knitting workshop at eleven. In the Lotus Room," Maggie called over her shoulder, "It would be nice to see a few friendly faces in the crowd," she hinted broadly. "And frankly," she added in a quieter tone, "I don't like the idea of any of us roaming around here alone. I think we should institute a buddy system. Nobody walks around without a partner . . . agreed?"

Maggie's friends glanced at one another. She wondered at first if they were going to make fun of her for being a worry wart. "I think that's a good idea, all things considered," Suzanne said. "You never know."

"I don't mind. I'm glad I had a buddy on the retreat last night," Lucy said, glancing over at Dana. "I would have run down the mountain."

"Same here. I agree, we have to watch out for each other if we're going to stay. It's only common sense."

"Don't worry, we'll be at your workshop, Maggie," Lucy

added. She glanced around and knew she was speaking for the whole group. Curtis Hill's death had shaken everyone up and they all felt the urge to stick together right now.

A few moments later, Maggie, Suzanne, and Phoebe headed off for their interviews with the police. They walked through the lobby, then to the check-in desk and down a short hallway on the side that led to the hotel's main office. They stood by the door and waited.

The area was surprisingly spare and utilitarian, a stark contrast to the sumptuous decor of the inn. The office was basically an open space with blue-gray walls, a few metal desks that held computers, and piles of folders and papers. Fluorescent lights hung from the ceiling, making it all look even bleaker. On a long wall behind the desk, Maggie saw a row of doors.

She noticed a brass name plate on one that read ALICE AR-CHER—GENERAL MANAGER. The corner office, she suspected. If there was a corner to be had in this arrangement, it would be assigned to Alice.

She didn't notice many hotel employees in the area, but quite a few policeman were milling about. A door opened and a man who Maggie assumed was a detective came out of one of the private rooms. He held a yellow legal pad. "Maggie Messina?" he called out, looking at the women.

Maggie raised her hand about halfway. "I'm here."

"I'm Detective Dykstra. Please come in. This won't take long." He walked into the office and Maggie followed.

When she was inside, he offered her a chair that stood on one side of a meeting table. He sat on the other side, flanked by another man, another plainclothes police officer, she guessed.

"This is my partner, Detective Michaelson," Dykstra said, introducing the other officer. "As you know, we're interviewing everyone who was at the inn last night in regard to Mr. Hill's death."

"Which was not an accident, I heard," Maggie finished for him.

His eyebrows rose a notch, but he showed little reaction otherwise. "Who told you that?" he said, without confirming if it was true or not, she noticed.

Maggie felt her face grow warm, remembering how Nadine had asked her to be discreet with that tidbit.

"I just heard it around the hotel. People have nothing to do but talk. You know," she shrugged.

He picked up a pen and wrote her name at the top of a page. "Can you tell us why you came to the inn this weekend?" he asked. Maggie felt relieved that he didn't try to learn her source for the inside scoop on Hill.

She went on to explain how she'd been invited last week by Nadine to teach knitting workshops because another teacher had canceled. And how she'd persuaded Nadine to let her stay in the cottage, instead of a single room, so that she could bring her friends. "We have a knitting group that meets Thursday nights," she explained.

Dykstra nodded, then double-checked the names of the group against another list. He already had this information, Maggie realized. Probably from Lucy and Dana.

It was important to learn every guest's reason—or alleged reason—for visiting the inn to find out if there was any connection to Curtis Hill.

His next questions proved that. "Did you ever meet Curtis Hill before you came here?"

"No . . . never." Maggie shook her head. "Though I have used those travel guides he writes for . . . used to write for, I mean," she corrected herself.

"Did you have any contact with Mr. Hill while you've been here?"

"Yes, I did." Maggie went on to explain how Hill had been part of the Random Knitting workshop yesterday. "He seemed like a nice man. He wasn't very good at knitting, but was a good sport and made some funny remarks. We didn't speak at all beyond that. I do remember seeing him with the others in the lobby getting ready to hike up the mountain."

Dykstra nodded, making some notes on the pad.

Michaelson leaned forward. "Did you notice him speaking to anyone in particular in the workshop, or in the lobby while he waited?"

Maggie thought about it a moment, then shrugged. "I'm sorry. I really wasn't focused on him. I'm here with my friends, who were joining the trip."

"Did you see him speaking to Dr. Flemming at all in the workshop or in the lobby?" Michaelson asked.

Maggie was surprised for a moment by the question. Not the question, exactly, but the pointed way he'd asked it.

"They exchanged a few words in the workshop, I suppose. Dr. Max was talking to all of us. He seemed to be making an effort, I thought, to give each person there some individual attention," she added. "I remember at one point, Dr. Max commented on something Mr. Hill said about having to use the Internet instead of actually traveling to write his articles. Dr. Max laughed and he said he found it ironic . . . or something like that."

Dykstra made another note. Michaelson sat back in his chair.

They asked Maggie more questions about her activities last night, and she told them about her meeting with Joy Kimmel. "She gave me an earful about Dr. Max and Alice Archer," Maggie confided. "Have you spoken to her yet?"

"Yes, we've interviewed Ms. Kimmel," Michaelson said, checking his list.

"What sort of an earful?" Detective Dykstra asked, looking interested.

Maggie felt uncomfortable repeating their conversation. "Oh, just about her relationship with Dr. Max and their past. They were married. You know that. It doesn't have any connection to Curtis Hill. She never even mentioned him."

"Please tell us what she said. We'll figure out if has a connection or not," Michaelson replied evenly.

Maggie paused, then tried to relate all that Joy had disclosed—that she was at peace with her past and the path she'd taken, and the things she'd said about her marriage to Max.

"Was there any reason why she confided all this personal information?" Detective Michaelson asked.

"I wondered about that myself," Maggie admitted. "Once she started talking, it all poured out. But she told me that it was all in Dr. Max's book. Have you read it yet?" she asked them.

"Not yet. We're getting to it," Dykstra said.

"Well, she said it's all in there. Of course, her opinions about Alice Archer, and Alice's relationship to Max, are not in the book. I think she's a little hard on Alice," Maggie added. "She could be a little jealous."

"How so, Ms. Messina?" Detective Dykstra leaned back in his chair, looking like he had all the time in the world to sit and gossip with her. But maybe that attitude was necessary if you were gathering information like this, Maggie thought. You never knew which strand would lead you out of the tangle.

"They're very different women. Complete opposites, it seems to me. Joy is so laid-back and . . . cosmic. Alice is all business. Even a bit uptight, you'd have to say. But she has a lot of responsibility here. A lot of pressure with the new spas Dr. Max has planned. He's close to her. He depends on her. Anyone can see that. Maybe Joy is jealous."

Not that it had anything to do with Curtis Hill's death, either, Maggie realized. How had they gotten onto this conversational track?

Detective Dykstra made a note. "Anything else you remember?"

"Not really. Oh, there was one thing. When Joy spoke about Alice and Max, she quoted a few lines from the *I Ching*. About a horse running away . . . something like that . . ."

Maggie's words trailed off as she tried to remember.

"The fortune-telling book, you mean?" Michaelson glanced at Dysktra, suddenly looking alert.

"That's right." Maggie nodded. "It's made up of hexagrams that correspond to different Chinese characters and each has a special meaning. Like happiness . . . or patience. That sort of thing. You ask a question and it tells you which hexagram to look up. It's a little complicated."

Dykstra opened a folder on the table and took out a small plastic bag. Maggie saw that it held a small white index card with a Chinese character written in black marker and a number was written above. Number eighteen.

"Like this?" He held up the card, then passed it across the table to her.

Maggie felt her mouth go dry, though she wasn't sure why.

She looked the card over through the plastic. It was an ordinary index card, the writing done in black marker. She noticed a tiny hole near the top, the perforation a pushpin or thumbtack would make?

"Yes, you might find that symbol in the book."

"Do you know what this one means?" Dykstra asked.

"I have no idea. I really don't know much about it, except what I've told you. That number on the top is important. I think you can look it up that way. They follow a special order," Maggie added.

Joy Kimmel probably knew the symbols by heart, Maggie thought. But she didn't say that to Detective Dykstra. He seemed pretty sharp and would connect those dots quickly, if he hadn't done so already.

She also guessed that the index card was evidence found at the crime scene. Why else would the detective have it in a plastic bag?

Maggie answered a few more questions about her conversation with Joy, then told the officers she'd gone to sit out near the lake before returning to the cottage.

"I did see something unusual out there," she said quickly. "Someone was walking in the woods, on the trail going up the mountain. They had a flashlight. It darted around a bit. The light caught my eye."

"What time was that? Approximately," Dysktra asked quickly.

"About eleven or maybe a few minutes past. I'm not sure. Joy and I finished talking at about eleven. I left the hotel right away and went out to the lake. I hadn't been sitting at the water very long when I saw the light."

"Did you see or hear anything else? The color of the person's hair or their outerwear for instance?" Dykstra asked.

"No . . . I'm sorry. It all happened so quickly. It was very dark and they weren't close by. I couldn't even tell if it was a man or a woman," she said honestly.

Maggie wondered if any of the guests had told the detectives that they had been out in the woods at that hour. The police would be able to cross-check that sort of fact easily, she thought, and figure out if it was significant or not.

"It could have been a guest out for some fresh air," she offered. "Did anyone mention that they took a walk last night?"

She didn't expect the detectives to tell her, but it was worth a try.

Michaelson saw through her ploy and smiled. "We'll have to look through all the interviews to check on that," he said, though she had a feeling he already remembered.

Michaelson glanced at Dykstra, then back at Maggie. "Is there anything else you'd like to tell us? Anything you saw or heard while you were outside last night?"

Maggie took a moment, then shook her head. "No, that's all. I stayed only a few minutes after that, then went into the cottage. I talked with my friends for a while and had some tea. Then we all went to sleep about midnight."

"You slept well? Nothing woke you during the night?"

"I heard a few sounds. A bird out on the lake. A loon, I think. Some racoons chattering in the woods. That was about it. I usually don't sleep well on vacation, but I did last night. Must be the mountain air," she added.

"Could be," Dykstra nodded. "I grew up around here so I'm used to the air by now."

He looked like a man who did not sleep well, Maggie thought. But considering the grim nature of his work, that was understandable.

When Maggie came out of the interview room, she found Phoebe waiting for her.

She'd just finished her interview with a uniformed policeman in another office. Then they called Suzanne in and she was still giving her statement.

"Suzanne said she would come to your workshop when she was done talking to the police," Phoebe told Maggie. "She said not to worry, she'll make it there safely on her own."

"My workshop . . . right." Maggie glanced at her watch. "We'd better get down there. It's in a meeting room. The Lotus Room, I think Nadine said."

"I know where that is. It's on the way to the spa." They quickly left the office and Phoebe led the way to the side of the hotel Maggie had not yet explored.

Chapter Eight

The meeting rooms were located in a wing of the inn that had recently been added on and was a bit off the beaten track. As the two women hurried along, Maggie consulted a small map of the hotel she had stashed in her knitting bag.

They walked down a long corridor that seemed to connect the older section of the inn with a new one. It was very quiet and desolate, Maggie noticed. So quiet that Maggie heard the sound of their shoes on the thick hotel carpeting. It was a bit unnerving.

"It's so deserted over here. Sort of spooky. Why did they stick you way back here?" Phoebe complained.

"I don't know. There must be other events going on in the lobby. Or maybe Nadine expected a big group to sign up for this."

"Right . . . you mean that big crowd that's locked in their hotel rooms, with the covers pulled up over their heads right now? There's not a soul in sight. And how will they ever find this place?"

Phoebe has the amazing talent to give voice to my every secret anxiety, Maggie reflected. Maggie actually felt the same, but would never have admitted it aloud. Now she got to play the voice of reason, while also quaking inside.

"Calm down, Phoebe. Everyone who wants to come will find the room. If we can," she murmured to herself.

They soon came to the end of a long hallway. A sign that listed the meeting rooms hung on the wall. The rooms all had clever names, Maggie noticed, hinting at eastern philosophies—the Shiva Room, the Feng Shui Room, the Lakshmi Room. Her room, the Lotus Room, was listed last.

"It's just down this hallway. Come on," Maggie told Phoebe.

Phoebe didn't budge. "That hallway is completely dark. Didn't you notice? I'm not walking down there. We should have asked a cop to come with us, or something."

That might have been a good idea. Half an hour ago. But it was too far to walk back now and ask for an armed escort. The long, dim hallway did look spooky and intimidating, but Maggie tried not to show that she was rattled.

"Maybe there's a light switch around here somewhere," she said, searching a nearby wall.

No luck. There were no obvious switches anywhere. "Must be a money-saving thing. Keeping the lights off in areas that aren't in use," she said in a logical tone. "There's enough light to find our way, come on." she told her assistant.

Phoebe didn't answer, just sighed and ducked her head as she followed.

All the meeting room doors were closed so that there was no natural light in the hallway, either. Maggie could only see a dim, shadowy light at the very end of the corridor, where it connected with another passageway.

As they walked along quickly, Maggie was tempted to break into a run and kept telling herself she was being silly.

Suddenly a tall figure slipped out of a doorway and blocked their path.

Phoebe screamed and clutched Maggie, nearly knocking her over. Maggie cowered, as the stranger, definitely a man, reached for the them.

"Get back . . ." Maggie said fiercely, holding out her knitting bag like an armored shield.

"Are you all right? What's the matter?" a deep voice asked.

Maggie realized she had her eyes squeezed shut and quickly opened them. "Dr. Max? . . . Oh, I'm so sorry . . . you scared us."

Maggie felt so embarrassed, she could barely look at him.

He peered down at her. "I'm the one who's sorry. I didn't mean to startle you. I just came down to check on this light situation. Seems a circuit breaker or something blew out." He glanced around, looking confused. "I'm not very handy. Someone will have to come and repair it later."

Maggie wasn't surprised. Dr. Max didn't seem the handy type.

"We'll find our way. I think our room is just a few more doors down." Maggie smiled up at Dr. Max, feeling relieved and silly.

She expected that Phoebe felt silly, too. She was just about to walk on when she noticed someone else, farther down the hallway. A slim figure slipped out of a room and practically sprinted down to the darkest end of the corridor, then disappeared from sight.

Maggie blinked. She looked back at Dr. Max, but he was facing in the opposite direction, the way she had come, and couldn't possibly have seen the elusive figure . . . unless he had eyes in the back of his head.

Before she could mention it, he held out a flashlight. "Here, take this," he said, offering the light. "Just in case. The lights are working in all the meeting rooms. It's just the corridor that blew out."

"All right. Thank you," Maggie said graciously.

"Not at all. Sorry I startled you. The atmosphere at the inn is highly charged today. So much negative energy."

Max shook his head, looking regretful and concerned, then headed down the way that Maggie and Phoebe had come.

"Turn it on, Maggie. Turn it on." Phoebe practically hopped up and down, waiting for Maggie to switch on the flashlight.

"Here, you hold it." Maggie handed it to her. "I think it will make you feel better."

"You got that right," Phoebe snapped. She held out the big flashlight like a weapon, as she slowly started to walk down the hallway again.

"Here it is, the Lotus Room. Amen." Phoebe sighed out loud with relief when they finally found the door.

"I hope it's unlocked." Maggie turned the knob, relieved to feel it turn. She opened the door, but both she and Phoebe peered in warily before they entered.

"Looks all right. At least it has a big window," Phoebe noted with relief.

"Yes, that is a plus," Maggie agreed. "Let's leave the door open. The light will go out into the hallway and help people to find us."

The room looked just as Maggie had expected—a big,

bare, carpeted square with windows on one side covered by vertical blinds. There was a long folding table near the windows, set up with Maggie's supplies, and a stack of folding chairs leaning against one wall.

Maggie and Phoebe put down their belongings and started to set out the folding chairs, making a circle. They had been at the task a few minutes when Nadine poked her head through the doorway.

"Oh, good. You're here. I was worried that detective was going to make you late."

"I was done just in time." Maggie unfolded one more chair, then walked over to her.

"How did your interview go?" Nadine asked.

"Fine . . . I guess." Maggie wasn't sure how private those interviews were supposed to be. The detectives hadn't told her not to discuss the conversation. Still, she felt awkward getting into it. "I didn't have that much to tell them about Curtis Hill," she said honestly. "He was in my workshop yesterday, but I'd barely spoken to him."

"Yes . . . I remember." Nadine nodded, then quickly changed the subject. Maggie guessed she was tired of talking about this whole depressing matter by now. "I think I brought all your supplies from the storeroom," Nadine told her, "but you ought to look them over, to make sure. Oh, and Joy just called me. She's not feeling well. She won't be able to teach with you today."

"Really?" Maggie was surprised. Joy had looked like the picture of health last night and seemed excited about teaching the workshop together. "What's wrong with her?"

"A bad migraine. She's prone to them. I think she's gone for acupuncture this morning, but it hasn't helped. It's all the stress from this unfortunate situation," Nadine said, nimbly tiptoeing around the plain truth—a guest at the inn had been murdered last night. "She's very sensitive. She gets upset easily."

"I understand. The situation is upsetting," Maggie agreed. "I'm not sure I can do this mindful knitting demonstration without her. The meditation segment is a big part of it. That was her territory."

"Don't worry. Just do what you can. Everyone will understand."

"I suppose so." Maggie glanced at Phoebe, who was arranging the supplies on the table. What could she do with the class? She could explain mindful knitting, what she knew about it, and they could try it and give them the handout that included the meditation instructions.

Or just stitch and chat, which was also amazingly relaxing. Maybe she would let them choose.

Nadine checked her watch, then sat on a chair and let out a small sigh. "It feels good to sit down a minute," she admitted. "What a day. And it's barely eleven o'clock."

"It does seem like a long day. We all got up at sunrise," Maggie reminded her. "It's amazing that you've been able to keep the schedule going, under the circumstances."

"Oh, tell me about it. It's hard enough to run one of these weekends. But this one is so important and now, this situation has cast such a cloud over everything." Nadine paused and took a deep breath. "I'm trying to keep things in perspective though. Max says all obstacles are illusions, paper tigers we create in our mind. And that this one is, too."

Tell that to Curtis Hill, Maggie wanted to say. Does Max think death is a paper tiger?

But instead Maggie just nodded and said nothing. Nadine seemed so nervous and worn-out. She obviously needed some-one to talk to right now, someone to just let her vent. Maggie didn't want to debate with her, what would be the point of that?

"We all feel terrible about Mr. Hill," Nadine added with a sad sigh. "But there's nothing to be done. It was simply his fate. Death is only one part of the great circle of life, you know?" Nadine paused a moment, then said, "Max and Alice talked about it and they decided to stick to the program, in-cluding the investors meeting tomorrow."

"It's a lot of pressure. Most people would cancel."

"Max and Alice are not most people," Nadine said with a small smile. "Max is very single-minded. Maybe that's why he's so successful. The architect's models are all set up. The PowerPoint presentation is ready to roll and the sites are cho-sen, one in Sedona and another in the Bahamas."

"Beautiful locations, both of them." Sedona in particular seemed a likely choice, famous for its red rock formations and breathtaking landscapes and also for the mysterious energy vortexes some believed were located in the hills.

"All he needs now is some capital. My sister Alice has so much on her shoulders," she added in a quieter, concerned tone. "She's a great help to him. A godsend, really. I don't think Max could have ever gotten back on his feet and come this far without her. He's very high maintenance."

"That must be difficult for her."

Maggie didn't know what else to say. She didn't like to gossip, but did wonder what the real relationship was be-tween Alice and Max. Last night Joy had said Max invited both Alice and her son to work for him when he bought the inn, but she'd also implied there was a romantic connection between them.

But Nadine seemed to be saying that Alice had been part of Max's life long before he wrote the book, made his millions, and set up shop at the inn. In fact, she'd implied Alice had given Max a hand up when he was struggling.

And what was their relationship exactly? It seemed more than a business partnership, but somehow less than a truly romantic one. The feelings were unevenly balanced, Joy had insinuated. Nadine's comment didn't really clarify one way or the other.

"Are many guests here this weekend interested in investing?" Maggie asked.

"Quite a few have come with that in mind. Max is always cultivating possibilities. I don't know what they're thinking now. I'm truly saddened about Mr. Hill. But it does seem unfair if this incident ruins things for Max and my sister. They've worked so hard."

Nadine's position seemed a bit selfish and even cold, Maggie thought. For goodness' sake, a man had been murdered. There were more important things than opening health spas. But she could see that Nadine was concerned for her sister, whose fortunes seemed deeply entwined with those of Dr. Max.

"Maybe Dr. Max can smooth things over at the meeting tomorrow. He does have a way about him."

He had quickly calmed her and Phoebe down when they met in the dark hallway. More importantly, he knew how to work a room, Maggie wanted to say.

"He has wonderful social skills. No doubt about that," Nadine agreed. "He really believes in his philosophy and the lessons he's learned, battling his own demons. He really wants to help others find their way. That's his calling. And his gift."

Maggie nodded. Luckily she hadn't voiced any serious doubts. She really wasn't sure what she thought of him yet. She could easily see how others were charmed and drawn in. He had a powerful personality. But she hadn't read his book and still wasn't very clear on his message.

Nadine's BlackBerry sounded. She quickly pulled it out of her sweater pocket and checked the number. "Alice . . . I've been summoned." Nadine rolled her eyes, but quickly jumped up from her seat. "I'll stop by later if I can. I really want to catch up with you some more, Maggie. We need to have a good long chat."

"Yes, we do." Maggie watched Nadine leave the room just as Helen Lynch walked in.

"Mindful Knitting workshop?" Helen asked, reading from her schedule.

"Yes, it is . . . well, it's supposed to be. We've had a little change in plans. Why don't you come in and have a seat. When the others arrive, I'll explain more."

Helen walked in and chose a chair close to Maggie's in the circle.

"I'm surprised there's anything going on today, with that guy found dead. I didn't sleep a wink on that camping trip and figured I'd just take a long nap this morning. But I couldn't. It's all sort of . . . creepy, you know?"

"It's upsetting," Maggie agreed. "But it helps to be occupied with a productive task. Like knitting. Would you like to pick up some needles and yarn from the table? I'll get you started on something."

"That's all right. I brought my stuff from yesterday. That's okay, I hope? Or are we supposed to start something new here?"

"You can keep going on your first project. That's a good idea." Maggie forced an encouraging note as she looked over Helen's random knitting project. Rarely, in all her days teaching the craft, had she ever seen such tight stitches. The few rows Helen had completed clung to the needle, practically puckered. Maggie wasn't even sure how the woman could fit the needle point under the strands of yarn.

She glanced at Helen, then back at her piece. "How is it going? Are you enjoying knitting?"

"Oh yes . . ." Helen let out a long ragged breath. "It's very relaxing, just like everyone said. Just what I need to unwind."

"Oh . . . good." Maggie smiled and nodded again. "We have plenty of different yarns. Maybe you'd like to change colors or textures soon. That's what the random technique is all about."

"Good point. I'll go up and check it out."

More students were coming in. Maggie recognized the Schumachers. They were wearing matching jogging suits again and baseball caps. Navy blue suits today, with white stripes on the arms and legs, and dark blue hats with the Red Sox baseball team emblem.

Rita walked in ahead of Walter, clutching her knitting bag. He followed slowly, using a cane. He didn't look well, Maggie thought, his face drawn with deep lines. Rita had told her that he was very sick and Maggie wondered what was wrong with him. Cancer, perhaps? He always had on a baseball cap, but now she noticed that he was totally bald underneath. The type of unnatural-looking baldness that comes with chemo or radiation.

They sat down side by side at the first chairs they came to on the side of the circle opposite Maggie. Rita fussed over her husband, helping him into the seat while he grumbled and batted her hands away.

Maggie briefly greeted them, then noticed Dana at the door. "It's just me, I'm afraid. Lucy felt too tired to leave the cottage. I made sure she locked herself in. And Suzanne ran off to try her free cellulite treatment. We walked most of the way together," Dana added.

"I'm glad they're both safe. But I feel positively abandoned."

"And the yoga woman called in sick," Phoebe told Dana. " 'No one-legged heron tonight, dear, I have a headache.'"

"A migraine," Maggie corrected, giving Phoebe a look. "I'm just going to wing it. Although what I know about yoga and meditation and how it relates to knitting could be inscribed on a button."

"Not to worry. I've got it covered." Dana patted Maggie's shoulder as she swept through the doorway. Maggie just stared at her. "I've been doing all of those things for years now and have often considered the similarities. I'd be happy to pull up the slack."

Dana was even dressed for the part, wearing a yoga outfit and toting her mat in the bag she'd knitted a few months back. She must have planned to take a class after the knitting session.

"If you don't mind, Dana, I'd welcome the help," Maggie said finally.

They all took seats in the circle. Maggie sat at the top with Dana right next to her. Just as they settled in, Shannon Piper appeared in the doorway.

"Am I too late?" She leaned in the room with a hesitant, million-dollar smile.

"We're just about to start. Come right in," Maggie invited her.

Shannon slipped inside and quickly found a seat. She looked as if she'd stepped off a page in a magazine, as usual, with her hair loose around her shoulders and held back with a wide white band. A chocolate brown hoodie and matching, wide-leg pants didn't look like they'd stand up well to a real workout, but the color was perfect for her gray-blue eyes and rich brown hair.

It was hard not to stare at her; so much beauty had been concentrated into one package. It almost didn't seem fair, Maggie reflected.

"Thank you all for coming. This morning, we're going to talk about mindful knitting. I will confess, this is not a topic I'm very familiar with. Though the more I learn about it, it seems to be something I've been doing automatically for most of my knitting career.

"Joy Kimmel was scheduled to teach with me, but she's not feeling well. So my friend Dana has offered to help explain the concept." Maggie cast an encouraging look in Dana's direction.

She seemed surprised to have been passed the ball so quickly, but she gamely smiled and glanced around at the wide-eyed students.

"Mindful knitting is just what the words suggest, a way of knitting that is a lot like mindfulness, meditation, and also like yoga. Yoga, meditation, and knitting have all been around hundreds of years and have all suddenly become very popular. It's not hard to understand. These activities are, at their core, a lot alike. All require that we slow down and focus, giving our busy minds a rest in the present moment. All encourage relaxation and contemplation. All help us cultivate inner peace and a kinder, gentler attitude toward the world at large . . ."

Warming up to her topic, Dana folded her legs beneath her in the lotus pose, balanced like a yogi on the folding chair. She took up her needles and began to demonstrate.

Maggie and her other friends stared at Dana, wide-eyed. Who knew? Maggie nearly said aloud.

"When we knit in a calm, focused manner and when we meditate and practice yoga, we have the potential to expand ourselves physically and mentally."

"How true. Why knit in the first place?" Maggie asked the group, jumping in. "Why not just buy a sweater or a scarf? Why sit and tie little knots in string?" she added, borrowing one of Dr. Max's lines. "Because knitting puts us in a creative and purposeful state of mind. Knitting is productive. When you're finished with a knitted object, you've made something useful with your own two hands and given something beautiful to the world."

"This practice is even easier if we're making a gift for someone. Focusing on each stitch as you knit, perhaps thinking about that person that you're knitting for, is also a mindful practice," Dana continued, slowly knitting as she spoke. "It's like saying a prayer for that person. Or simply sending out waves of goodwill."

"What a lovely thought." Shannon tilted her head to one side. "Dr. Max says that positive thoughts raise the vibrations of the whole world. Even the entire universe."

"It's like sending waves of love, like radio waves," Rita offered. "That's the way I feel when I'm knitting things for the family, my kids and my grandchildren. I've been meditating all along and I never realized."

"If you've cleared your mind and focused on the process, stitch by stitch, and felt that you've lost all track of time, and even your surroundings, then you are in a mindful state," Dana clarified.

"Knitting nirvana," Maggie said simply. "It's a beautiful thing," she promised.

Helen Lynch shifted in her chair. "Well, I didn't get a thing from that damned campout. Nothing but the willies," she murmured. "Guess I'll give this a try."

"Let's knit a while," Dana suggested. "Then we'll do a short breathing meditation."

Maggie nodded in agreement. "That's a good plan. Let's start with the knitting. I see you've all brought along projects."

Dana was brilliant at this, but of course she would be, Maggie realized. She was so poised and well spoken.

Once again, Walter was the only one who was not knitting. He had taken out the newspaper when Dana started speaking and had been reading it ever since.

Everyone else was able to knit on their own, except for Helen. Maggie sat in the empty seat next to the businesswoman and took her under her wing.

"Your stitches are even but they're very tight. You need to work the yarn a little looser."

"I've been trying, but it's just my style or something. Then with that Curtis Hill turning up dead this morning and the police crawling all over the place? How is a person supposed to relax with all that going on?"

"It's been a difficult day, to be sure," Maggie agreed.

"Yeah, well . . . I have a feeling this is all going to get worse before it gets better." Helen twisted her mouth to the side as she aimed her needle at the next stitch like a dart at a board. "I was in the hotel office, waiting for a word with Alice Archer, and I heard that Hill wasn't even a travel writer. He was a reporter for some TV news magazine. *Expose*, I think the police said."

"*Expose*? They're always chasing some unscrupulous businessman with a video camera. Or doing an undercover story about puppy mills. Is that the one?" Phoebe asked her.

"That's the one, all right," Helen replied.

"Geez . . . a reporter? Really?" The information had even drawn Walter's attention. He put down his newspaper and stared at his wife.

Rita made some clucking sounds and shook her head. "Who would have guessed? How did they find out?"

"I couldn't really hear that well, but seems that when the detectives went through his room, it was obvious. It looks like he was here to do a story on the spa . . . and Dr. Max. And not a puff piece, either," she added in a dour tone.

"*Expose* doesn't do puff pieces, that's for sure," Maggie agreed.

This news changed everything. If Curtis Hill was an investigative reporter . . . well, then you make a lot of enemies in that sort of job. Serious enemies.

His true identity also explained his penchant for secretive photography, with this camera phone, which Lucy had observed. That made perfect sense now. He was trying to catch Dr. Max in some outlandish, absurd act or presentation. The moonlight meditation retreat was the perfect place for that.

But what else was he investigating? Max's business practices perhaps? The way he courted new investors? The plans for the new spas?

Maggie's head spun with possibilities, but she had no time to consider all the angles on this now. This was a juicy morsel to talk over with her friends later.

Maggie looked up to find Dana staring at her with an alarmed expression. But she quickly recovered.

"This isn't really a time to dwell on negative thoughts," Dana told the group. "The idea is to focus on the knitting and put all worries and troubling thoughts aside."

Helen just ignored her. "It's too bad for Dr. Max. This kind of publicity will really impact his branding. I was concerned this morning when they found the body. But this is very disconcerting. It doesn't bode well."

It doesn't bode well for the new spas, Maggie guessed she meant. But perhaps she was concerned about Dr. Max, too.

Shannon had been sitting quietly, knitting in a calm, focused way. She looked up suddenly and stared at Helen.

"I'm concerned for Dr. Max. What have we learned if we desert him now? Nothing. Can't you see? This isn't a disaster, Helen. It's an opportunity. A chance to answer the negative energy in the universe with love," she added. "A chance to hold your sacred space."

Helen shifted in her seat, but wouldn't meet Shannon's gaze. "It's all that, I'm sure. *And* a publicity nightmare."

"Well, I'm not jumping ship now," Shannon snapped back. "I wouldn't even be sitting here if it wasn't for Max. I have an eating disorder," Shannon confessed to the group. "I've battled it most of my life. But when I read Max's book, something happened. I found the key to my recovery," her soft voice trembled. Maggie thought she might start to cry. She sighed and returned to her knitting. "He changed my life. I owe him so much."

Helen sighed, staring down at her knitting, then answered Shannon's passionate declaration in a tired tone. "Maybe you ought to write a book, Shannon. People love that stuff . . . beautiful celebrities with secret afflictions. It really sells."

A cold reaction to Shannon's heart-baring moment, Maggie thought. Maggie had a feeling that the two women had already covered this topic. Up on the mountain maybe? While they waited to give their statements to the police. They had covered it and locked horns over Dr. Max.

"I'm just being honest. No drama. Just the facts," Helen said bluntly.

Shannon ignored the jab. "You're still going to the meeting tomorrow, aren't you?"

"Yes, yes . . . if he still has one, I'll be there. I'm curious to hear what he has to say. Such a big secret. They won't give you a scrap of information in advance," Helen complained to the others.

Never underestimate the element of surprise. Maggie remembered the quote but wasn't sure where it had come from.

"I'm surprised he's even having that meeting. Not only does that poor fellow Hill die, but now he doesn't even turn out to be who he said he was." Walter turned the page of his paper and took a wheezy breath.

"What a shame." Rita shook her head again, looking a little teary, Maggie noticed. "How could a thing like that happen? Up here, I mean. In this beautiful place? Do you think the police can figure this out? Do they have any idea who did it?"

Walter patted her shoulder. "Calm down, Rita. You're getting yourself all worked up again."

"Yeah, I know." She swallowed hard. "Better not to talk about it. I lose my head."

"You said it. I didn't." Walter gave her another look and returned to the sports page. "When it's your time, it's your time. The only one who knows is the Big Guy upstairs."

"That's true. You never know." Rita agreed and turned her knitting over.

The knitters worked quietly for a few minutes. Then Maggie thought Dana should wrap things up with the breathing meditation exercise, before they all got talking again about the murder and this latest twist in Curtis Hill's story.

"I hope you got a taste of the mindful knitting method this morning. Now Dana is going to close the workshop with a breathing meditation exercise."

"Let's just dim the lights in here a bit," Dana began. Phoebe jumped up and closed the blinds.

"Just put your knitting aside. Sit up straight in your chair and rest your hands in your lap," Dana instructed. She sat up straight with her feet on the floor and did the same.

In a soothing, quiet voice, Dana led the group, step by step, in a short session of meditation, focusing on the in-and-out flow of their breath.

Maggie tried it and felt herself drifting off. She knew that napping wasn't the objective, but it had been a tiring day, and it was only half over. At least she'd finished her obligations for today. She only had one session left, a walk-in workshop in the lobby again, tomorrow morning. She could relax for the rest of afternoon, maybe even get down to the spa.

She wondered if the police had made any progress. Now that they knew Hill's real identity and reason for being here, that must have given them some ideas and leads.

Too bad Joy had not come today, Maggie thought. I could have asked about the *I Ching* symbol. Maggie decided to look it up herself, when she had a chance. She remembered it was number eighteen. There had to be a copy of the *I Ching* around the inn somewhere. The gift shop probably had a whole shelf of books like that.

A few moments later, Dana's soothing voice cut into her rambling thoughts. "Now let's slowly open our eyes and take another deep breath. There's no rush. Just come back slowly. Stretch. Breathe. That's right. That's all there is to it."

The guests in the knitting circle roused themselves and stared around, blinking and flexing their shoulders. They looked a lot like newly hatched birds, Maggie thought.

"Well . . . that was interesting. I liked it." Helen said, a slightly softer edge to her usually clipped tone.

"Thank you, Maggie. Thank you, Dana." Shannon rose, picked up her tote, and quickly left the room.

Phoebe opened the shades and Dana stepped over to help. The Schumachers took their time, standing up, straightening out their jogging suits. Walter kept folding his newspapers, making a rattling sound, then finally tucked it under his arm, and picked up his cane.

"I'm starting off. It takes me longer," he told his wife.

"Go ahead. I'll catch up." Rita had strolled over to the supply table and was sifting through the basket of yarns. "Mind if I take a few? I didn't bring much of a stash."

"By all means, help yourself." Maggie walked over and looked through another basket for good finds. "Here's a nice one. Alpaca." She held up a ball of pale blue yarn for Rita to see. "That's hand dyed."

"That is nice." Rita took the soft ball of yarn and fingered the strand. "I've used a lot of this. It's nonallergic, so you don't have to worry. Nice and soft, too. Great for baby gifts."

"It is. I often recommend it for baby patterns."

"Was a time when I could only find the alpaca at a little shop in Cambridge, the Yarn Tree. Now you see it all over, all these exotic yarns. Lately I've seen yarn from camel, possum, buffalo, even from bamboo. What happened to the poor sheep? Did they fall out of fashion or something?"

Maggie had to laugh at her recitation. Alpaca weren't even sheep. But it was true. There were so many amazingly exotic fibers out there now and fiber blends. But when she started knitting, the choice was either/or . . . wool or acrylic.

"I know the Yarn Tree. Lovely little shop. I still go there whenever I get into the city. Do you live in Boston, Rita?"

"We're from Worcester," Rita replied, mentioning a medium-size city in central Massachusetts, about an hour west of Boston. "I used to visit the area pretty often, though. One of my grandchildren went to college around there . . ." Rita hesitated a moment, then said, "Harvard. Ever heard of it?" she joked.

Maggie was impressed. "I believe so. Your grandchildren must be brilliant."

"Runs in the family." Rita smiled and put the ball of alpaca in her tote, then picked out two others. "I'd better catch up to Walter, before he gets in trouble."

Finally, Maggie was alone with her friends. Dana and Phoebe were putting away the folding chairs and she gave Dana a big hug. "You pulled my turkey bacon out of the fire that time, Dana. Bravo . . . you're a natural."

Dana shook her head. "It's just a topic I know a little about. I was happy to help. Though I'm not sure I really captured their attention."

"Not with that Helen Lynch yakking away. Sheesh, what is her problem?" Phoebe asked the others.

"Helen's a little abrasive but I really don't think she's so awful," Dana offered, "though Shannon seems to bring out her dark side."

"I'll say. But Helen has a valid point about Hill's death bringing bad publicity. How could Dr. Max avoid it?" Maggie asked the others. "And now we hear that Hill was a reporter for *Expose,* obviously at the spa to research a story. Sounds like Dr. Max was already in line for some damaging press."

"Damaging and brutal. That show tars with a wide brush . . . and it sticks a long time," Dana added. "Was that the reason Hill was killed? But it doesn't really make sense. If Hill knew some nasty, damaging information about Max or anyone close to the spa, getting him out of the way would—temporarily, at least—brush it under the rug. But his murder still puts the spa in a bad light. Am I missing something here?" Dana asked the others.

Maggie felt just as puzzled. Maybe more so. "It is confusing. Hill could have been a blackmailer. But again, killing him in such an obvious way seems self-defeating . . . and not very clever."

"You guys both seem to think good old Dr. Max did the dirty deed," Phoebe pointed out.

"It is a possibility," Maggie had to admit, though the thought was extremely chilling. Especially after bumping into him, face-to-face, in the hallway only an hour ago.

"Well, he had the most to lose from Hill's investigation," Dana pointed out.

"Yeah . . . Max and his entourage," Phoebe agreed. "The thing is, someone could have killed Hill just to smear this place and tank Max on the verge of the big meeting."

"Out of the mouths of babes," Maggie murmured.

Phoebe laughed. "Me? A babe? Wait till I tell Josh. He never gives me any good compliments lately."

"You are a babe, in more ways than one." Dana reached over and gave Phoebe's ponytail a playful tug.

"Oh dear . . . this is all confusing. My head is spinning," Maggie admitted.

"One cure for that. Let's grab some lunch and head over to the spa," Dana suggested. "It will be much easier to figure this after a dose of roughage and a soothing massage."

"An excellent plan," Maggie replied. "But let's let the police untangle this tale. We've got more important things to do here."

Chapter Nine

*L*ucy was tempted to join her friends when they called from the reception area of the spa. They were indulging in special treatments and even offered to share their coupons for freebies, compliments of Alice Archer. She had refused. "I'm sorry. I'm too tired," she told Suzanne.

"Okay. Be like that. Party pooper," Suzanne scolded her.

"Just make sure everything is locked up," she heard Dana say. "Especially if you take a nap. The police just announced that everyone is free to go if they want to, but we still need to be careful," she reminded Lucy.

Lucy was relieved to hear that the lockdown had been lifted. Even though her group was in for the duration, she didn't like the feeling of being trapped. The whole situation was very stressful . . . and tiring.

She did plan on taking a nap. A long one. The night on the mountaintop had worn her out. She showered, put on clean clothes, and flopped on a big, lovely bed, where she quickly fell into a deep, dreamless sleep.

Afterward, even a stroll around the lake seemed too ambitious. She'd ended up on the porch with a cup of green tea, reading Dr. Max's book—and trying not to check her phone for messages . . . or give in and call Matt.

Luckily, Max's book—*Confessions of a Lost Soul: One Man's Journey to Reunite Mind, Body, and Spirit*—drew her in from page one. The doctor had a strong voice and an interesting story to tell. The autobiography opened at the height of his success as a well-known and respected psychiatrist with a thriving practice, describing his carefree, affluent lifestyle. Then the tale quickly grew darker, turning to the tragedy that ended that cushy life and his enviable career, when a patient under his care at the practice he shared with Edward Archer committed suicide.

The young woman, who was not named, was being treated for depression with talk therapy and well-known antidepressants. She was not Dr. Max's patient, but he and Dr. Archer consulted with each other about many of their patients. Max took an interest in her case and felt a strong bond with her. Something about her touched him in a deep place, he confessed. She seemed a symbol for youth, beauty, and unlimited promise.

The young woman's death was a devastating blow to both Max and his partner. Archer eventually drank himself to death, Lucy already knew, and Max told how he lost the practice and his personal holdings in a lawsuit with the girl's family. He was ruined and practically destitute. Even his wife of over twenty years, Joy Kimmel, left him, too.

Looking back, Max believed it was not just personal failing or Archer's miscalculation of the patient's state of mind, but a cruel lesson in the limits of conventional, traditional medicine and psychiatry, which he now deemed to be tragically limited and "as primitive as medieval medicine, at times."

He pointed out that with all our advances in technology, even putting a man in outer space or sending instant messages around the globe in the blink of an eye, doctors and psychiatrists persist in treating only the symptoms of an individual's inner torments, never getting to the root of the vine that eventually chokes and kills the soul. Modern medicine and psychiatry fragment the body and mind, Max claimed, and totally ignore the spirit, the source of our emotions, thoughts and creativity.

He asserted that most people see their existence in a concave mirror that reverses the single most important fact: We are not material beings, having the occasional spiritual experience, but spiritual beings, having a material experience, he wrote.

Very true, Lucy thought. But hadn't she read that some place before? Maybe during some college philosophy course? Or maybe in an old Star Trek movie. Her ex-husband had been a big fan.

Max went on to claim that once you fully understand and master that fact—once you understand the dynamic laws of energy that control the universe—the sky is the limit. Every intention and desire can be fulfilled—perfect health, fulfilling relationships, financial abundance. It is all within reach.

Lucy set the book aside and stared out at the lake. This was powerful stuff, more profound that she'd expected. She could also see why people were drawn in. Follow me to complete happiness and fulfillment. Just do as I say, and it's all yours. Every wish, every desire. His promises were hard to resist.

She took a sip of tea and continued.

The night the young patient died, Max made a solemn vow. That he would never forget her and he would never allow her death to be in vain. He went on to describe the hard road he had to follow in order to purge his sick soul and make himself worthy. Losing all his material possessions and status in society. Traveling around the globe with just the clothes on his back and a few coins in his pocket.

Lucy had come to the end of a chapter and paused again. No wonder Max got the call from Oprah. She wouldn't be surprised if he had his own show pretty soon.

She heard footsteps on the gravel and looked up, expecting to see her friends. Instead she saw a young man wearing a dark blue sweatshirt with the inn's logo on front and carrying a toolbox. The same guy she'd run into yesterday, when the group had first arrived and she'd wandered off, looking for the restroom. The man who had been arguing with Alice Archer.

He doesn't seem to remember me, though, Lucy thought. If he did, he was very adept at hiding it.

"Sorry to bother you, miss. But we have to check all the heating units in the hotel. I need to take a look at the wood-burning stove. Make sure it's working properly."

"Oh right. Go ahead in . . ." Lucy stood up, suddenly remembering that Suzanne had told her a repairman from the inn would be coming by. Even though Hill's death had not been an accident, the hotel management was trying to assure guests they were vigilant and on top of things.

The maintenance man walked up on the porch and entered the cottage. Lucy followed, grabbing her mug and the book.

"Sorry to interrupt you," the young man said as he glanced at the book cover. "I hear that's a page-turner."

Lucy smiled. "It's not required reading for hotel employees?"

"I just flipped to the good parts. I'm waiting for the video."

Were the film rights sold? Lucy hadn't heard about that. Then she realized he was just making a joke. A dry, sarcastic one.

She smiled, but he didn't smile back.

He stood in front of the wood-burning stove and put his toolbox down. Lucy noticed that his name was embroidered on the sweatshirt: Brian.

"I'm pretty sure this stove is fine. This is just a precaution," he explained. He knelt down, opened the stove door, and peered inside. "Have you tried this yet?"

"I'm not sure. I wasn't here last night. I went on the campout, on the mountain."

"You're a brave one. Did Dr. Max beat on his drum and howl at the moon?" He was looking into the stove and Lucy couldn't see his expression. Once again, she couldn't tell from his tone if he was joking or not.

"He did beat on a drum. And he only howled once or twice," she reported. "It was a little . . . out there. But his book is different. I'm enjoying the book. So far, I mean. It's better than I expected."

She wasn't sure why she felt inclined to shade her opinion so carefully for this repairman. It was just a certain feeling he gave off. She could sense he didn't like Dr. Max much.

Brian leaned back on his heels and glanced at her. "Well, Max had some help with that. He always has some help."

Lucy shrugged. She could tell from the cover that the doctor had a cowriter. All the celebrities did that. Lucy had the feeling this guy meant something else. He said Max's name in such a familiar tone, there was definitely some subtext here. "Do you have a paper bag or some newspapers? I need to clean this thing out."

"Sure. There's some newspaper around somewhere." Lucy found a stack of papers Dana had brought along and handed them down. He had already opened the toolbox and pulled on a pair of heavy work gloves, tan leather, she noticed.

He set up the paper around the hearth, then proceeded to scoop out the ash with the fireplace tools.

"So, you were up on the mountain when Max found that guy."

"Curtis Hill. Yes, I was. It was pretty awful. A real nightmare."

"I'll bet. It's Max and Alice's worst nightmare, that's for sure. Especially this weekend, with that big meeting planned." He sounded almost happy about that, Lucy noticed. "Bad karma . . . real bad."

"You could say that, I guess." Lucy stood with her arms crossed over her chest, watching him work. "You sound as if you know Max well. And Alice."

He laughed. "I hardly know them at all, to tell you the truth. Alice is my mother. That must count for something," he added.

Lucy was surprised by his glib answer. Then the pieces fell together. She'd heard that Alice's son worked at the inn. It was right in the book. When she'd seen them together arguing, she hadn't gotten it. But the way they'd spoken to each other made more sense now.

"I don't think the police are going to sort this mess out that easily." The stove was cleared of ash and Brian removed a small grate and set it aside. "They had a real long talk with me.

I'm the only one who can screw in a lightbulb around here, so I guess that makes me a suspect. I worked on those heaters, but the company that supplies the gas does the real maintenance and signs off on all that stuff. The units were working fine the night before last. No problems."

"Really? Was there another meditation hike? I thought they only did that once a month."

"We had a hiking club from town up there. My mother's always looking to pull in a little extra cash. The temperature dropped, and the heaters must have kicked in fine. Everybody got up the next morning, ate their granola, and hiked back down," he said casually.

"So you're saying someone must have tampered with the mechanism last night, or even yesterday? But if they were after Hill, they would have needed to wait, to see which hut he chose. So it had to have been sometime last night," Lucy added, working out the timing in her mind, "after we all went to bed."

"Sounds about right to me. I think you're on the right track," Brian Archer said lightly. "Which lets me off the hook since there's a string of bartenders in town who will give me a solid alibi for that shift. I'm a good customer. They know me well."

Lucy didn't know how to answer that. Was he trying to explain himself to her? To answer a question she never asked? Or was it just more of his peculiar, bleak humor?

What motive would Brian Archer have to do away with Hill? Lucy couldn't think of any that was obvious. Of course, motives for murder seldom were.

"Hey, look at this. Something's clogging up the works. Lucky you didn't make a fire last night. It might have gotten smoky." Brian pulled out a large piece of charred wood and put it with the rest of the ashes. "Ashes to ashes, dust to dust . . . sorry I've made such a big . . . muss?"

Lucy forced a smile at his lame poetic attempt, then watched as Brian carefully rolled the paper, took off his gloves, and put his tools back in his box.

"Well, my work is done here. Thanks for the interesting conversation . . . miss?"

"Lucy . . . Lucy Binger. Good to meet you." She held out her hand, but he just waved.

"My hands are dirty from the stove," he said with a smile. A genuine smile this time. "See you around, Lucy. I'll be interested to hear your review of the book."

"I'll be interested to tell you," she said honestly.

She watched him head down the path, swinging the box. He was smart, attractive . . . and troubled, she thought. Though he tried to mask it under that cool, irreverent attitude. It almost worked, too.

Lucy made a fresh cup of tea and headed out to the porch with Max's book again. She settled down and opened it, but realized she felt different about Max's tale, now that she'd met Brian Archer. It was hard to say why and it wasn't anything Alice's son had said, exactly. It was just his attitude, she realized, and what he hadn't said. And maybe the unspoken fact that Brian, though ten years younger at the time, had been a witness to all the trauma and tragedy Max related.

Lucy returned to *Confessions of a Lost Soul,* but hadn't made much progress before she heard her friends returning to the cottage. She looked up and saw the group on the path, walking two by two. Phoebe waved and ran ahead.

"You missed a real spa splurge, Lucy. We all had sugar scrubs and shiatsu."

"Shiatsu . . . isn't that a type of miniature dog?"

"You're thinking of a shih tzu," Maggie corrected her. "We had these terrific massages. The real deal. I feel like a new woman."

"It was fabulous," Dana agreed, bringing up the rear with Suzanne.

"And check out my thighs . . ." Suzanne was so proud of her legs, she lifted the hem of her skirt to show them off. "Much better, right?"

"Suzanne . . . your legs have always looked great to me," Lucy insisted.

"That's sweet, Lucy. But be honest. I'm starting to get that dimply, cottage cheese thing going on. I'm going to get one these treatments every week," she vowed. "I just have to hit the lottery or something."

"I'm hitting the fridge. Time to take out those gourmet treats we brought along." Maggie had gone straight to the kitchen and was setting up a tray with appetizers, cheese, crackers, and a bottle of white wine. "Having a massage makes me hungry. Is that odd? You're not doing anything, just lying on a table."

"The relaxation lowers your inhibitions," Dana explained, swiping a cracker off the tray. "Don't you remember how boys in high school always wanted to give you a shoulder rub?"

Maggie laughed. "Is that what was going on? I was naive, wasn't I?"

Lucy rolled her eyes. "I've got news. You still are, Mag," she said, making everyone laugh.

She joined her friends in the sitting area, happy to have company again. She poured herself a glass of wine and sat back in the big couch cushions.

"So what have you been up to all this time, Lucy?" Dana

asked her. "Did you make any progress on your knitting or take a nap?"

"I napped for a while. Then I started Max's book." She held it up for the others to see. "I'm not that far into it. But it's not bad. He comes off as very likable and even modest."

She placed the book on the table and sat up a bit. "The funny thing was, while I was reading, Alice's son came by to fix the wood-burning stove."

"That's right. He works at the hotel doing maintenance. Nadine told me that," Maggie said. "What was he like?"

"Smart and sarcastic. A classic underachiever. Sounds like he doesn't like Max much . . . or even his own mother, for that matter."

"Hmm, interesting," Maggie murmured through a mouthful of cracker.

"Listen to this . . . remember when we got here and you all went into lunch and I went off in search of a restroom? Well, while I was wandering around I saw them, Alice and Brian, having an argument. They weren't raising their voices very loud, but they were both steaming. He even picked up a vase and threw it on the floor."

"Wow. Guess he has a temper . . . and a violent streak," Suzanne said.

"Think so?" Dana asked blandly. "What were they saying to each other, do you remember?"

Lucy had to think back. "It all happened so fast. I was embarrassed to barge in like that . . . so I was trying not listen. I think she was ordering him to do something. Or telling him that after he did some job, he couldn't leave. He said that wasn't part of their deal and he was angry. She said something about him drinking too much and not remembering. And he just told me that he drank a lot, more or less . . ." Lucy realized she was rambling a bit, but it was hard to remember. "Oh, I remember now. She told him he could leave it he wanted to, but he wouldn't get paid. That's what really sent him over the edge."

"For someone who didn't mean to listen, you did a pretty good job remembering," Maggie remarked.

Lucy felt herself blush. "It was intense. I couldn't really help it."

"I wonder what they were talking about," Suzanne said. "Maybe some special job at the inn, some overtime situation?"

"It's impossible to guess, isn't it?" Maggie shook her head.

"It's not hard to guess why he's so angry," Dana told them. "He's been hurt by the way he lost his father and maybe he feels somehow . . . humiliated by the way Max has helped him and his mother. If Alice and Max are romantically connected now, he must resent that too," she added.

Lucy had already considered that. "He started talking about Hill's murder, telling me he'd been questioned but had a good alibi. Oh, and he had a good handle on when the murderer must have fiddled with the heater. He said the heaters had been working fine the night before last. So it must have been tampered with yesterday, or last night sometime, especially if Hill was the intended victim and it wasn't just a random incident. We all just fanned out and picked out our huts. There were no advanced assignments," Lucy told the others.

"That's right," Dana confirmed. "If the killer was after Hill specifically, he or she would have needed to wait to see which hut Hill ended up in."

"Which means that the murderer might have been with you, in the retreat group," Suzanne said. She reached for a bite of cheese, then put it down. "That gives me goose flesh."

"Saying the words 'goose flesh' gives me goose flesh," Phoebe chimed in. She sighed and stretched out on the floor, tucking a big silk pillow under her head. "But whoever knocked off Hill didn't even have to be part of the retreat group. They could have come up on their own," Phoebe pointed out.

"I did see a light on the mountain and heard someone in the woods," Maggie reminded them.

"It's a long way up that mountain in the dark. Even with a flashlight," Dana noted.

"Yes, but not if you've done it a lot and know the way," Lucy suggested. "I don't know . . . there are just too many possibilities here. And who would want to murder Curtis Hill? He was just a travel writer."

Her friends looked at one another. "You didn't hear? Hill lied about his reason for coming here," Dana quickly explained. "He was really a reporter for that TV show *Expose*. He was probably here gathering research for a report that would have smeared the spa and Dr. Max."

"Wow . . . no, I didn't hear that. Who told you?"

"Helen Lynch, in the workshop." Maggie said. "She overheard the police telling Alice."

"That does change things," Lucy agreed. "Though I'm still stumped."

"We've already ruled out blackmail," Maggie told her. "Just doesn't make sense."

"No, it doesn't," Dana agreed. "Though there are a lot of members of this ersatz little family who do have a motive to protect Max. He's at the center, the hub of the wheel, and they're all revolving around him. Alice, Brian, Joy Kimmel . . . even the former model, Shannon Piper, could qualify for that list. She made an emotional plea on his behalf at the workshop."

"Did she ever. The woman would take a bullet for him," Phoebe called up from the floor.

"So you're saying it wasn't Max. It was someone who wanted to protect him. That makes sense. But protect him from what?" Lucy asked her friends. "I'm not even a third of the way through this book. The man discloses everything. I don't know that there was any dirty linen left over to embarrass him with," she told she others.

"Lucy, there's always more dirty linen tucked away somewhere. Trust me on this," Dana answered. She crunched down on a carrot stick to underscore her point.

Before the group could speculate on Dr. Max's dirty secrets, a sharp knock sounded on the glass door.

They all jumped in their seats and Phoebe popped up from the floor.

"What was that?" she practically shrieked.

Chapter Ten

$\mathcal{L}$ucy quickly turned and saw Detective Dykstra standing on the porch, peering inside.

She let out a quick breath, trying to hide her attack of nerves. "I'll let him in," she said. She was nearest to the door and walked over to open it. "I wonder what he wants."

"Maybe we're being summoned up to the inn again. Maybe the police have an announcement," Suzanne said.

"Or they're staging a scene out of an Agatha Christie play. When all the prime suspects are gathered together in the manor house drawing room, and Miss Marple pins the murderer," Maggie offered.

"Where is Miss Marple when you really need her?" Dana asked.

"She knits a lot. She'd fit right in here," Phoebe added.

Lucy had opened the door, spoken to the detective briefly, and led him over to her friends. "Sorry to disturb you, ladies."

Lucy noticed him looking over their wineglasses and hors d'oeuvres platter.

"We're just relaxing. Trying to figure out what happened to Curtis Hill," Dana answered.

"Hit on any good theories?" he asked.

"Not yet, but we're coming along," Suzanne said. "We've ruled out some duds."

"You're welcome to join us. Would you like a glass of wine?" Maggie said.

He smiled and Lucy thought for a moment he was going to accept. Then he shook his head. "Thank you. But I'm on duty right now. Actually, I came down to see you, Mrs. Messina. I have something to show you . . ."

Maggie sat up and looked at him alertly. They were all looking at him now, Lucy noticed.

He reached into his pocket and took out a plastic bag. Lucy saw a scrap of knitting inside. Only a few, uneven-looking rows with a loopy edge where a needle had fallen out.

He held the bag out to Maggie. "Do you recognize this?"

Maggie stared at it for a moment, then nodded. "Yes, I do. It's one of the random knitting projects the group did on Friday. This one was started by Dr. Max."

"Dr. Max Flemming," he repeated. "You're sure about that?"

Lucy saw Maggie swallow, looking suddenly nervous. "Yes, I'm positive. I noticed the yarn he chose. This blue shade and the fiber. It's a memorable merino. We were talking about the color blue, too. How it stands for optimism and the imagination." The detective nodded, listening to her. "And also, when he was working, he asked me for help at one point. I noticed his stitches. The way he was mixing them up . . . does that convince you?"

"Yes, it does." The detective put the plastic bag back in

his pocket. "What did he do with this when the workshop was over, did you notice?"

"He put it in his pocket. He told me he was going to work on it and show me his progress." Maggie's expression turned grim. Lucy guessed that she just realized she was giving the police information that tied Max to the murder somehow.

"Did you find that at the campsite?" Maggie asked bluntly.

"Yes, we did."

"Not just at the campsite, but you must have found it at the murder scene. In Hill's hut," Dana guessed.

Detective Dykstra's mouth twisted to one side. "I can't tell you anything more. I don't know if this scrap of yarn has any significance yet. It would be foolish to speculate."

It would be, Lucy agreed. Though that wouldn't stop most people around here, she thought.

The detective looked back at Maggie. "Thanks for your help. If you recall anything more, about conversations you had with Mr. Hill yesterday or at the retreat"—he looked over at Dana and Lucy now—"or anything you saw or heard during the night up there, let me know."

"We will," Lucy promised.

Detective Dykstra turned and headed for the glass doors. "I'll show myself out. Have a good evening, ladies." He was stepping out the porch when Dana suddenly jumped up from her seat. "Detective? Wait . . . I have something else to tell you. I think."

He quickly turned and stared at her. Dana stared back, her blue eyes wide.

"Yes . . . what is it?" he asked curiously, walking back toward the group.

Everyone was quiet, wondering what Dana had to say.

She took a breath and touched her forehead. "I didn't even think of it this morning when I gave you my statement. But it was so early and the situation was so stressful . . . and you did keep saying that Curtis Hill was found in his hut . . ."

"Yes? What is it exactly, Dr. Haeger?" The detective leaned toward her, his body tense as a bow string.

"Well, when you showed us that piece of knitting just now, it made me think. Last night, when we all went in to bed, I looked out the little window in my hut. I could see the first hut, directly across the campsite from mine. The one where Hill was found in the morning. You kept saying 'we found Mr. Hill in his hut.' Well, the door opened for a moment and a lantern was on inside. I saw the person who had gone in there to sleep. It wasn't Curtis Hill . . . it was Dr. Max."

Lucy and her friends exchanged glances, but no one dared break the silence.

"Max Flemming? Are you sure?" Detective Dykstra stared at Dana, his eyes narrowed.

Dana nodded solemnly. "I'm positive. The men look nothing alike and the huts aren't very far apart. It was easy to see that it was Max."

"Was he alone?"

"Yes, I think so. He left the door open a minute. I think he was putting something outside the hut. His drum maybe? But the door was wide open. There was no one else in there with him."

The huts were so small, you could barely swing a cat, as the saying went. You couldn't even hide a cat in there, Lucy thought.

"Then what happened?" Dykstra asked.

"He went back inside and shut the door. And the light

went out. I remember that, as well. I was looking around because I hadn't seen where my friend, Lucy, went," she added. "I don't remember seeing which hut Curtis Hill chose. But I'm certain now. He didn't start off the night in the same place where he ended up."

Ended up dead, she meant, Lucy added silently.

Dykstra didn't answer. A muscle twitched along his jaw. "Why didn't you tell us this before? Any reason?"

His tone wasn't accusatory, Lucy noticed. Merely curious.

"I don't know. I feel stupid now for not remembering. It was the sort of thing you watch, but don't realize it's significant at the time. It took my mind a while to put it all together, I guess," Dana tried to explain. "And the shock this morning, of hearing that Mr. Hill was dead. I guess I was more rattled than I thought," she admitted.

He seemed to accept her explanation. "Thank you for the information. We may need to ask you more about this."

"I'm not going anywhere," Dana answered with a shrug.

After the detective left, the group of friends collapsed on the sofa again and let out a long, collective sigh.

"Dana . . . I think you just let the dogs loose on Dr. Max," Suzanne said.

"Maybe the dogs should be set loose on him," Phoebe said.

"His random knitting project . . . going into the same hut . . . this is all meaningful, I'm sure. But it still doesn't mean Max killed Hill," Lucy insisted.

"Lucy, I think you've just softened on Max from reading his book," Suzanne said.

"That's not true," Lucy insisted. "I'm just trying to look at this objectively, like the police do. What are the facts here?

They can be arranged and rearranged in a lot of different patterns, too."

Maggie's expression grew serious. "Lucy is right. There are a lot of players on this small stage and we hardly know the full story. I'm sure the police know more, too. Which reminds me, there's another piece of evidence that Detective Dykstra showed me this morning. I think it was also found in the hut, or maybe even tacked on the door."

"Tacked on the door? Was it a note?" Dana asked curiously.

"Not a note, but maybe the murderer's calling card?" Maggie said in an eerie tone. "A plain white index card with a Chinese hexagram written on it. From the *I Ching*. That was all. But I noticed a little thumbtack hole on the top, so I assume it was pinned somewhere in the hut where Hill was found."

"Why did the police show you that? They didn't show it to me," Suzanne said, looking around at her other friends.

"Me, either," Dana chimed in. Lucy and Phoebe said the same.

"Let me see . . ." Maggie thought back to the interview. "Oh, right. I was telling the detective about meeting Joy Kimmel last night and how she'd quoted something from the *I Ching*. That's why."

"That's not surprising. It's sort of a new age bible," Dana told the others. "What did the hexagram look like? Can you remember?"

"I don't remember the lines exactly, but I do recall the number on top. Eighteen. That's significant, right?"

"Yes, very," Dana confirmed.

"I was going to look in the gift shop for a copy of the *I Ching* and look it up. Guess I got distracted at the spa," Maggie told the others.

"If we had a computer handy we could search it right now. Too bad I made everyone promise to leave the laptops at home." Dana glanced around at the group, her gaze resting on Suzanne.

"Yeah . . . too bad," she agreed. "Good thing I have Internet access on the horrible BlackBerry that you hate so much."

Suzanne grabbed her purse and pulled out the BlackBerry, then searched the meaning of the *I Ching* symbols.

"Let's see, number eighteen. 'Decay. Work on what has been spoiled,'" Suzanne read aloud. She looked around at the others with a puzzled expression.

"That's heavy," Phoebe said.

"Yes, it is. Let me read a little more." Dana peeked over Suzanne's shoulder. "The symbol represents a bowl of rice where worms have been breeding."

"Ugh! That's gross," Phoebe jumped up from her seat and walked away.

"It's a symbol of corruption, guilt, a mistake in the past. But one that can be corrected," Dana continued. She took the BlackBerry from Suzanne and scrolled down some more. " 'What has been spoiled by man can be restored by taking the right action.'"

Lucy felt chills hearing the words read aloud.

Dana shook her head and smiled. "Wait, it gets better. Each of the lines in the symbol has a meaning. But it seems they are all related to the same story—a son taking action to correct a mistake made by his father . . . or mother."

Dana looked up to check everyone's reaction. Lucy felt the gooseflesh pop out again on her arms and knew that her friends felt it too.

"Now what do we think?" Maggie asked the others. "Is this about Max . . . or Brian Archer?"

"Or someone trying to frame one of them?" Lucy offered.

"Or purposely tossing dust in everyone's eyes," Suzanne added.

"Or none of the above?" Phoebe said succinctly.

"Phoebe's right," Maggie said. "It's just one more juicy tidbit. We don't know where it fits."

No one spoke for a moment. Finally, Suzanne sat up and looked around at the others. "Let's face it. We're stumped on this one. It's not only a juicy tidbit, you've made me hungry for Chinese food. Anyone ready for dinner?"

"Some dinner—and the latest gossip down at the inn sounds good to me." Maggie stood up from the couch and stretched.

The plan sounded good to everyone and they scattered into their rooms to get ready. Lucy had a feeling that they were getting very close to figuring out who killed Curtis Hill and why.

But solving the mystery was starting to seem like a chess game. All the pieces were dangerous for different reasons— Dr. Max, Brian, Alice . . . Joy? Each of them was capable of striking the final blow, if moved into the right position.

Lucy had no idea who did it. She also doubted that the police did, either.

The dining room at the inn was busy, but they didn't wait long before a hostess led them to a table. The mood seemed subdued, Lucy thought, as she glanced around at the other groups of guests. And why wouldn't it be?

As they were ordering their dinner from the menu, Nadine came by. "Do you have time to sit a minute?" Maggie invited her.

"I do. Just a for a second, though," Nadine said, taking a chair.

"How did the Mindful Knitting workshop go? I'm sorry, I never got to check with you."

"It went very well," Maggie reported. "My friend Dana helped. How is Joy doing? Is she feeling better?"

"She's made a full recovery. She's even about to do some belly dancing . . . see?" Nadine glanced at the far side of the room.

There was a circle of varnished wood that must have been used as a dance floor from time to time. Tables had been cleared away and Joy was fiddling with a boom box perched on a chair.

"She thought it would be a good distraction for the guests," Nadine added.

Before anyone could reply, they heard music coming from the boom box, a syncopated, Middle Eastern rhythm, and a throaty female voice singing in a high-pitched, foreign tongue.

Dressed for the dance in what looked like a harem girl costume, Joy even wore finger cymbals and bracelets of tiny bells on her wrists and ankles that tinkled and chattered as her hands waved softly around her body.

Her wide, swaying hips reminded Lucy of the Egyptian boat ride at the county fair. But she still managed to look exotic, sexy, and even dignified somehow.

"Wow . . . she can dance," Dana said quietly.

"She moves very gracefully," Maggie agreed. For a big woman, she didn't say, but everyone was thinking it, Lucy knew.

"I don't think she worries much about her cellulite, Suzanne," Lucy remarked.

"She has a lot of body confidence," Suzanne agreed. "Score one for the big girls."

Joy danced for a few minutes, swaying and twirling on the small patch of dance floor. Then she tiptoed on her bare feet, out among the tables, urging the guests to join her. She stopped at a table where Helen Lynch sat with a guest whom Lucy didn't know.

Joy yanked on Helen's arm, but the businesswoman shook her head so hard her glasses nearly flew off.

"If Helen gets up, I really do need to get the camera going on this thing." Suzanne pulled out her BlackBerry, puzzling over the settings.

"Helen would pay good money to keep that video off YouTube, I bet," Lucy noted. "Good for the college fund."

But Joy soon gave up on Helen and danced on.

She danced from table to table, but all her hip shaking and bustier shimmies were for naught. She couldn't seem to elevate the flat mood in the room or inspire any volunteers to join her.

Except for Walter Schumacher, who sat with a silly grin as Joy twirled around him. At one point his hand shot out and Rita slapped it back just in time.

"Thanks, honey. He's had enough," Rita said kindly, as if telling a waitress to remove an extra serving of dessert.

Finally, Joy gave up. With sweat beads on her forehead and her long hair plastered flat, she took a quick bow, shut off her sound system, and hopped out of view.

"Poor Joy. She's only trying to help. Everyone wants to help Max, even after he wipes his feet on them. It's really quite amazing," Nadine said. Her words were calm, detached, and vicious, Lucy thought. She thought Nadine was on the doctor's team. She wondered if anyone else at the table had noticed.

"Where is Dr. Max?" Maggie asked. "I haven't seen him all day."

Nadine sighed and leaned closer to answer in a confidential tone. "Getting hell from Alice. I was working at my desk in the outer office, but I could hear everything. The detectives stopped by and had another chat with him just a little while ago. About the sleeping arrangements on the mountain. It seems the moonlight inspired a game of musical huts."

Lucy looked over at Dana. Detective Dykstra had not lost any time confronting Max with Dana's recollection. Max and Alice, it sounded like. So maybe that's why Nadine sounded so angry at Max right now. She didn't like the way he treated her sister.

"I was the one who noticed that Max started off the night in the hut where Curtis Hill ended up," Dana told Nadine.

Nadine shrugged. "The police would have figured it out sooner or later, don't you think?

"What did Max say? Why did he switch huts with Hill?" Maggie asked.

"Max claims Hill was complaining about his cot. Max leads those retreats several times a month and always takes the same hut, which has a more expensive cot with an extra air mattress. Max told the police he thought it would help the review of the inn if he gave the writer the better bed."

"That sounds logical." Suzanne looked around at her friends to see what they thought.

Dana wasn't buying it. Lucy could tell just from the way she patted her mouth with her napkin. "Why didn't he tell the police that initially?" Dana asked.

"He says he didn't think of it. He says he just assumed the man died in his sleep, maybe from heart failure or some other natural causes. He didn't think the switch in sleeping huts was important."

"But the police must have told him that the heating unit had been tampered with. They discovered that early this morning," Dana persisted.

"So he claims he switched huts with Hill sometime during the night, is that right?" Maggie asked.

"That's what he says. Of course, once the police start checking sleeping bags for Max's DNA, no telling what they'll find." Nadine's tone of voice was tired and not just because of the long hours she kept at the inn, Lucy thought.

She stood up and picked up the ubiquitous clipboard and pile of folders. "The coast should be clear by now. Guess I'll creep back to my desk. See you later, ladies."

"Seems our fearless retreat leader was wandering," Dana said once Nadine had left. "I'll bet you a belly dance in front of the breakfast crowd that's what he and Alice are arguing about."

"I know who it was, too. I mean, I have a good guess," Lucy said quietly, looking around the dining room.

"Shannon Piper," the rest of the women whispered in unison.

"No-brainer," Phoebe added. "I mean, filling in the name. Not *her*, necessarily."

"She's not stupid. Just so sweet or something," Suzanne said, defending the former model.

"I think the word your looking for is 'gullible.'" Maggie took a final bite of her dinner, then pushed the dish aside.

"How about vulnerable?" Dana offered. "She seems to have more than her share of blessings—looks, wealth, fame. But there are still deep insecurities. And an eating disorder."

"Maybe Max and Shannon were together last night. But

maybe she just wanted to talk to him, like a counselor or something," Lucy speculated. Her friends answered with a chorus of groans and eye rolls.

"You're kidding, right?" Suzanne asked her.

"Maybe Max is gay?" Phoebe ventured.

Lucy tried to tell if she was joking, but she looked perfectly serious.

"The situation would cause serious temptation for Elton John," Dana pointed out. "It's possible, but not likely. Especially when you consider the size of those huts," Dana added. "Factor in the passionate speech Shannon made today, defended Max to Helen Lynch. It adds up for me."

"Me, too," Maggie agreed. "I don't see her down here tonight, either," she noticed, gazing around.

Lucy hadn't seen Shannon around, either, and wondered what that could mean, if anything.

After dinner the group wandered around the lobby for a little while, but there was not much going on. Lucy did spot the speaker who worked with sock puppets giving an informal workshop off in one corner.

"Uh-oh . . . sock puppet therapy alert," Phoebe whispered to Maggie and Lucy.

"Let's get Dana out of here, before the police have another crime scene to deal with," Lucy said.

"Good idea," Maggie answered eagerly. She quickly walked over to Dana and Suzanne, who were admiring a Zen flower arrangement on the fireplace mantel.

"I don't have any workshops schedule for tonight. Why don't we just go back and knit?" Maggie told them.

The idea immediately appealed. The atmosphere at the inn did seem heavy and dark tonight, Lucy thought, as if a storm were about to break.

* * *

The walk back to the cottage alongside the lake was refreshing, Lucy thought. Like a splash of cool water on her face . . . and fevered brain.

Once inside, they quickly shed their dinner outfits for loungewear and fluffy bathrobes. Lucy and Phoebe made a fire and even found some packets of hot cocoa in the kitchen cupboards.

Phoebe waved a cocoa envelope before tearing open the packet. "This is probably considered an illegal substance around here. I hope the police don't barge in again for a white sugar raid. All the miniature marshmallows and preservatives. We could do hard time."

"A risk I'm willing to take," Suzanne called back.

They'd decided to take a break from talking about Curtis Hill and the clues that had piled up so far. Lucy's head was starting to ache from the information overload that didn't seem to fall into any recognizable pattern so far.

But it was hard not to think about it as she sat and knitted, even if she and her friends didn't speculate aloud. As the night went on and the fire in the wood stove dampened down, one by one, the Black Sheep Knitters headed for their beds. First Suzanne, who was used to an early-to-bed, early-to-rise schedule with her kids, then Maggie, and even Phoebe, who claimed the massage had worn her out.

Only Dana and Lucy remained, sitting and knitting, occasionally exchanging a few words, but still avoiding conversation about Curtis Hill's murder.

The problem was, if she didn't think about that puzzle, all Lucy could think about was Matt. That brain twister was almost as confusing. And even more heart wrenching.

"Hear back from Matt at all today?" Dana asked, as if reading Lucy's thoughts.

"He sent a text this afternoon. He says Tink is fine. Not to worry. But he thinks the dog misses me."

"The dog misses you? How about him?" Dana looked up briefly from her work and took a sip of tea.

"He didn't get into that," Lucy answered glumly, without looking up.

"Isn't he worried about you, up here at an inn with a murderer loose? Jack is sending me texts every five minutes . . . well, in between holes," she amended.

Lucy smiled at the image. Some women wouldn't have the patience for Jack's golf obsession, but Dana not only understood but seemed to find it amusing.

"I didn't tell him what was going on. I couldn't explain in a text message and he hasn't called me. So . . ." Her voice trailed off and she gave a careless shrug, though inside she was simmering.

Dana shook her head. "Wrong move, Lucy. That's a bit . . . passive-aggressive. How could you be mad at him for not showing concern about you if he doesn't even know there's trouble up here?"

Dana's words made sense . . . on a certain level, but Lucy still felt entitled to her feelings. "I'm not mad at him." Her words came out stronger than she intended, but Dana only smiled a "gotcha" kind of grin.

"Yes, you are. You don't fool me. Besides, you're a terrible liar."

"Thanks . . . I'll take that as a compliment." Lucy put down her knitting and stretched out on the couch. Plenty of room now that the others had turned in.

"What should I do now? Tell you my dreams?" she asked Dana in a teasing tone.

"I'm not shrinking you, pal. Not for free," Dana teased her back. "I'm just giving you some friendly advice. I know you hate confrontation and avoid it like a root canal. But when we get back on Sunday you have to take a deep, calming breath and have a heart-to-heart with your boyfriend . . ."

"If he still is my boyfriend by Sunday night," Lucy cut in. She glanced at her watch. "He could be out with someone else right now, for all I know."

"Lucy . . . get a grip. Matt's not that type. But holding all these doubts and little grudges inside is only going to backfire. You've been seeing him for six months. You know him well enough by now to have an honest talk. It's time to clear the air."

Lucy turned her head on the silk pillow again and stared up at the ceiling. "Get the toxins out, as they say around here?"

"Exactly. Think of it as a healing conversation . . . or something like that."

Lucy was silent a moment, considering her friend's advice. Dana was right. There was no use sitting with her doubts and issues, feeling awful and blue. Waiting for Matt's other size-eleven jogging shoe to drop. She had to confront him—in a calm, reasonable way, of course—and talk this out.

"I wonder if the inn will empty out tomorrow, since the police said everyone was free to go."

"I was wondering the same thing," Dana replied. "I was surprised to see so many people in the dining room. If we weren't sticking with Maggie, I don't think I'd be here right now," Dana admitted.

"Me, either. The police don't seem to have a clue who did

this. But they must know more than we do. Things we haven't overheard or figured out on our own." Lucy turned her head to look at Dana, to see if she agreed or not.

"Maybe, maybe not. I think we've found a pretty good pipeline in Nadine Gould."

"What do you think the police are doing now? Still searching for a connection between Hill and his report for *Expose,* and Max and the spa? Or a connection between Hill and someone else at the spa?"

"Those both sound like reasonable tracts to follow. Maybe some other guest had crossed paths with Hill and had a motive to kill him. Those *Expose* pieces are strong. They can ruin a business or tank a career," Dana mused. "The thing is, we have to remember the *I Ching* symbol. That seems to bring it back to Max or someone connected to the spa, in my mind."

"I agree." Lucy sat up again, the conversation waking her from her dozy state. "But to me it seems like someone is trying to send a message to Max. Or about him. The *I Ching* symbol seems to rule Max out as the murderer. I don't think he'd leave something so obvious. It's like a big sticky handprint."

"Exactly," Lucy agreed. "But what was the killer trying to say about Hill? What was spoiled that Hill had to work on? One of his stories about some corrupt businessman? About Max maybe?" she speculated. "Taking bribes to hush something up? Or to purposely slander someone?"

"What was Hill investigating here, you mean?" Dana replied. "I've wondered about that myself. Whatever it was, it couldn't have been good. Maybe Max's entire chain of health spas is a huge, phony investment scheme. He does seem to be preying on the vulnerable and infirm," she noted. "Like Shannon Piper and the Schumachers."

"I thought of that, too," Lucy agreed. "But Max is so visible, such a well know face and name. It would be very hard for him to grab the loot and disappear into the woodwork somewhere. Unless he changed his identity, had plastic surgery and all that," she hypothesized wildly.

Dana had just finished a large section of the wrap dress. She sat listening to Lucy as if tuned into a radio show. She held up her knitting, calmly examining the stitches, and snipped off an extra strand of yarn that trailed from one corner.

"Yes, I think you're right about that. But the card isn't a message about Hill, Lucy. It's about Max." She looked at Lucy with her steady blue gaze. "It just came to me while you were talking. We've been so hung up on Hill, his secret identity and muckraking job, that we missed the elephant in the room. Or rather, in that tiny wooden hut . . ."

Lucy realized it, too, and nearly jumped out of her seat.

"The murderer didn't expect Hill in that hut. That was the hut Max always slept in." She paused and took a shaky breath. "The killer was after Dr. Max."

Chapter Eleven

hat should we do? Detective Dykstra might still be up at the inn. I think we need to tell him."

Lucy jumped up from the couch and looked around for her shoes. She was wearing big flannel pajama bottoms imprinted with poodles and a gray hooded sweatshirt, her hair gathered in a ponytail on the top of her head. She knew she looked insane, but this was an emergency . . . wasn't it?

Dana stood up, too, then placed a gentle hand on Lucy's shoulder. "Slow down, pal. I doubt Dykstra is still around. It's after eleven. Even he has to sleep sometime. If we reached this square on the game board, don't you think the police have gotten there already?"

Lucy took a breath. "Well, probably. But not necessarily. You know that as well as I do, Dana."

Lucy had never known much about police work beyond what she'd seen on TV, that is, until recently. She and her friends had been closely involved in two investigations in their hometown within the last year.

The first, when a shopkeeper named Amanda Goran had been found bludgeoned to death in her knitting store and the second, when a good friend of theirs and honorary member of the knitting group, Gloria Sterling, had drowned in her own swimming pool. Neither of the official investigations that had followed up the murders had inspired Lucy with great faith in the deductive powers of the police force.

But that was just Plum Harbor and Essex County. Maybe they were sharper up here in the Berkshires?

"If it makes you feel any better, I'll call the hotel and see if Detective Dykstra is still around," Dana offered. "But this revelation is still just another possibility. If I saw into Max's hut, maybe someone else was watching the hut, too, and saw Hill go in," she pointed out. "We all know of one person who definitely knew Hill was in there. Who had practically tucked him into his sleeping bag."

"We're back to Max again." Lucy didn't mean to sound tired, but she knew she did. After her burst of excitement, she felt the wind slip out of her sails.

"Looks like it." Dana packed up her knitting needles and yarn, then neatly folded the piece she had completed. "I think we should just go to bed now and leave this all for tomorrow morning."

Lucy nodded. "You're right. No need to call Detective Dykstra." Lucy felt embarrassed now for even suggesting it. "I'm sure he's got this covered."

"I'm sure, too." The two friends said good night and Dana headed for her room.

Lucy shut the lights and made sure the fire was out, then grabbed Max's book off the lamp table as she left the room.

Talking over the murder again had made her mind restless

and she hoped a few minutes of reading would settle her down for sleep.

Lucy was the first one up the next morning, despite the fact that she'd made a good dent in Max's tell-all. The rambling redemption tale did keep you hooked.

She made some coffee, then dressed in her running clothes and headed out for a jog around the lake. A thick mist clung to the lake and mountain, like a smoky cloud. The waterfront was perfectly quiet, except for the sound of birds chirping or splashing in the water and animals rustling through the tall grass.

Lucy left the cottage behind and was soon on the far side of the lake, with the inn in miniature on the opposite shore. The path was a bit overgrown on this side of the lake and there were no other hotels or houses in sight.

She was used to running through the streets of Plum Harbor, which wasn't exactly Manhattan, but she never failed to pass fellow joggers or the health walkers, who usually traveled in pairs, chattering away with arms wildly pumping.

If the sun had been out and the fog burned off, the scene would not have appeared so eerie, she thought. But it did seem eerie and lonely. Especially with Curtis Hill's killer still on the loose.

Lucy's steps unconsciously sped up and she found herself practically sprinting down the path that bordered the shore-line opposite the inn. It was pretty dumb to come out here all alone this morning, she realized now. She'd forgotten all about the pledge with her friends to use the buddy system.

And nobody knew where she was . . . and she hadn't even pocketed her cell phone.

She could be dragged into the woods, screaming her lungs out. Who would hear her? Who would even know where to look?

I hope you're happy when you find out what happened to me, Matt, Lucy thought, sending a silent message to her neglectful boyfriend. Then you'll be sorry you didn't call . . . sorry you weren't nicer to me . . . but it will be too late. I'll be . . .

Lucy felt herself stumble, lose her balance, and fly into the air.

The only way to avoid landing face-first on the gravel was to block her fall with her hands. She slid for a moment on her stomach and finally came to a full stop, her head stuck in a clump of reeds.

Lucy let out a long breath, just a second before the pain set in. She felt like a bug that had slammed into a windshield and lay on the ground, getting her bearings. She hadn't been watching, and the toe of her jogging shoe had gotten caught on a root.

She rolled to her back and groaned, surveying the damage—scraped palms, imbedded with sand and grit and bleeding a little. She gingerly touched her chin, where she felt a little blood and lump. Her knees hurt, too, but at least her jogging pants were thick and she hadn't ripped through the fabric.

She sat up slowly, feeling every bone ache.

I don't even need some stranger to come along and murder me, she thought. I can do enough damage on my own . . .

"Hey . . . are you all right?"

Lucy's heart skipped a beat at the sound of a voice. A man's voice, coming from the edge of the woods.

She jumped to her feet, totally oblivious to her pain and

bruises. She had often heard that happiness was a natural anesthetic, but never knew that fear could be, too.

She looked around and quickly spotted Brian Archer coming out of the woods, walking slowly toward her. He'd been out bar crawling again last night, Lucy guessed. His eyes were puffy, and his face unshaven. He carried a jagged-edged saw in one hand and a short, keen-edged ax in the other, looking a lot like the star of a slasher film, she suddenly realized.

Lucy took a deep breath and stood frozen to the spot.

Saints preserve me. No one will ever believe this . . . if I ever see them again.

He came closer, staring at her with a puzzled expression.

"Hi, Brian!" Her hand popped up at her side, like a broken marionette. "How are you?" She tried to sound natural, but only succeeded in a chipmunklike voice.

"I'm all right. How are you?" he asked curiously. He leaned the ax on one shoulder. He was stronger than he'd first looked. She'd seen him in a baggy sweatshirt yesterday, but this morning he wore a snug thermal shirt and fleece vest that showed off impressive muscles in his shoulders and arms.

Lucy knew a little self-defense and wondered if she could take him. And get away with all her limbs still attached . . .

"I saw you fall. Are you okay?"

"I'm all right. Just stupid. I caught my toe on a root or something." Lucy gestured with her hand, then quickly covered the scraped palm.

"You seem a little shaken up. What happened to your hands?" Before she knew what was happening, he was reaching out and grabbing her wrist.

Lucy jumped back and screamed.

He stared at her. "Does it hurt that much? Maybe you broke your wrist."

"I don't think so . . . just a sprain," she said quickly. She rubbed her wrist and avoided looking at him.

Had he been trying to yank her into the woods . . . to chop her up into little pieces? Or just checking her scraped hand?

"You ought to wash those cuts off in the lake. The water is clean enough."

"I'll be okay. I'll just wait," she insisted.

Right, I'm going to walk over to the lake, lean over, and let you push me in, or grab me from behind. How stupid do you think I am, pal? Lucy stared at him, watching every move.

Her hands did hurt, though. Her entire body hurt mightily.

It was going to be a long walk back. A very long, achy walk. What if she had to make a dash for it? He looked like he could run fast, too.

I could climb a tree and wait for help, she thought desperately. Like they do on nature shows when the narrator gets chased by a wild boar?

But he has an ax and saw. He might just chop it down . . .

"Are you all right?" he asked again. "You didn't hit your head, did you?"

He took a step closer and Lucy stepped back, folding her arms over her chest. "I'm good. Really . . . what are you doing out here so early?"

"Clearing some branches that were blocking the path. I didn't get to the stray roots yet. Sorry."

"Oh, that's all right. I should have watched where I was going."

"Do you want some water? I have some with me." He walked a bit farther down the path and put the saw and ax into the toolbox, then took out two bottles of water.

Lucy did feel thirsty, and now that he was unarmed she dropped her guard a notch.

"I'll walk back with you," he said, handing her a bottle of water. "I have a few final touches to make on the meeting room."

"So the big meeting is still on?"

"That's right." Brian opened his water bottle and took a long swallow. "Short of a meteor strike, the show must go on. A sucker is born every minute, you know."

His bitter edge was showing even more this morning. Lucy wondered if that made Brian more likely to be Hill's murderer, or less. If he really was guilty, wouldn't he be less vocal about his resentments and try to show a happy face?

She wondered if he'd heard yet that Max and Hill had switched huts. News like that had a way of getting around quickly. But she decided it was best not to get into that conversation. Not with Brian.

"I guess I have no right to complain around here," he continued. "I get my slice of the pie. We all do. What's good for Max is good for all of his pilot fish. I'm not quite as innocent and unmercenary as I seem," he added, glancing at her.

Lucy didn't doubt that. He didn't seem innocent at all. "If it all works out, will you move to one of the new spas?"

"Are you kidding? This is my last tour on Planet Max. It's amazing I've lasted this long. I'll make what I can here, then head down to Florida or Texas maybe. Where I can gorge on burgers, fries, and beer until I bust a gut. I never want to see another bean sprout in my life."

Lucy laughed. He seemed as amusing now as he had seemed ominous just a few minutes ago.

"Don't make me talk about that damn meeting anymore. It just ticks me off."

Lucy was thankful for the warning. She'd already seen him angry. He liked to break things.

"So, did you finish the book?" he asked. "I'm waiting for your review."

"I'm not done yet, but I made a good dent. The story does draw you in."

"He can spin a good tale. Quite an imagination, I'll grant him that."

He seemed angry again, masked beneath a cool, snide attitude.

A thick, dry branch blocked their way. Brian picked it up and easily snapped it in half, then tossed the pieces into the brush. The sound of the breaking branch echoed in the stillness, like the sound of a bone cracked in two. The vase-smashing incident was just a warm-up, she realized. She wouldn't want to be around when this guy really popped his cork, which she suspected did happen from time to time.

Lucy was glad to see that they had rounded the bend and the cottage was coming into view. She wasn't sure how she'd limped along so quickly. The conversation had certainly helped distract her from the aches and pains.

"So the book is not a truthful version of events?" Lucy asked quietly. A touchy subject. As touchy as the meeting.

Had she gone too far? She hoped not. But she did want to know.

Brian shrugged. "Now we're getting into philosophical territory, Lucy. What is the truth? What is reality? That's more Max's turf, not mine. I deal in the nuts and bolts around here. The clogged drains and cracked windowpanes." He paused and glanced at her.

And the gas heating units behind the huts on the hilltop? Was that task on his to-do list, as well?

Had someone—Max or even Alice—persuaded Brian to kill Hill, for the good of all connected to the great man? The ersatz family, as Dana had called them?

While these wild accusations swirled through Lucy head, Brian continued talking.

"Everybody has their own version of the truth," he continued. "And their own version of the past. I will tell you one thing, Max never believed any of this new age crap back then. That was my father's thing. He was the one into all that. That girl who committed suicide? Max blames my father in the book. But I know Max dealt with her directly. My father was away at some conference. He couldn't be reached easily and left Max on call for his patients. Max doesn't tell you that part. The girl called him repeatedly, and he told her to go to an emergency room and call him again from there. He was too busy to see her out of hours. Or she could wait until my father got back, the following week, which to her must have sounded like an eternity. That's what Max told her," Brian repeated again. "I heard him arguing with my father afterward. I heard everything," he added, just in case Lucy had any doubts.

"She didn't feel like waiting for my father. She didn't feel like sitting in an emergency room, either. Who can blame her? Those places are real downers. Especially when you're down already. Believe me, I've been there. She preferred to stay home. And stick her head in a stove and turn on the gas. That seemed like a better solution to her problems and she did it that very same day."

Lucy gasped at his cold recital of the facts. But were they the facts or just Brian's version? Either way, the image was chilling. No wonder the event had shattered so many lives. Brian's included, it seemed.

"If Max's version of the story is so off the mark," Lucy

asked, "how does he get away with putting all the blame on your father?"

"It was all settled out of court and the family signed a confidentiality agreement, so the truth will never come out. I think the family just doesn't want to go there anymore. Revist all that pain. It won't bring the girl back," Brian pointed out. "What does it matter? Max landed on his feet. He's rolling in money and has bought off everyone who knows the truth. Including me and my mother." His tone was bleak, fatalistic.

And if he'd taken the blame, your father might still be alive, Lucy wanted to say. But she didn't know Brian nearly well enough to offer that insight.

It's a sad story, she thought. She didn't know what to say. She knew that Brian has a vested interest in shifting the blame from his father to Max. And who could even say if the patient would be have survived, despite anything anyone did for her? But Lucy could see that if Brian's version were true, Max had misrepresented himself and exploited the tragedy for his own profit and advancement.

"But if all this new age thinking didn't work for your father, why is Max taking up that banner now? That doesn't make sense to me."

"He claims he believes in it now. The transformative experience made him see the light." Brian rolled his eyes in disgust. "But Max always believed he was smarter than my father. He thinks he's smarter than everyone. He can see there's money in it. My mother thinks he's smarter. She thought my father was a screwup. I guess that's why she's overlooked the way Max trashed my dad. The truth is, my dad *was* a bit of screwup," Brian conceded. "And Alice likes a safe bet. She plays the odds, and Max is a winner. Anyone can see that."

Lucy couldn't argue with that observation. Max did seem to have "the magic," as Helen Lynch would say.

They had come to a fork in the path. One side led to the cottage, the other up to the inn.

"This is where I get off," Lucy said gratefully.

"Hey, 'when you come to a fork in the road . . . take it.'"

"Yogi Berra?" It sure sounded like the late baseball great's brand of wisdom.

"That's right. That's the only kind of yogi I'm into." Brian waved and headed up his side of the path, ending their outing on yet another snub of Max, his nemesis and benefactor.

Lucy walked into the cottage and could tell it was empty. Suzanne had left her a note, propped on a coffee mug:

Fitness Freak—
You've shamed us all, going out jogging at the crack of dawn.
We figured it out when we saw your shoes and iPod missing. You
shouldn't have gone without a partner. But who would have gotten
up at that hour? We went to the inn for breakfast. Maggie has a
workshop in the lobby at 10:00. Catch up to us.
XXX
Suzanne

Lucy wished that at least one of her friends had been around. She was dying to tell someone about her strange, frightening encounter with Brian Archer and his unauthorized version of the Max Flemming story. She felt as if she'd just interviewed a murderer . . . Had she?

She realized now that she ought to tell the police about the argument she'd witnessed between Alice and Brian. It may have been very innocent, just a squabble between a mother and a difficult, trouble son. But then again, maybe not, Lucy speculated.

It was probably best that she had hobbled in alone. She needed to check her injuries and bind her wounds in private. Suzanne would have been fussing all over her and Maggie insisting she needed X-rays.

Lucy found an ice pack and some ibuprofen and hobbled into the bedroom. A hot shower, some Tiger Balm, and she'd hardly be limping at all by the time she met up with her friends.

Lucy reached the inn a few minutes after 10:00, but Maggie hadn't started the workshop yet. She spotted her friends sitting near the hearth again, with the baskets of yarn and needles set up for the session. Everyone but Phoebe, who had gone out on a nature walk called "Incredible Forest Edibles," they'd told her.

"Forest edibles? What's that? Anything like a scavenger hunt?"

"You go into the woods with a guide and they point out all the wild edibles . . . mushrooms, tree fungus, ferns," Dana explained. "Seeds and berries, that sort of thing."

"It sounds like a chipmunk buffet . . . and possibly dangerous," Lucy said.

"It sounds crazy," Suzanne replied. "Even I couldn't get that hungry."

"You were out early," Maggie said, changing the subject. "How was your run?"

"It started off fine, but I wasn't watching the path and tripped on a root or something."

"Did you hurt yourself?" Maggie asked with concern.

"A little. Nothing too bad." Lucy held up her hands and

they all sighed sympathetically. "I think I'll skip the knitting today. I brought a book instead."

Lucy took Max's book out of her knitting tote and set it on the table. "I'm almost finished . . . but now I'm wondering if this should have been classified as a novel."

"A novel? What do you mean?" Dana was casting on stitches for another section of her dress and counting to herself.

"I met Brian Archer on the other side of the lake. He told me a completely different version of the story."

All of her friends looked up from their knitting now, ready to hear more.

"I'm sure he has his own ax to grind—" Maggie began.

"Tell me about it. He had it with him, slung over his shoulder. Freddy style," Lucy cut in. Her exclamation was answered by a puzzled stare.

"Lucy . . . what are you talking about?" Dana's tone was suddenly alarmed.

Before Lucy could even begin to explain, Shannon Piper arrived. She flashed a brief, well-practiced smile before settling down in an armchair at the far side of the circle.

"Hello, everyone. Sorry I'm late."

"That's all right. We haven't even started yet. You're the first one here. Except for my friends," Maggie added with a smile.

Shannon Piper didn't answer. She seemed distracted and rummaged around in her large tote before pulling out a project, a toddler-size sweater with blue, purple, and white stripes. Lucy recalled that the former model had three children. It was hard to remember that. She didn't look very motherly, today especially.

Her look was more what Lucy would call aloof and dramatic—a black cowlneck tunic sweater, leggings, and high, cuffed boots. Her hair was pulled back in a tight, ballerina-style bun. Her large eyes were heavily outlined with makeup and her high cheekbones and pale skin took on a skeletal cast.

She looked as if she'd hardly slept, or perhaps spent the night with her head hanging over the commode. Was her eating disorder rearing its ugly head again? Maybe Max could help with that. Or perhaps he was the cause of its return, Lucy mused.

Helen Lynch appeared, coming up to the circle of seating from the opposite side of the lobby. "Here I am. Back again. Not too much going on today until the meeting starts. Mind if I sit in?"

Before anyone could answer, she chose a seat near Maggie and dropped her big leather purse on the table.

Helen was also dressed in black today, Lucy noticed, a V-neck cashmere sweater and slim woolen pants. The silk Hermès scarf draped around her shoulders had a black background with a gold and red print, her only concession to color the entire weekend.

"So what's on for today? Some random, mindful, free-range technique?" She stared at Maggie, looking alert and expectant.

"Just plain old-fashioned knitting, Helen. No additives, no extra ingredients," Maggie quipped in return.

"It's all the same to me," Helen said honestly. "I'm going to start again. I had to throw the last one out."

Needles and all, Lucy wondered?

Shannon suddenly scooped up her knitting, tossed it in her bag, and got up from her seat. "I have to go. Thanks."

Then she turned and practically ran across the lobby.

Maggie sat back and looked over at Lucy and her other friends. "What happened? Was it something I said?"

Dana and Lucy both shrugged.

"I didn't see anything happen." Suzanne had been knitting also and stared around in surprise.

"It was me. Obviously. The skunk at the garden party. The supermodel's garden party," Helen clarified.

She was sifting through the selection of needles and this time chose the largest she could find, number twelves.

If she couldn't make loose stitches with those babies, the woman should just pack it in, Lucy decided.

"She's gotten this . . . thing about me. I'm trying not to take it personally. The woman is more than a little neurotic. Beautiful-but-crazy type?"

"Oh, that's a cliché," Dana said evenly. "But Shannon does seem sensitive."

Helen answered with a look, as if she knew better and could argue the point, but decided to let it pass.

She picked up some yarn, stuck one needle straight up, clamped between her knees, and got to work. "Okay, let me see if I can cast the line myself this time."

Cast the line? Did she think she was going deep sea fishing? Lucy glanced at Maggie, who was trying not to laugh.

No one had noticed Rita Schumacher ambling over with her Red Sox knitting bag. "Good morning, ladies. Room for one more?"

"Of course, Rita. Have a seat," Maggie said, welcoming her. "We're not trying any special technique today, just straight knitting."

"Stitch and kvetch . . . I love it." Rita seemed chipper this morning, Lucy noticed, and a little more dressed up than usual, with a dash of bright pink lipstick and dangling, beaded earrings that matched her purple velour jogging suit.

When Lucy imagined Walter in a matching suit, she couldn't help but wince. But he probably *was* wearing one.

She expected to see him bringing up the rear with his cane, but he was nowhere in sight.

"Where's Walter?" Lucy asked.

"We had a rough night. He's resting in the room." Rita's cheerful expression darkened. She shook her head with concern. "I thought he had a little heartburn, or a reaction to his treatments, but it seems like something more."

"That's too bad. Maybe you should ask the police to let you leave. I'm sure they would let you go home if you wanted to," Dana told her.

Rita had started knitting and didn't answer. "I told him that. He wants to stay for the meeting. He thinks he's getting in on a good deal. Something to leave our kids, he tells me." Rita shrugged. "Besides, he'll feel sick at home, too. What's the difference? These spa treatments seemed to help him the last time. But I'm not so sure now. Things are taking a turn, you know what I mean?" she asked, finally lifting her head.

Lucy didn't know what to say. Nobody else answered her, either.

"What time is the investors meeting?" Maggie asked her.

"Twelve noon, I think they said. They give you a special lunch," Rita added.

"Right. Dr. Max said something about that this morning," Maggie recalled.

"You saw Dr. Max today?" Lucy was surprised. She'd thought he would have been in seclusion, centering himself for his presentation. Clearing his aura and his toxins . . . or whatever.

"He was making the rounds at breakfast. Keeping up morale," Dana told her. "I guess you just missed him."

"I guess so." Now that she'd read most of his book and heard Brian's side of the story, Lucy was interested to see Max again. Up close and personal. To try to discern if he was a demon or an angel. Or a mixture of both.

"I thought he'd be meditating all morning. Resting his chi," she quipped.

"He did say something about taking a special treatment at the spa," Suzanne told her. "A quick kelp wrap. I tried it yesterday. It really works."

Mind over seaweed, Lucy decided.

"He thinks the police are making progress and will close the investigation soon," Maggie added.

"I hope so," Rita said in a worried tone. "I can't take much more of this."

"Much more of what?" Walter suddenly appeared, standing beside Rita's chair. He leaned heavily on his cane, looking peaked and shaky, Lucy thought.

He sat down next to his wife with a wheezy sigh. Everyone greeted him.

"Hello, Walter. How are you feeling?" Maggie asked.

He shrugged. "Same old, same old."

As Lucy had expected, he also wore a purple jogging suit. But he looked like he'd had a rough night, and rough morning, too. His jacket and pants were rumpled and stained, compared to Rita's set.

Rita cast a concerned glance. "Why didn't you stay in the room, Walter? You'll wear yourself out."

"I'm fine, Rita. Stop worrying." He patted her hand. "Everything is A-okay, kiddo."

Rita sighed and gave him another look, but she didn't say anything more.

Everyone in the circle continued to knit without much conversation. Even Helen Lynch seemed to be making some progress today on her giant needles. The graceless way she still held them, one clamped between her knees, made Lucy wince and was probably making Maggie sick to her stomach—but she seemed content, so no one corrected her.

"Time to wrap it up, everyone," Maggie announced finally. "Any questions?" she asked, looking around. "Let me give you both a card, in case you're ever in Plum Harbor," she said to Helen and Rita Schumacher. "Stop by the shop and say hello."

Rita was quickly picking through Maggie's basket of yarn, selecting more freebies for the road, Lucy noticed. She took the card with her hands full and a ball of wool rolled onto the floor.

"Oh boy . . . get that for me, will you, Walter. It's a good one," Rita told him. He bent over and picked it up, then gripped his stomach, stifling a little moan.

"What's the matter? Are you sick again?" Rita turned to him quickly.

He nodded, his face gray. "Let's go back to the room. I need to lie down."

Rita quickly picked up her things and grabbed his arm.

"Do you need some help?" Lucy asked, jumping up from her seat. "Let me call a bellman. They must have a wheelchair around here somewhere . . ."

She chased after the seniors for a few steps, but they were moving at a decent pace, considering the situation.

"It's okay, honey, I've got him," Rita called over her shoulder. "He hardly weighs a thing anymore. We'll be fine."

Lucy hung back, watching them for a moment, then returned to Maggie and her friends. Helen Lynch had left, too.

"She took my number twelves," Maggie remarked, straightening out the empty chair at Helen's place. "She wasn't supposed to take them with her. And Rita forgot all that yarn she picked out. I'll give it to her later, I guess."

She started to put the balls of yarn back in the basket, then put them in an empty bag and put them in her own knitting bag, so they wouldn't get mixed up with the rest, Lucy realized.

"Well, that's it for me. That was my last session for the weekend," Maggie announced.

They strolled out of the lobby and found seats on the stone terrace, near the lake. The sun had burned off the morning mist and the sky was deep blue with high, fluffy clouds. The branches of the tall trees surrounding the lake swayed in the breeze. The brilliant fall colors were reflected in the smooth water.

"It's a perfect autumn day," Lucy said.

"Absolutely. Should we head back now, or stick around?"

"We have to wait for Phoebe, of course," Maggie said, glancing at her watch. "As beautiful as this place is, I'm looking forward to leaving," Maggie admitted.

"I'm almost tempted to sign up for that meeting," Suzanne said, before anyone answered Maggie's question. "All this hype has me curious."

Lucy was curious, too, but not nearly enough to sit through some long, drawn-out lunch and presentation. And that meant staying here a few more hours. Which wasn't her preference, either. Like Maggie said, it was a beautiful place, but something was rotten in Denmark.

"I wonder if the police have any idea yet who killed Hill. I saw both detectives around today. They must still be investigating," Lucy said to her friends.

Were they really going to leave without an answer? Possibly, she realized. Some murder cases take months, or even years, to close. And some are never solved.

Before anyone could speculate, a screaming siren made them suddenly sit up, alert and alarmed.

Lucy could tell it was coming closer to the hotel. "An ambulance. Maybe it's for Walter," she said to the others.

No one bothered to answer. They quickly got up from their seats and went back into the lobby.

EMS workers were already coming through the big front doors, carrying a stretcher and a black box with resuscitation equipment.

Nadine ran toward them. She was holding her hand over her mouth, as if trying not to scream. "He's down in the spa . . . I think it's too late," she said, choking on the words.

The emergency crew ran past her and down the hallway that led to the spa. Nadine stood in the same spot, looking stunned.

"I think she's in shock," Maggie murmured. She quickly approached her friend and gripped her shoulder. "Nadine, what's happened? Is it Walter Schumacher?"

Nadine stared at her, her mouth agape.

"Walter? . . . No . . . no . . . it's not Walter. It's Max. Max is . . . dead. He's stone-cold dead."

Chapter Twelve

Maggie managed to grip her friend's shoulders just as Nadine's legs buckled. With the help of the others, she led Nadine to a chair.

Lucy could hardly believe what she'd heard. Max was dead? It didn't seem possible. Maggie didn't seem to believe it, either.

"Are you sure it was Max?" she asked gently. "Perhaps there's been some mistake."

"Oh, I'm positive. I saw him with my own eyes. I was meeting with the spa manager. The receptionist ran in to get us. Joy was down there, too. Having some aroma therapy for her headaches, I think. We all ran into his treatment room. He'd been there for a kelp wrap. The treatment was over. He was just lying on the table, in the dark, resting a while. When the attendant came back to get him, he didn't wake up. He didn't . . ."

She swallowed hard and covered her face with her hands. "I tried to give him mouth to mouth. No response."

Lucy noticed a smear of green paste on the front of Nadine's sweater and sleeves. Max's kelp treatment, of course.

"How awful." Maggie shook her head.

No one said a word. People rushed all around them in the lobby. News was spreading quickly, Lucy noticed. There was practically a panic, with a crowd of guests already massing at the front desk.

Nadine stood up suddenly. "I have to find my sister. I have to tell her. I don't know what to say. Dear heavens . . . She'll be devastated . . ."

Lucy felt so sorry for Nadine. What a terrible duty to perform. Alice seemed so cool and detached, bloodless in a way. But Lucy suspected that her feelings ran deep, especially for Max. Right to her core. This news would crush her.

Nadine headed off toward the back office, but she was too late. Before she'd even reached the front desk, Alice rushed out into the lobby, her face as pale as paper, her eyes wide with shock.

"What happened to him?" She grabbed Nadine's shoulders in both hands, her fingers digging into Nadine's flesh like claws. "Did you see? They said you were down there . . . what happened?"

"Alice . . . please." Nadine could barely support her sister, who suddenly broke into deep sobs and clung like a dead weight in Nadine's arms.

Then she fell to her knees in the middle of the lobby, sobbing into her hands. "Oh, Max . . . oh, my poor boy . . . why did you do this to me? Why?"

Maggie ran over to help Nadine. They quickly lifted Alice into a chair, then left Nadine to comfort her.

Lucy and the rest of her friends huddled together. They didn't know what more to say or do to help the women.

"How do you think he died?" Lucy whispered to Dana and Suzanne.

"Could have been anything," Dana whispered back. "A heart attack, a stroke, a hemorrhage . . ."

"Right. Just like Curtis Hill?" Suzanne asked slyly.

Lucy didn't answer, but she was thinking the same thing. Dr. Max may have died of natural causes, but she *so* doubted it.

The police doubted it to. Detectives Dykstra and Michaelson rushed into the lobby. Dykstra headed at a brisk pace toward the spa. Detective Michaelson walked over to the women.

"Mrs. Gould. Mrs. Archer. I'm sorry for your loss," he said grimly. "We realize this is a difficult time, but I need to ask you both some questions. Can you come with me for a few minutes?"

Alice nodded quickly, her head bowed. Her expression looked blank now, catatonic, Lucy thought. Her neatly arranged hair hung wildly around her head. She didn't seem to notice.

Nadine took hold of her elbow and helped her up, then the sisters walked arm in arm as Detective Michaelson led the way to the hotel office.

Lucy noticed a pack of irate guests had rushed the front desk. A rattled-looking assistant manager tried to field their questions, but was clearly overwhelmed.

"For goodness' sake, Dr. Max just passed away. You'd think people would just take a decent break before they started complaining," Lucy said.

"They're scared and confused. And feel out of control," Dana said quietly. "Max was the hub of the wheel here, no question."

"And now we're all trapped in a hotel where the wheels

just fell off, and a killer may have struck twice," Maggie added. "That could have something to do with everyone's distress."

No doubt, Lucy added silently.

"Look, the mushroom hunters are back." Suzanne pointed to the doors at the back of the lobby where a group of guests, dressed for hiking and carrying big paper bags, were just walking in.

"I wonder if they know," Maggie murmured.

Phoebe waved and quickly walked over to them. Her hair was parted down the middle and fixed in two long ponytails that bounced on the side of her head. She looked like a punk-style hiker in her baggy green shorts, red high tops, and a military-style jacket covered with brass buttons. A pair of binoculars were slung around her neck and she carried her paper bag proudly.

"Hey, guys. You should have come. It was awesome. I found a lot of great stuff," she said, shaking the bag. "I don't have to go food shopping for a week."

"I'm glad you had a good outing," Maggie said mildly.

"What's going on here? What are all the people doing in the lobby? Is Alice giving out more coupons?" Her eyes lit up hopefully.

"Actually, we have some bad news." Maggie sighed and faced Phoebe squarely. "Dr. Max passed away this morning. He was having a treatment at the spa and apparently expired right on the table. That's why all the guests are down here," Maggie added, gazing around, "and the police are back in force."

"Dr. Max? Really?" Phoebe's voice rose on a note of alarm. She pressed her hand to her forehead and her eyes got glassy. "I can't believe it. He was like . . . so alive, you know?"

A good way to describe Max Flemming. He was "so alive," blessed with more than the usual share of vitality, Lucy thought.

"It's been a terrible shock," Maggie agreed. "Nadine and Alice are shattered."

Maggie had merely mentioned the two women by name when they both came into view. "Look, there they are now. Coming out with police," Suzanne whispered. Nadine walked behind them.

"That was a fast interview." Dana's tone held a curious note. "Record time, I'd say."

Lucy thought it had been fast, too, considering that both women were probably among the last to see Max alive and Nadine was one of the first to see him dead.

Alice was walking slowly between Detective Michaelson and a uniformed police officer. A female officer with a long, dark braid hanging down behind her cap, Lucy noticed.

Alice's head was bowed, her chin to her chest, one hand clamped on the strap of her shoulder bag. Her expression was blank and numb. She almost seemed to be sleepwalking.

Nadine looked much more animated and distraught, following behind in an erratic manner, walking from side to side, as if trying to get Alice's attention. But her sister remained with her gaze fixed forward.

At one point, Nadine touched her sister's shoulder. "Please don't do this. You don't have to, Ali," Lucy heard Nadine say.

Alice shook her head without turning around.

Detective Michaelson and the female officer seemed to be urging Alice forward again. But Brian appeared, flying through the front door of the inn and blocking their path.

"Mom? What's going on . . . where are you going?"

Alice didn't answer him. She reached out and touched his shoulder, holding him at arm's length. "You stay here, Brian. With Aunt Nadine. I'll handle this," she said firmly, the old "take-charge" Alice emerging from the wreckage for a moment.

"What do you mean? What the hell do you think you're doing?" Brian was upset with his mother, Lucy noticed, but beyond that, she didn't notice any signs of shock or grief over Max.

Doubtlessly he knew by now. From what he'd told her this morning, his reaction, or lack of one, wasn't a surprise.

"I need to speak to the police. Don't worry. It will be all right," she promised him in a softer tone. She touched his cheek a moment, then allowed the police to escort her out.

Brian turned and stared, but didn't follow her. "Why is she going with the police?" he asked his aunt.

Nadine looked up at him, suddenly angry. "To help you. Why else? Why does she do anything?"

Then she turned and stalked off, heading back to the hotel office, but was immediately confronted by the wave of irritated guests who were waiting there for some answers.

"I have to help her. This is too much," Maggie told her friends.

She walked up to Nadine and took her arm. "Mrs. Gould is off duty right now," Maggie said politely. "Our assistant manager is over there . . . and a concierge. They'll be happy to answer your questions."

Maggie shooed the pesky guests aside, directing them to the front desk as she ran the gauntlet with Nadine.

A bit breathless and frazzled, Maggie returned to the group with Nadine at her side. "Come back to the cottage with us, Nadine. You need a break from this mayhem, and a nice cup of tea."

"I will come," Nadine said, hurrying along with them. "But I need a good lawyer for my sister even more."

Back at the cottage, Nadine went into one of the bedrooms to contact a local attorney who often represented the inn. It didn't take long for her to explain the situation. He agreed to meet Alice at the police station immediately and promised to keep Nadine updated.

When Nadine returned to the sitting room, she sat down in the middle of the largest sofa. The rest of the women were waiting for her, with their knitting out and cups of tea at hand. Maggie gave Nadine a mug, then handed her a damp towel to clean off her sweater. The sticky green paste from the kelp treatment hand clung in small patches.

She finally looked up and put the towel aside.

"Alice confessed. She told the police that she killed Max."

Dana leaned forward. "The police know for sure that Max was murdered?"

Nadine nodded solemnly. "It was very obvious. He was smothered on the treatment table with a pile of towels, pressed down over his face. The kelp solution from his face was on the towels. There are other signs, too. He seemed to have struggled a bit. But the muslin wrapping from the treatment constricted his limbs. Long enough anyway, I understand," she added quietly.

"I had a feeling it wasn't natural causes," Maggie replied.

"I think we all did," Dana added. "A bad feeling."

Lucy had read about the kelp detox treatment. The solution, a purified seaweed cream, was smeared all over your body and then you were wrapped in layers of gauze, as if in a cocoon, and left to rest for a while, a half hour or maybe more.

She imagined the lights in the room were dimmed and some electronic, Zen-like music was playing to enhance the mood.

Max must have been lying there with his eyes closed, maybe even asleep. Maybe even practicing some positive visualization for his upcoming meeting?

It would have been easy for the killer to creep in and smother him with the towels. Someone who knew their way around the spa, knew the timing of the treatments, knew where they would find him.

Since he was lying on a table, caught unaware, that person didn't even need to be very strong. Just focused and . . . persistent.

He must have reacted, purely by instinct. But the element of surprise could not be underestimated here.

"Alice told the police she couldn't stand it anymore. He tortured her. All his flirtations and affairs. I saw it, but there was nothing I could say to change her mind. She would never leave him. I told her more than once that she should." Nadine's voice was flat, resigned.

Maggie glanced at her friends, but made no comment. "So you overheard her conversation with Detective Michaelson?"

"I heard everything. I was right in the next room. Besides, I already know most of the story. She is my sister," Nadine added sadly. "It was that model, that Shannon Piper. When Max told the police he'd switched huts with Hill, Alice stood by his story about the better cot. But she didn't believe him. They had a huge fight. She badgered him until he told her the truth. He'd been with the model. After he'd sworn he was going to change. Max had finally promised Alice they'd get married. But I doubt he would have ever gone through with it. As soon as they found investors for the new spas, he said. They decided it all last week. But I was the only one who knew. Me and my nephew, Brian," she added.

"How did Brian take it," Lucy asked her.

"How do you think? You saw how he acted in the lobby." Nadine shook her head and took a sip of tea. "He hated Max and was enraged with Alice for staying with him."

"So he opposed the marriage?" Dana asked to clarify.

"Oh yes, made a big scene. Last week, while we were all preparing for this weekend. Maybe Alice shouldn't have told him. But she wanted to be honest, I guess. Personally, I wonder if Max was ever going to follow through on that engagement. Maybe Brian lost his head for nothing. I think it was just as likely that once the business took off, Max would toss my sister aside."

"Did Alice think that, too?" Maggie asked in a sad voice.

"She was always afraid he would leave her. She told the police this misstep with the model was the last straw," Nadine added quietly.

Lucy found that scenario very believable. Alice was devoted to Max, but everyone had a limit.

"What about Hill? Did she tell the police that she killed Hill, too?" Dana asked.

"I don't know about the reporter. The police think she killed him by accident, assuming Max was in that hut," Nadine speculated. "Alice was very confused about that. She claims she had some sort of blackout."

Lucy was getting a little confused now, too. Today was Sunday; wasn't it only last night that Alice had discovered Max

212 / Anne Canadeo

had been fooling around with Shannon? Was she already mad enough to kill on Friday night? Had she planned this out and messed up on Friday, so she tried again today? And with even more reason, too?

"She told the police she went up to the campsite to spy on Max. I think that part of her story is true."

"That part? You mean, you don't think her entire confession is true?" Dana asked quickly.

"I saw someone hiking up the mountain late at night," Maggie confirmed, "but I didn't see a face. I couldn't even tell if it was a man or a woman."

"I wouldn't be surprised if she did hike up that mountain to spy on him. She had all that insecurity and jealousy about Max and more. But I still don't think she killed him. She screamed and yelled and threatened. But she was hopelessly in love, no matter how he treated her. There was only one person in the world she loved more."

Nadine let out a long, sad sigh and took a sip of her tea.

"Her son, Brian," Lucy said.

"That's right. My nephew. So damaged and troubled. His life is a mess. It's everyone's fault but his own, you know." Nadine's tone was suddenly arch and cool. "She's trying to protect him. It's obvious to me."

"That's what any mother would do. I'd do the same in her situation," Suzanne said sympathetically.

"It's a little more complicated with my sister. She carries a lot of guilt, I think, for taking up with Max. I know she always had a thing for him, even when she was married to Edward," Nadine confided. "After Edward died, she went over to Max's side pretty quickly. I know Brian was hurt. He thought it was very disloyal to his father's memory." She paused and took a breath.

"My nephew has made an art out of punishing her for all of that. Even his drinking problem and the way he dropped out of college . . . it's all tied in with the past, the twisted, sad events."

Lucy knew that much was true. Brian had expressed those same sentiments to her just this morning.

"Now she sees a chance to make it all up to him. Like some tragic heroine," Nadine concluded. "That's what I think."

Dana handed Nadine a box of tissues and rested a hand on her shoulder. "Don't worry, Nadine. A false statement won't stand up for very long. If Alice is really innocent, the police will see that very quickly and she should be back here very soon."

"Oh, I hope you're right. It would be a very sad day if my nephew were found guilty of killing Max Flemming. The finishing blow for my sister. But I can't sit by and see her take the blame for a crime she didn't commit. I just can't." Nadine cried in earnest now, covering her eyes with a tissue.

Maggie leaned forward and rubbed Nadine's shoulder. There was little anyone could say.

"The problem is, I think my nephew had far more motive to kill Max than my sister. He's always hated him. Always," Nadine insisted.

Before anyone could comment, Nadine's cell phone sounded. She checked the number, then picked up the call. "All right. Yes, I know. I'll be right there."

She slipped her phone back in her pocket and stood up. "The police need to speak to me again and the guests are about to storm the castle walls. Thank you, ladies, for whisking me away and bringing me here. And letting me pour my heart out. I appreciate your kindness."

"Oh Nadine, we wish we could really help you," Maggie

said sincerely. "Would you please let us know if there's anything we can do?"

"There's only one thing that can help me now, Maggie. If someone can figure out who really killed Max Flemming."

She said good-bye with a sad smile and headed out the cottage door.

Chapter Thirteen

*L*ucy and her friends could barely wait until Nadine was out of view before they began to speculate.

"I think she's right. I don't believe Alice did it. I've been thinking about the timing. It doesn't add up," Lucy told the others. "Alice said that Shannon Piper was the last straw, but she didn't find that out about that tryst until last night, Saturday. Hill was killed the night before."

"She may have killed Max, but not Hill," Dana pointed out. "Hill may have been killed for completely different reasons and by someone else entirely."

"That's possible, Dana, but highly unlikely, don't you think? What are the odds that two murders would happen in one weekend at this little inn?" Lucy challenged her.

Dana usually had the upper hand in these conversations since her husband had done police work and she was so well-versed in the investigation process. But this time Lucy felt very strongly that she was on the right path.

"I think we have to assume that Hill was killed by accident

Friday night. He was in the wrong hut at the wrong time. Someone was after Max and they screwed up, then tried again today and hit their target," Lucy concluded.

Dana shrugged. "All right. Let's just go on that track for a while," she conceded. "I'm still not ruling Alice out, even though her story has some inconsistencies. You forget, it's been presented in the best possible light by her sister, who doesn't want to believe Alice was capable of killing Max," Dana reminded them.

"Even so, there's still a good case for Brian," Maggie argued, taking up Nadine's position. "The police must see that, despite what his mother tells them. He resented Max, knows the mechanics of the heaters, and could have easily slipped up to the mountain on Friday night. He made a mistake with Hill, but got it right this morning in the treatment room. He hated seeing Max succeed when his father was such a failure. When his mother and Max got engaged, maybe that was *his* last straw."

Maggie turned to Lucy. "Did you ever tell the police about that argument you witnessed, between Brian and his mother?"

"No, I didn't have any reason to," Lucy replied. "It didn't seem to have anything to do with Curtis Hill. But I should definitely tell them now."

"Yes, you should," Dana agreed. "It is a real Hamlet scenario, isn't it?"

"Is it ever," Lucy agreed. "And there's even more than Nadine told us. Brian gave me an earful this morning. He claims that Max's book is a pile of lies. He remembers the past much differently."

Lucy quickly related Brian's version of the story, giving her group even more to think about.

"Brian resents Max for surviving and even thriving, when his father wasn't strong enough," Lucy summed up. "He claims Max unfairly blames his father in the book for the patient's death and exploited the story of the tragedy—even the story of Edward's demise and death—for his own selfish gain. He told me he felt guilty himself from benefiting from Max's success. That seemed to upset him, too."

"I don't know about you, but I need to knit while I process all this." Maggie continued working steadily on her project, another sweater coat for her daughter, Julie, who was away at college, Lucy noticed.

Sometimes Lucy wondered if Julie had opened a sweater boutique in her dorm room, for a little extra pocket change. Maggie certainly supplied her with enough inventory.

Dana, Phoebe, and Suzanne were also still knitting, but Lucy's hands hurt too much from her fall. She was content to watch the others and just talk the puzzle through.

"I feel as if we're missing something," Dana insisted. "Brian told Lucy he was in town on Friday night and has witnesses."

"I've spoken with him twice now. He's pretty sharp. If he was really trying to murder Max the whole weekend, would he be walking around bad-mouthing the guy so openly?" Lucy asked the others. "That doesn't seem to make any sense."

"You have a good point, Lucy. Unless he's a total nut job. Excuse me for throwing around medical terms." Dana flashed a smile. "And there are other candidates. Joy Kimmel, for instance. Didn't Nadine say she was down in the spa this morning, when Max was killed? She had good reason to resent her ex-husband. She'd been cut out of his recent run of good fortune and was jealous of Alice's proximity and power. She was probably jealous of any woman who got close to Max these days. And there seemed to be plenty of them."

"She looks pretty strong," Phoebe noted. "I could easily see her shimmying over and pressing a pile of towels on his face."

"Phoebe . . ." Lucy gave her a look.

Phoebe shrugged. "Well, I could. I'm just being honest."

Now that Phoebe mentioned it, Lucy could, too.

"When we talked on Friday night, she sounded almost too easy and accepting of her lot in life," Maggie decided, "which isn't much, really. Maybe she wanted Max back and he rebuffed her? Then he tried to make it up to her with this menial job at the hotel. And let's not forget the *I Ching* symbol the police found," Maggie pointed out. "She was the one who referred to that book and speaks that new age lingo so fluently."

"So we can't rule out the belly dancer, is that what we're saying?" Suzanne had taken out the faithful chulo hat and was making another stab at it. "I just want to keep my score card straight."

"I haven't checked her off mine," Dana noted. "I suppose Joy could have tampered with the heating mechanism, too. I don't think it's hard to do if you know how. We can't rule her out on that point, either, just because she's a woman."

"Certainly not. I've always done the little home repairs. Even when Bill was alive," Maggie said.

Lucy agreed. It would be sexist—and plain dumb—to think a woman would not have been capable of killing Hill because of the mechanics involved, though a guy like Brian, touted for his talents as a handyman, would jump to the top of the list.

The phone in the cottage rang and everyone flinched. Maggie put down her knitting and ran over to pick it up.

"Yes . . . oh, really. Well, that's something, Nadine," she

said quickly. She listened some more and her expression grew serious.

"All right. Tell the police they don't have to send an escort this time. We'll be there."

She hung up the phone and turned to her friends.

"The police have finished interviewing Alice. Her attorney said that he's waiting now to see if the police want to detain her. They haven't booked her yet on any charges."

"I wonder if they will," Suzanne said.

"They might, if they know something that Nadine doesn't know about it."

Lucy was thinking the same. It was still hard to predict.

"And Detective Dykstra wants everyone up in the lobby in fifteen minutes. He must have an announcement to make."

"An announcement. Praise the Lord." Suzanne stood up and stretched, wriggling her lower back. She glanced at her watch. "I can't believe it's only one o'clock. What a day this turned out to be. I told Kevin I'd be home for dinner. I hope the police let everyone go by then."

"He might say we have to stay for more interviews, about Max's death this time," Lucy pointed out.

"I don't know about the rest of you, but I've had enough conversations with police officers for a while. And enough pampering and free-range vegetables. This place is giving me the willies," Maggie finally admitted. "I'm ready to head back to cozy old Plum Harbor, with or without any answers."

Lucy felt the same, though she did hope they left with some hint about the culprit behind these nasty deeds.

When they walked into the inn a short time later, the lobby was crowded. There was no place to sit, so they just stood and waited for the detective to appear.

Nadine was wandering about with her clipboard, which looked even more like a prop this afternoon, Lucy thought. Her expression was dark and deflated, her eyes puffy and red-rimmed. No longer fit to play the role of social director, she was carrying on bravely.

She walked over to Maggie and touched her arm. "I have some news. The police have released my sister. I guess they didn't believe her story any more than I did."

Maggie's expression brightened. "You must be relieved."

"It's not all good news. They've asked my nephew, Brian, to come in for questioning. Now his neck is next on the chopping block. Alice is beside herself. I could hardly understand a word she said over the phone."

"Oh, that's too bad. That's awful," Maggie replied sincerely. She shared a look with Lucy and the others. Bad news, but not totally unexpected.

Still, something about Brian being singled out didn't work for Lucy. She wondered if anyone else had any doubts. She was the only one who had spent time with him. Wasn't he too smart to be so vocal about his disdain for a man he planned on murdering? Or was he just obsessed? So filled with hatred he couldn't control what he said . . . or did?

The group on the other side of the lobby, closer to the main entrance, parted and Lucy noticed a stretcher coming through, carried by two emergency medical technicians. Rita Schumacher trotted alongside. Her purple jogging outfit and white walking shoes, as big as pillows, finally suited her activity.

When the crowd parted a bit, Lucy caught sight of Walter strapped on the stretcher under a blanket. An oxygen mask covered most of his face. All she could see was his shining bald head. It was hard to tell if he was even conscious.

"Rita Schumacher called the front desk a few minutes ago. Walter collapsed in their room," Nadine explained. "All the stress must have gotten to him. Luckily, there was an ambulance on the grounds already, parked at the spa wing. Waiting to take Max's body away," Nadine added in a quieter tone.

She paused, taking a breath. Lucy could tell it had been hard for her to explain that part. "But the medical examiner isn't finished yet, I understand," she continued, "and this need is definitely more pressing."

"Rita said that Walter has been feeling poorly all weekend," Maggie replied. "All the stress and excitement must have gotten to him. First Curtis Hill . . . then Dr. Max."

"Walter looks awful, poor man." Suzanne shook her head. "I think Rita said he has cancer."

Lucy suspected that was it, too, though Rita had never told her specifically.

"I guess the treatments and philosophies here can't cure every ill . . . yet." Maggie's tone was philosophical.

Nadine sighed. "No, not yet. But some people do come with a lot of hope. It's hard to turn them away or tell them not to bother, you know?"

Lucy could see that would be difficult, a real ethical dilemma. Who could really say? There were many studies that had shown a positive attitude, meditation, and visualization techniques had change the course of serious illness, even cancer. Maybe Dr. Max was not a complete fraud and soy bean Svengali. Just ambitious and able to rationalize the ethical gray areas.

A few minutes after the Schumachers departed, Detective Dykstra walked out from the back office. He took a position near the front desk and the crowd of guests pressed around him.

As everyone hoped, he told the guests that they were free to leave. "We will continued to investigate the deaths of Mr. Hill and Dr. Flemming, but believe we're coming very close to closing this case. We ask that everyone confirms their valid contact information with us. There may be a need for more follow-up questioning in the coming days and even weeks."

The entire group seemed to give out a collective sigh of relief. Lucy and her friends immediately took their places in the long line to check out. The hotel had added extra staff at the desk, she noticed, to shorten the wait.

She had to find one of the detectives and relate the argument she'd witnessed in the lobby between Alice and Brian, Lucy realized. But after that, they were free to go.

It wouldn't be too long before they'd be on the road, heading home. Lucy felt relieved, though she expected to be talking over the murder with her friends the entire way back. The alternative wasn't that attractive, either: mulling over her problems with Matt for two hours.

With all the drama around here, she hadn't thought about that crisis very much. Maybe she could solve that case by the time they reached Plum Harbor.

A short time later, Suzanne's SUV was packed and everyone climbed inside, taking their seats for the ride home. By silent agreement, the others allowed Maggie to ride in front again.

They rode in silence for a while, through the dappled, late-afternoon light as Suzanne steered the SUV down the curving mountain road, toward the village and the highway.

Maggie was the first one to speak. "Nadine seemed so sad when I said good-bye. She's going to the police station to wait with Alice while Brian is questioned."

"What a choice to be faced with, either believing that your sister is a murderer or your nephew." Suzanne shook her head in sympathy.

"Not one I'd ever want to face," Maggie agreed. She slipped on her glasses, then picked up her knitting bag. "Well, this weekend has been an experience, I must say. Not exactly the relaxing break we planned, was it?"

"No comment. But that just means we have to plan another," Lucy said decidedly. "If you don't get something right the first time, you just have to try again."

"How true," Maggie agreed. "But I still want to apologize for leading you all up there. I have to do a little more research before I agree to any last-minute teaching jobs at hotels, no matter how tempting the website and free accommodations."

"No apologies necessary, Maggie. We all wanted to go," Lucy reminded her. "Didn't we?" she prodded the others.

"I wouldn't have missed it for anything," Dana insisted. "Actually, even knowing what I do know, I still would have come along. If all of you were going," she added.

"I can't say that it was fun exactly," Suzanne added. "But if I have to be trapped in a hotel for the weekend with a killer on the prowl, I'd always want to be with you guys."

There was silence for a moment, then they all laughed. Suzanne's logic was a bit convoluted, but Lucy knew that they all shared the same warm but twisted feelings.

Chapter Fourteen

When they finally reached Plum Harbor, several hours later, Dana was the first to be dropped off. "Anywhere along Bayview if fine," she told Suzanne as they cruised into the village. "I'm meeting Jack and Dylan for dinner at that little Japanese place across from the dock. They'll tell me all about their golf tournament and I'll tell him all about our wild weekend. I'm sure my story will be much more interesting," Dana added as she grabbed her bags from the back. "But you never know. There may have been some psycho golfer out there, knocking people out with his sand wedge."

"Let's hope not," Maggie said. "I hope Jack had a far more peaceful weekend than we did."

Phoebe was next. Suzanne parked in front of Maggie's shop and Phoebe climbed from the very backseat, dropping kisses and hugs all around as she worked her way out. She sprung out onto the sidewalk, hoisting her tote bag a notch higher on her shoulder, then made a beeline for her car, a banged-up VW Bug that sat parked a short distance up the block on Main Street.

"You're not even going inside?" Maggie asked. "I thought you might go down to the shop later and water the plants."

"Sorry, Maggie. I promised Josh I'd come straight over tonight. He claims he missed me so much, he wrote me a song. Isn't that sweet?" Phoebe stopped and turned to look at them again, smilingly dreamily.

"Very romantic," Maggie called back. "See you tomorrow." She waved as Suzanne pulled away.

"Have you ever heard his music? I don't know how it could be either sweet or romantic," Suzanne said.

"It's the gesture that counts," Maggie replied. "Beside, dogs hear sounds that we can't hear . . . so do the fans of the Babies, apparently."

"At least one fan," Lucy clarified. That was love for you. She didn't want to go there.

But she did want to get home and was thrilled and relieved when her house came into sight.

The small cottage was only a few blocks from the beach in an area of town known as the marshes. The place had been left to Lucy and her sister, Ellen, by their aunt Laura when she'd died two years ago, unmarried and childless.

Every summer while growing up, Lucy and Ellen had spent long visits in Plum Harbor, as if Aunt Laura's house were some free, exceptionally exclusive sleepaway camp. Lucy had many happy memories of the cottage and village. It was only natural that she'd gravitated here, two summers past, when her marriage had broken up and she'd quit an office job to work from home as a graphic artist. She'd come out to the cottage to rest and regroup and had ended up a year-round resident of the beach town.

The cottage was small and had never been renovated or

expanded, like so many on the street, but it suited Lucy and her dog, Tink, perfectly. These days, she couldn't imagine living any place else.

Lucy quickly climbed out of the backseat and grabbed her bags.

"When do you pick up Tink?" Suzanne asked.

"I'm going over to Matt's in a little while." Lucy tried to strike a casual note, though she was actually nervous to face him.

She knew that they had to have a serious conversation and she was the one who had to initiate it. She hated that. She didn't want to talk about a relationship, she just wanted to have one. But that wasn't always the way it went, she knew by now.

"Well, good luck," Maggie said lightly. "I'm sure everything will work out."

"One way or the other," Lucy added. "What was that Joy Kimmel said to you about Dr. Max? 'If your horse leaves the corral and doesn't come back, maybe it's not your horse'? Well, maybe Matt just isn't my horse."

"Yes, but maybe he is. You just need to train him better," Suzanne insisted. "And toss him a few carrots."

Maggie looked puzzled for a moment, then shook her head. "That advice is actually not in the *I Ching*. But she has been happily married for over twenty years," Maggie reminded Lucy. "I wouldn't discount it."

Maggie's house was nearby and Suzanne dropped off her last.

"Home sweet home." Maggie sighed as they pulled into the driveway. "We've barely been gone three days, but it feels like weeks for some reason."

"It was an event-filled weekend," Suzanne said diplomatically.

"No argument there." Maggie gathered her things and climbed down from the high seat. The two women said good night and Maggie headed for her front door, picking up the Sunday newspaper from her driveway on the way in.

The news of Dr. Max's murder would surely be in tomorrow's paper, she realized. She wasn't looking forward to reading that article. In fact, she decided not to read the paper at all tonight . . . not even turn on the TV. She was going to sit by her own fire and knit. Maybe call her daughter and catch up on her news.

She unlocked the front door and went inside, feeling comforted by her plan. Everything was just as she'd left it; the empty house seemed to greet her with its familiar sights and sounds.

Maggie switched on a lamp in the foyer and then another in the living room as she made her way back to the kitchen. She was glad to be home at last. In her own, safe, sacred space. Alone, but not lonely.

As Suzanne walked up the path to her front door, she thought about Maggie. It must feel odd to come home after a trip to an empty house. Of course it had happened to her once. She was sure of it. She just couldn't remember when.

Especially when the two faces of her twin boys appeared in the living room window. Ryan waved wildly and smiled until his cheeks seemed strained, his braces sparkling in the dim light. James immediately disappeared. Moments later, as she stood at the front door, she heard him running through the house, shouting, "Mom's home! Mom's home!"

She was sure the place was a disaster area and it would take her the entire week to clean up. But when the boys tackled her as she walked through the door, and she saw her husband, Kevin, in the kitchen doorway, it all seemed worth it somehow.

"I tried to cook you something, but it didn't come out right. How about some pizza?" he asked as she kissed his cheek.

"Pizza sounds perfect to me," she answered. And it truly did.

Lucy had dashed into her house, dumped her bags in the living room, then ran upstairs for some quick repairs to her appearance before she headed to Matt's house to pick up Tink.

She wanted to look good, but not like she tried. There was a fine line, that was for sure.

After a few minutes spent in her bathroom and bedroom, touching up the shadows under her eyes and trying on a pile of sweaters, she managed to clean up just enough to look attractive.

If he'd been cheating on her, she just wanted him to regret it.

Just as she grabbed her car keys, she heard her phone ring in the kitchen. She waited for the message to come on, expecting her mother or sister with their usual Sunday-night phone call.

Instead, she heard's Matt's voice.

"Hey, Lucy. I really want to see you tonight, but I have to get going. I have to go to my folks' house and help them put up their new computer, you know how it is. It's getting sort of late and I have an early day tomorrow. I left you a key, it is under that blue flower pot on the porch. If you have any trouble getting in, just call me. I'll call you tonight, if I don't get back too late. Tink is all ready for you. I think she really missed you," he added in a teasing tone.

Oh, great. Thanks a bunch. How about you? No comment, right?

Lucy felt so frustrated and disappointed, she nearly started crying. Then she took a breath, swept out of the house, and set off to pick up her dog.

Maybe it was better not to see Matt tonight, she decided after a few minutes of fuming and driving along. Her emotions were still worked up from her crazy weekend. If Matt had been at home and she cornered him for some relationship talk, she might say something she'd really regret.

Lucy kept reminding herself of that insight as she walked up the path to his house. The porch light was on and also one light inside, back in the kitchen. He never left the dogs alone in the dark. Matt had a dog, too, a chocolate Lab mix named Wally. Tink and Wally got along well, luckily. Probably better these days than their owners, she reflected while looking around for the key.

She found the extra key just where Matt had left it and let herself in. Then she slammed the door shut and braced herself. The thunderous sound of dog paws galloping through the house filled the rooms. Wally only had three legs, but still kept up with the best of them.

Wally appeared first. He ran up to her barking and stopped, then sniffed her leg and barked again, though not very ferociously. More of a hello bark. He was too well trained to jump, Lucy knew. Also, too old now.

The Lab had been hit by a car and brought to Matt for surgery. But his owners never came back for him. Matt had grown so attached, he couldn't give Wally to a shelter and just took him home.

"Hello, Wally. Good dog," she said, patting his head.

Tink soon appeared at the top of the stairs. The fur on her head and ears stuck out like feathers. Doggie bed head, Lucy noticed, and figured that the mutt must have been napping on one of the comfy human spots up there.

Tink spotted Lucy and let out a joyful yip. All was forgiven as the big dog flew down the stairs. At the last step, she leaped up and flung herself into Lucy's chest, trying hard to lick her face or any exposed area.

"Tink, get down . . . down, honey," Lucy knew her tone was highly unconvincing. Tink paid no mind at all, and never stopped dancing around on her hind legs for one second.

Finally, Lucy just put her arms around the mass of moving fur and hugged her back.

"I missed you, too, sweetie. I really did. Hey, at least someone around here is happy to see me."

True to his word, Matt finally called, but Lucy had fallen asleep in her favorite armchair while watching TV. She'd been waiting for the late news, sure there would be a story about the dark events at the Crystal Lake Inn and Dr. Max Flemming's mysterious death.

But she'd missed the report, along with a chance to talk to Matt and tell him about her strange, frightening weekend.

He'd left a brief message saying he was home, but had to go straight to bed. He had a long day in the surgery room tomorrow but would try to touch base in the afternoon.

Lucy sighed and then deleted the message. She'd wait to see if he would call her back tomorrow. She wasn't holding her breath.

She was annoyed at herself for missing his call. She wasn't quite sure how that had happened. The entire weekend had caught up with her all at once and she'd drifted off, Tink's head resting on her shoe and her knitting in her lap.

Lucy roused herself and headed for bed. If their relationship didn't work out, she'd survive just fine. Worse things had happened to her, that was for sure. At this point, any answer would be a relief.

But somehow, the thought wasn't very comforting. The idea of breaking up with him did seem painfully bleak.

Once she got in bed and shut the light, her thoughts jumped from Matt back to the Crystal Lake Inn and the horrific events of the weekend. It was hard to sleep, though she felt bone tired. She glanced at the clock. It was midnight. Too late to call one of her friends, to commiserate and speculate again about the murders.

Maybe tomorrow she would catch up with Maggie or Dana and hear more news. She wondered if she would be able to get a decent night's sleep until this case was solved.

At some point on Monday morning, Lucy remembered why she avoiding going away for long weekends. It took time to get ready beforehand and then even more time to dig out and catch up when you came back. Even though you'd just been gone a weekend, the pile of mail, newspapers, and laundry always seemed worthy of a real vacation. Why even bother?

That was a cranky and negative way to look at it, she knew. But that's how she felt today, no help for it.

She didn't even have a spare half hour to take Tink for a long walk into town before heading for her computer. She probably needed the walk and fresh air even more than the dog. It would have definitely improved her mood.

But work came first and she had plenty of it, an annual

report for a nonprofit organization based in Boston. The pay wasn't great, but it was a simple job, just time-consuming. Enough to keep her glued to her computer for the rest of the day and even into the night.

By the late afternoon, she felt a bit brain dead. The graphic images of bar graphs and pie charts made her head swim. Lucy knew she needed a break or risked messing up the entire layout.

She rose slowly from her chair, unfolding her body very slowly, like a paper airplane that hadn't come out right. Tink had been stretched out under her desk for hours and now jumped up as if someone flipped a switch. She trotted to the back door and grabbed her leash in her mouth, her tail beating like the propeller on a military helicopter.

"Yes, yes . . . you can take me for a walk," Lucy told the dog agreeably. "Just don't pull my arm off. I might need it later."

Lucy was tugged down the winding streets as if she were on water skis and Tink were a motorboat. The dog already knew the way to town and Lucy hardly needed to direct her. Instead of going all the way down to the harbor on their usual route, they came out on Main Street, a few blocks from the knitting shop.

Standing on the porch, Lucy could see the shop was nearly empty inside, but she still didn't think of bringing Tink inside. She never did, fearing the baskets of yarn and other goodies, displayed at snout level, would be far too tempting. She tied the dog in her spot on the porch and gave her a chew toy she'd stashed in her purse.

"Be a good girl. I won't be long," she promised.

She found Maggie in the back of the store, searching

through the drawers of the tall hutch on the back wall that held buttons and other types of trim and accessories.

"Hello, Lucy. Didn't think I'd see you today. Don't you have a deadline?"

"Sort of . . . they sent me a file this morning with more charts to fit in. So I have a little more time on it." Lucy noticed a new issue of a favorite knitting magazine and started paging through. There was also a copy of the *Boston Globe* on the table, but she purposely avoided it.

"Have you seen the inn on the TV news?" she asked Maggie. "I missed it last night, but I saw a short story this morning."

"Oh, I saw it all over. Last night, this morning . . . and the *Globe* has an article, too," she added. "Brian Archer was released late last night, but he's still a person of interest. The reporters make it sound like the police are just trying to gather more evidence before they issue a warrant for his arrest."

"I can't say I'm surprised," Maggie added. "The deck seemed stacked in his direction."

"Your friend Nadine seemed to think so," Lucy replied.

"I spoke to Nadine today." Maggie put a handful of button cards on the table and then started sifting through them. "I thought I should call, just to see how she was holding up. Sounds like she's been left to run the place, though there's practically no one staying there right now. All the weekend guests checked out last night and with the bad publicity, she's had a ton of cancellations."

"I guess that's just as well, with everything else they have to deal with. How is Alice Archer doing?"

"Alice is a wreck. She's even too upset to plan Max's memorial and the police haven't released the body yet, either. Nadine is very worried about her. Alice has always been such a rock for everyone else. Even when her husband, Edward, died. But losing Max . . . and the way he died . . . well, she's fallen to pieces." Maggie sighed and shook her head in sympathy.

"That's too bad. Isn't there anyone around to help Nadine? How about Joy?" Lucy asked.

"Joy Kimmel's been no help," Maggie replied. "She's flown the coop. With the investigation still pending, she can't go very far, but she's left the hotel. She claims that she's heartsick and says the place is still filled with pockets of Max's energy and she just can't take that. It 'drains her life force.'"

Maggie glanced at Lucy, but didn't comment further.

"That's a new one. I wonder if she qualifies for unemployment checks," Lucy mused. "Seems like she's quitting for health reasons."

"Sounds like she might need a little extra income. She also found out she's not named in Max's will. Nadine thinks that news drained her energy, too. The only heirs named are Alice and Brian, who have inherited practically everything. Except for a large donation to some foundation that researches holistic cures and all these new age theories."

"Sounds about right. I guess Max had some conscience after all and some deep feeling for Alice and Brian. He did try to take care of them. Maybe to pay them back for the past? For the way Edward died and for using the story of that patient they lost?"

"Maybe. I'm sure Alice would like to believe that. But I guess we'll never know for sure," Maggie said wisely.

"No, we won't. Neither will Alice and Brian, I guess. Though they do have a small fortune to comfort them now. They could easily sell that inn for zillions, if they want to."

"Yes, they could. Nadine says Alice has no idea what she

will do. She hasn't given any of those issues a thought. Nadine told me it was hard to tell if the news about the inheritance even registered, she's so completely focused on Brian right now."

"I can understand that," Lucy said quietly. She closed the magazine and pushed it aside. "Now that Brian stands to benefit big time from Max's death, the police will count that as a motive, too."

Maggie had returned to sorting out the buttons, but now her head popped up and she stared at Lucy. "Yes, I guess they will. I didn't think of that. It does strengthen their case."

There was a strong case to be made for Brian as Max's killer—he had the means, the motive, and the opportunity—but Lucy still didn't see him as the one. Maybe just because she'd spent time with Brian alone at such close range, the idea of him killing not just one, but two people, was simply too frightening.

"I'll be interested to see if the police find some really conclusive proof. Some physical evidence. DNA? Whatever," Lucy said. "I think if they had some already, they would have charged him. No matter how much he hated Max, it still doesn't mean he did it."

"Yes, I know," Maggie agreed. "I thought once we came home we'd get out from under that mess. But it's hard to stop talking about it, isn't it?"

"It is," Lucy agreed, taking a seat. "Especially since the police haven't arrested anyone yet. We did meet a lot of memorable personalities," Lucy added, thinking over the varied roster. "What happened to Walter Schumacher? Did Nadine ever find out?"

"She did mention the Schumachers. She said she called the nearest hospital a few hours after he was taken away. They said he was in the ER a while, but had never been admitted. So I guess he wasn't as bad as he looked."

That was some good news, Lucy thought. She also wondered about Helen Lynch and Shannon Piper, but before she could ask about them, another voice broke into the conversation.

"You're open today . . . thank goodness. I came here on Saturday and then again on Sunday. The place was shut tight as Grant's Tomb. You didn't even leave a note on the door. What's the idea of that?"

Normally, Maggie would have raced over to a customer who had entered with that complaining speech. But she hardly raised her gaze and then simply smiled.

"Oh . . . hello, Edie. I was away for the weekend. There was a note on the door. Didn't you see it?"

Edie Steiber ran the diner a few blocks down on Main Street. The Schooner was a town treasure and historic landmark. You might say that Edie was, too, Lucy thought. She had all the necessary characteristics and bearing. She dressed like a parade float most of the time, in large flowered shifts and a beehive hairdo, and always moved through town as if on official business, though she'd never held public office, to the best of Lucy's knowledge.

Edie was sort of an unofficial mayor, with no term limits. Or maybe even the Queen Mum of Plum Harbor, holding court from behind the long counter at the diner, seated on her throne behind the cash register. Her watchful eye overseeing the kingdom, taking in all the news, granting her favors, overseeing the realm. There wasn't much that Edie missed. In fact, Lucy was surprised that she didn't already know where the knitting group had been.

"I didn't see a damned thing. Maybe it blew off. I didn't know what happened to you." Edie waved her hand in the air as she walked slowly through the shop, stopping to check out some new yarn—cashmere-silk blend—that Maggie had put on display. "I thought someone was dead in here or something."

Quite a leap in logic, Lucy thought, though such a thing had actually once happened in town. A woman who had owned another knitting shop had been murdered in her store and no one had known until her husband found her. So the gruesome fear wasn't entire unfounded.

"Don't be silly. I went away for the weekend. With the knitting group." Maggie glanced at Lucy and didn't say more.

"The whole group? That sounds nice. Where did you go? Leaf peeping?"

"We were in the Berkshires, but not for the foliage, exactly. We went to a spa." Lucy could tell Maggie was trying to decide if she should tell Edie that they'd been at the Crystal Lake Inn, the one that was all over the news today.

Edie would probably find out anyway. But once she did know, she'd spread the word like a ladle of brown gravy over a meat loaf special and pretty soon that's all anyone would be talking about, especially here in the knitting shop. Lucy could understand why Maggie was hesitating at full disclosure.

But finally, Lucy could see that Maggie was going to give in. Edie sat down at the oak table with a grunt. "So, how was it? Those places look nice, but they are pretty pricey. I wouldn't bother. The beauty pageant's over for me," she said with a laugh. "You girls are still in the game. God love ya. Was it worth it, you think?"

"It probably would be . . . under different circumstances,"

Maggie began carefully. "We didn't have an altogether wonderful time. It was in the news, maybe you heard? That famous psychiatrist Dr. Maxwell Flemming was found murdered and the day before that—"

"Holy cow!" Edie gasped and covered her mouth with her hand. "You were up at that place, where the doctor and that reporter got killed? For crying out loud, what kind of hotel was that? Sounds like *The Shining*," she added, naming the famous horror film set in a deserted ski lodge. "Hey, when you saw Jack Nicholson at the front desk, that should have given you a clue, girls."

Maggie glanced at Lucy, her expression deadpan. "So you've heard about it on the news, then. I won't bother going into the details."

"I heard all about it and read the article in the newspaper, too. You girls are lucky you got out alive. That must have been real weird, sleeping in a place that had a murderer running around loose."

The way Edie described it, the situation sounded even worse that it actually had been. Well, maybe it was bad, but they were all in denial, Lucy thought.

"It was very . . . stressful," Maggie agreed. "But we hung together. What could we do?"

"Not much but watch your back, I'd say. I'm surprised you didn't keep the place closed today, just to recover from the ordeal."

"Oh, I'm okay. It's good to get back to work." Maggie returned to her button sorting. She did seem focused and relaxed today, back in her routine.

"Do they have any idea who did it? I know the papers can't report the whole story," Edie added.

"They suspect someone. A young man who knew the doctor for most of his life. But the police aren't sure. They have no solid evidence yet," Maggie explained.

"They'll figure it out. These killers always leave something behind. Now that they have all those high-tech, scientific tests, it's hard to get away with anything. Why did you go up there? Was there some special deal or something?"

"Sort of," Maggie said. "We got the hotel accommodations for free and a break on the spa treatments. The inn is sort of new age and I was invited to teach some artistic, spiritual knitting techniques. Random knitting, for instance. I'm going to teach it here soon, too. What do you think, Edie? Want to try it?"

There was a random knitting sample in a basket on the table, one that Maggie had not unpacked yet after the weekend classes.

Edie took the abstract-shaped piece of stitchery, examined it, and turned it over in her hands a few times. "What the heck is this supposed to be? It looks like the dog's breakfast," she said bluntly. "What do you do with something like that? I couldn't even use it for a pot holder."

Maggie took no offense. "You put a few of these together and make a coat or a handbag or a fiber art piece. It's more about the process, Edie. Knitting from the heart and intuitive center, without someone else's pattern imposed on you."

Edie sat with her mouth hanging open a second, then said, "What a crock of cheese. I'm surprised at you, Maggie. You're going to charge good money for that?"

Maggie shrugged. "I don't teach special techniques for free." Lucy knew that she did hold beginner classes several times a year for free. Maggie felt very strongly that spreading the joys of knitting was a public service.

"Well, don't expect me to sign up for that one." Edie tossed the sample across the table in Maggie's direction. "Thanks very much, I'll just stick with plain old patterns. I don't need to express my little self that badly and end up with a big mess," Edie told them plainly. "I like to know where I've been and where I'm going. I'm not a random sort of person."

"I had a feeling you'd say something like that," Maggie replied mildly. Lucy could see the humorous glint in her dark eyes.

"What did I come in here for in the first place? All this chitchat makes me forget." Edie delivered the words in a scolding tone, as if Maggie and Lucy were purposely trying to distract her, when in fact she was the one who encouraged the chitchat. Not only encouraged, but socializing did often seem her real purpose for visiting.

"What do you need today? You didn't say." Maggie walked toward her, taking on her alert shopkeeper expression.

"A circular needle. That's it. I had a few and misplaced them all. I think I loaned my last one to my daughter. I should have kissed that baby good-bye. She never returns anything. Her house is filled with junk, piled to the ceiling. She could be on the TV show, about the hoarders . . ."

Edie rambled on as she followed Maggie to the front of the store, where a display of tools stood across from the cash register—straight needles, circular, crochet hooks, and other knitting sundries.

Lucy went into the storeroom to get Tink a cup of water. Just as she shut the faucet, Phoebe came downstairs from her apartment. She was wearing baggy camouflage pants and a Big Fat Crying Babies T-shirt that Lucy had never seen before.

"Hey, Lucy. What's going on?"

"Not much, Phoebe. How about you? Is that a new T-shirt?"

Phoebe tugged the T-shirt and looked down at it. "Yup. Josh gave it to me. It's a sample. Do you like it?" She turned so Lucy could see the back. The title of the group's new CD, *Can't Stop Crying. Really*, was written in ragged type.

"It's very cool." Lucy smiled and nodded.

"Josh said he was so worried about me, he wrote me a song. He wants to record it. But I told him not to."

"That's really sweet. Why not?"

"Mainly, because it sounds tragically familiar. Like something I've heard on the radio . . . inverting a few chords and stuff. Second, because it really stinks," she said frankly.

"Oh, too bad." Wasn't anyone's relationship working out? "Well, it's the thought that counts. You're pretty lucky. Nobody has written a song for me lately."

"Yeah, well, you get free health care for your dog. That counts for a lot."

"It does. Speaking of dogs, I'd better get out there before she taste tests Maggie's new Knitters Welcome Here doormat."

"Good idea. She had to send away for that. It was custom made." Phoebe rolled her eyes.

Maggie was still engaged with Edie, talking about the Main Street Preservation Committee, whatever that was. Lucy waved good-bye as she passed and let herself out.

Tink was stretched out in a shady spot under the bay window. She looked up at Lucy with a doggie smile.

"What a good dog. How could I even suspect you'd be up to mischief." Lucy held out the cup of water and Tink lapped it up gratefully. Then Lucy untied her and they headed for home.

Phoebe had made fun of Josh's song, but Lucy was sure that secretly she'd liked it. What woman wouldn't want a man to write a song for her? Or a poem? Or a love letter?

Matt had done none of the above lately. He hadn't even sent a flirty e-mail, come to think of it.

Bad sign. Especially the last.

They kept missing each other with phone calls. Mostly because she'd been trying to play it cool and not seem so eager to see him, if he wasn't eager to see her. But if they spoke later today, she'd just ask him point blank to come over so they could talk. The conversation was long overdue.

Chapter Fifteen

*L*ucy finally spoke to Matt later that day and asked him if they could get together and talk. "There's something on my mind," she said vaguely.

He didn't seem surprised nor did he ask what it was about. Lucy wasn't sure if that was a bad sign or a good one.

Bad, she decided. He's relieved. He's been looking for a way to break up with me and I've just opened the door.

"How about tomorrow night? I'm sorry . . . I have that class tonight. I'll get back too late."

"A class? Oh, right. What was that again?"

"Canine Dentistry?" Just the way he said it, she could tell he was lying. "I'm trying to get certified, remember?"

"Sure. I remember. Okay. See you tomorrow night, then."

She hung up the phone and sighed. So be it. It's probably better to just get this over with.

She ate a quick dinner, then worked past midnight, determined to finish her project. The next morning Lucy would have liked to stay in bed just a few minutes more, but Tink was not buying. She nudged Lucy's arm and sniffed her neck and, when that didn't work, came back with a shoe and dropped it on her stomach.

"Okay, Tink. I get your point." Lucy stumbled out of bed and got her robe and it was time to get up anyway. She had to finish the annual report she'd been working on and send a final file today by noon.

She didn't have that much more to do on it. A few corrections and cleanups. But you never knew what could happen at the last minute. Sometimes that was the trickiest part.

Lucy finished the project without any unexpected disasters, which she was thankful for, and sent the file off at about twelve, just as she'd planned.

It was a beautiful day, a bit warmer than it had been, a taste of Indian summer. She decided to take a well-deserved break with a walk downtown. Tink deserved a walk, too. She'd been shortchanged last night and then again this morning, just left to romp around the backyard.

They were soon outside, heading down familiar streets, all the way to the harbor. It seemed the entire world was out, joggers: walkers, bikers, women pushing strollers or running after toddlers on big plastic bikes. It was a challenge to maneuver the extremely friendly dog around the moving, living obstacles, but Lucy was used to it.

She bought her lunch at the bakery across from the harbor, nearly fainting at the buttery, sugary smell within. She virtuously resisted a tempting row of cupcake. She even surprised herself by resisting the free cookie that came with her wrap sandwich. "Can I have a dog biscuit instead?" she asked, pointing to the bakery dog biscuits in a jar near the register.

"I bought you something," Lucy said, joining Tink again.

With their lunch in hand in a white paper bag, they walked up Main Street to Maggie's store.

Lucy left Tink on the porch and gave her the biscuit alongside a portable bowl of water. She had already noticed Dana sitting at the oak table in back, with Maggie and Phoebe, already eating their lunch and knitting together.

"Hi, guys. I must have gotten a psychic message or something about a lunch date?" Lucy walked in, waving the bakery bag.

"And you made fun of that moonlight meditation," Dana teased. "I think it's kicking in."

Dana had finished her lunch, a mixed green salad with grilled chicken and chickpeas. She tossed out the dish, washed her hands, and started on her knitting again. "We were just hanging out. Talking over the investigation again."

"Any news from Nadine?" Lucy asked curiously.

"Not really," Maggie said. "If the police are making progress, they haven't told her. It's sort of a big tangle, if you ask me."

"And we know something about that," Dana added. "Case in point, my sweater dress. At least we can try to figure that out today. Here's the messy part, Maggie . . . I'm not sure what went wrong."

Dana showed Maggie a section of her black sweater dress. It looked like it might be a sleeve to Lucy. Maggie put her glasses on and examined the stitches. "I think I see it. You might have to rip this all out. Maybe I can catch it with that very thin hook," she said hopefully. "I'll try . . ."

She looked around the table for her handy crochet hook, then picked up a tote bag that was on the sideboard and started rooting around in it. "I took it with me on the weekend.

I know it's in here somewhere. Why do crochet hooks always fall to the bottom of the bag? Why is that? It's so annoying."

"It's called gravity?" Lucy reminded her.

"It's still annoying," Maggie mumbled. She pulled things out of the overloaded bag and piled them on the table. Needles bunched together with rubber bands. Skeins of yarn, a chain of diaper pins she sometimes used as markers, then several small balls of wool in a plastic bag.

"Oh . . . Rita Schumacher's yarn. I never got to give it to her. Maybe I can mail it or something. She seemed so happy to see this alpaca," she noted.

She set the bag on the table, then stared at it. She picked it up and turned it over carefully in her hand. Then she quickly put her eyeglasses back on to get a better look.

"Look at that . . . do you see that?"

She twisted around and held out the bag of yarn, specifically a light blue ball of alpaca, showing it to Lucy and Dana. They both leaned closer, but Lucy had no idea what she was looking for.

"Alpaca?"

"Yes . . . alpaca. One of Rita's favorite fibers. What else?" Maggie asked intensely.

"I don't know . . . some green stuff sticking to the wool?"

"That's right. I thought I'd imagined it for a second. But it's definitely there." Maggie snatched the yarn back, looking shocked and amazed.

"What's there? What's going on, Maggie? Can I see the yarn?" Dana reached out to take the bag, but Maggie snatched it from her reach.

"Don't touch it! It's evidence . . . we need to call Detective Dykstra. Immediately."

"Evidence? What are you talking about?" Dana tried to take the bag again, but Maggie wouldn't let her.

Maggie held the bag up and pointed at the ball of alpaca. "See those little green stains? It's kelp. From Max's treatment room, I'll bet. I wonder if kelp has a DNA imprint. It was a living thing. It must, right?"

Maggie looked around the table to gauge her friends' reactions. Phoebe walked out of the back room holding a dish of food. Lucy could tell from the smell it was her usual lunch, a frozen taco zapped in the microwave. She practicaly lived on them.

"Every living thing has DNA. It's the fingerprint of life," Phoebe recited as if from a textbook. "Intro to Biology; a pretty interesting course. What are you talking about anyway?" she asked, sitting down at the table.

"We're talking about Dr. Max's murder," Lucy explained. "Maggie thinks she's found evidence."

"I don't think. I know. If Walter didn't leave any of his own fingerprints in the treatment room, this should help the police place him there."

"Walter Schumacher?" Phoebe stood up straight, looking surprised. She practically dropped her plate. "Wow, you think he did it? No way . . ."

"Just eat your taco, Phoebe, and stop interrupting, please." She let out an impatient sigh. "Do you remember when Walter came to the workshop this morning? He had stains on his jogging suit," she reminded them.

"I saw that, too. I thought it was just his breakfast or from a smoothie," Lucy said. An easy assumption. There was a lot of green, slimy cuisine at the inn.

"Rita dropped this ball of yarn and he picked it up for her.

I distinctly remember because I was just about to lean over and get it. I was surprised that he moved so fast and easily, come to think of it," Maggie added. "He left these bits of kelp cream on it. I'm positive."

"Maybe he'd been down in the spa," Dana answered.

"I think he was. While we were in the workshop, he was in the a treatment room, suffocating Max. Even the alpaca she picked out from the yarn basket is significant," she continued. "Rita told me that she liked to knit with this fiber, but for a long time could only find it in a little knitting store in Cambridge. She said that she used to shop there about ten years ago, the same time as the suicide of Edward Archer's patient. She said she used to visit the neighborhood to see her granddaughter who was a student at Harvard." Maggie looked around at the other woman. "Max Flemming and Edward Archer's practice was in Cambridge, and the patient who committed suicide was a student at Harvard. Didn't you just read that in the book, Lucy?"

"I did." Lucy nodded quickly. It was all coming together in her mind, too. "Or maybe Brian told me? I'm not sure, Maggie, but I think it all fits. The Schumachers have stayed at the spa before, so they know the routine. They must have come in the summer to figure things out. They even said that they went on the moonlight retreat. So they would have known the hut that Max usually slept in."

"And Rita said that Walter used to be an engineer," Phoebe remembered. "So he would have easily known how to rig the heater."

"And nobody saw them the night of Hill's murder. They stayed in their room," Suzanne recalled.

"Rita said Walter had been sick, but he must have felt well enough for a hike up the mountain." Lucy rubbed her forehead. It was falling into place so quickly now, she almost felt light-headed.

"And the same thing Sunday morning," Maggie reminded them. "Rita was just covering for him when she told everyone her husband was too sick to leave their room. He was down at the spa, giving Max his final treatment."

"Everybody knew Max's schedule for the morning. He'd been walking around the dining room at breakfast, spreading the bliss. Trying to get guests to come to that meeting," Dana recalled. "I think I saw him sit down with the Schumachers and schmooze them up."

"I did, too," Maggie said quickly. "They must have asked what he was going to do before the meeting. Time was running short. The weekend was drawing to a close and they'd already messed up once and accidently killed 'that poor fellow Hill.'"

Dana imitated Rita's voice so perfectly, it gave Lucy a chill. "I remember that now. Rita seemed so shocked and upset. No wonder. Her husband had killed the wrong man."

"But sneaking up on Max alone in a spa room was an ideal opportunity. Hard to screw up that job," Phoebe chimed in.

"I bet Walter doesn't even need that cane," Lucy said suddenly. "He must have used it just to throw everyone off the trail, acting weak and harmless. Crafty old couple, aren't they?"

"Very," Maggie agreed. "The *I Ching* symbol left at Hill's murder scene was a nice touch, too. They were just mocking all this new age stuff and trying to point the police toward someone in Max's circle."

"I think you're right," Dana nodded. " 'Decay . . . work on what has been spoiled,'" she added, recalling the meaning of the *I Ching* symbol. "By killing Max, they meant to right a wrong. To avenge the death of their granddaughter."

"Even the way they first tried to kill him—and mistakenly killed Hill—by inhalation of gas. That was the way their granddaughter had committed suicide," Lucy said sadly.

"Wow, those Schumachers are wicked clever," Phoebe said, shaking her head in amazement.

"They *are* wicked clever, Phoebe," Maggie agreed in a far more serious tone. "I'd bet my entire stock of hand spuns even that medical emergency was staged, just a clever way to escape the inn before the police caught on."

"I thought of that, too, just now, when you were talking about the cane," Dana's eyes widened in amazement. "Wow . . . that one takes the cake."

"It sure does," Maggie agreed. "I wonder if the police will catch up with them. They could be anywhere by now. But that's their job. First I have to do mine . . ."

Maggie found Detective Dykstra's card in her wallet and quickly dialed the number. The others waited around the table, listening to her conversation, barely able to breathe.

"Detective Dykstra? It's Maggie Messina. I was at the inn last weekend? Yes, that's right." She nodded. Lucy guessed he had remembered her. "I'm calling because I have some important information for you. Some evidence. I just found it in my supply bag . . ."

She paused. "Well, it's yarn. A ball of alpaca actually. That's a certain type—Yes, it is evidence, I'm sure of it. I saved it in a plastic bag," she noted. "Very carefully."

She listened again for a few minutes, then suddenly said, "Listen, I know who killed Max Flemming and Curtis Hill. It was not Brian Archer. It was Walter Schumacher. And perhaps his wife helped him," she added. "The yarn? Well, that pulls everything together . . . as yarn usually does."

Maggie slowly but succinctly related the pieces of the story to Detective Dykstra, the same as she had done for her friends a few minutes ago. Lucy, Dana, and Phoebe sat by. Lucy and Dana were working on their knitting. Phoebe was still working on her taco.

Lucy could tell by the tone in Maggie's voice that the detective was finally listening to her and taking her seriously.

When she hung up a few moments later, she seemed satisfied. "He started off pretty skeptical. He thought I was some sort of crank. But once he really listened, I think I convinced him. I think he's been stumped by this double murder. I mean, who wouldn't be?"

"Doesn't he want the evidence?" Dana asked.

"He does. He's coming down here to get it himself," Maggie said. "He has to be in the area tomorrow, to interview someone involved in another case. He'll be here sometime in the evening, he told me."

"Maybe we should move our meeting up a day for this," Dana suggested.

"I was thinking the same," Maggie said. "More psychic energy, you think?"

Psychic energy or not, Detective Dykstra's schedule did bring him to town a little after seven o'clock and the knitting group agreed to move their meeting up a day in order to witness Maggie's moment of glory, handing over the crucial evidence.

Lucy had to cancel on Matt. As much as she wanted to get to the bottom of their problem, she couldn't stand the idea of missing Detective Dykstra's visit.

Let Matt stew a little, she thought, and wonder what I want to talk about.

* * *

Everyone in the group was prompt and already settled in with their projects by the time Detective Dykstra arrived.

Maggie saw him at the door and opened it for him. He entered the shop and looked around curiously. "Very interesting. I don't think I've been in a knitting shop before."

"You've led a sheltered life for a detective, haven't you?" Maggie's tone was teasing.

Lucy thought he might be offended, he was normally so serious, but he smiled at her and took off his hat.

When he reached the back room, he politely greeted the other women.

"Here it is," Maggie said, drawing his attention again. "See that smudge of green? I'm sure it's kelp. Nadine had it all over her sweater, after she tried to give Max mouth to mouth. I know that Walter Schumacher touched this and then handed it to his wife. She was with us the entire time, but he just—"

"Mrs. Messina," Detective Dykstra cut her off with a serious look, "this is important evidence and I thank you for holding on to it so carefully. Acting on your information, we located the Schumachers this afternoon. We brought them in for questioning and they have signed a full confession. I probably shouldn't say this," he added, "but I think Mr. Schumacher was even proud of what he did."

"They confessed? So quickly?" Maggie pressed her hand to her chest in surprise.

"They started talking as soon we found them. In a bed-and-breakfast up in Maine. Seems they had some idea of crossing over to Canada on the ferries up there, then decided not to run, because of Walter's illness mainly. They told us everything. Rita Schumacher could hardly stop herself."

Lucy didn't find that hard to imagine.

"Well . . . I'll be. I was right, then, wasn't I?" Maggie sat down hard in her seat, looking a little surprised. But pleased, as well.

"Yes, you were. We were looking at Brian Archer. He looked very good on paper, you might say. But it seems we almost arrested the wrong man."

"But how did he do it exactly? When did he fool with the heater?" Lucy was curious about that part of the story. "Brian told me that the huts were used the night before Curtis Hill's murder and everything was in perfect working order."

"Good question. The heaters were working the night before Hill's murder. And no one saw anybody else go up on the mountain once those hikers from the club in town came down," Dykstra explained. "But here's where Mr. Schumacher really shined. He came into town a few days early and stayed over at a small bed-and-breakfast. He already knew about the hiking club outings and went along the night before the moonlight retreat with that group.

"Not only was Mr. Schumacher far more fit that he acted at the inn, but he really looked very different," the detective continued. "He had a full head of hair and a beard, dyed dark brown. No one would have recognized him returning to the inn, even if they'd noticed the townies."

"So he went up to the campsite the night before and damaged the heating unit in Max's hut before he came down?" Dana asked.

"That's right. Max always used that hut. It had the better camp bed and other special touches. Walter was sure he'd stay there."

"So who was walking through the woods that night?" Maggie asked. "You know, when I saw the light on the hillside."

"That was Alice. She told us that she'd started up the mountain, intending to surprise Max, then felt foolish.

'Disgusted with myself,' I think were her exact words," the detective recalled.

How sad, Lucy thought. But love drove people to extremes, the wrong kind of love.

"Walter Schumacher is a clever man, I'll grant him that. But he didn't figure Max would wander," Suzanne said. "But Max told you he had offered Hill the hut, so the writer would be more comfortable? Was that part at least true?"

"No, it wasn't exactly." Dykstra laughed. "You know how the inn didn't serve hard liquor? Seems Mr. Hill didn't like that rule. He'd brought along his own flask of bourbon. Had it up in his hut with him. We now think he started off in his own hut, which was right next door to Max's. Drank the bourbon and got up in the middle of the night to relieve himself, then wandered into Max's hut on the way back by mistake."

"And by that time, Max had gone to visit Shannon Piper," Dana remembered. "So the hut was empty and Hill fell back to sleep undisturbed."

"And when the temperature got low enough, the heater turned on and filled the hut with carbon monoxide," Lucy finished for her.

"That's how it happened, more or less," the detective confirmed.

"An unlucky mistake for Curtis Hill," Maggie murmured. "Mr. Schumacher made a grave miscalculation. What did he think about that?"

"Schumacher expressed remorse about killing Mr. Hill," Dykstra told them. "But he also said it couldn't be helped."

"He was determined to get Max. He was obsessed with avenging the death of his granddaughter," Dana said.

"That was his motive," the detective confirmed. "Plain and simple. He was angry at his daughter and son-in-law for settling out of court and signing a confidentiality agreement. I don't think he ever spoke to them again."

"What will happen to the Schumachers now?" Phoebe asked. "Will they go to jail? They're so old."

"It's hard to say. A judge will take all those factors into consideration."

"Is Walter really sick," Lucy asked, "or were they faking that, too?"

"He is ill, but not as frail as he acted."

"His illness must be serious, though, for him to have acted so recklessly. He obviously doesn't care what happens to him," Dana said.

"That's very possible," the detective said. "Well, I have to get back on the road. I've said enough about the case. Probably too much."

He took the bag of yarn, looked it over again, and tucked it in his jacket pocket.

"Thank you for your help, ladies. I think that's the whole ball of wax."

"The whole ball of alpaca, you mean," Maggie corrected him with quiet satisfaction.

He laughed. "Right again, Mrs. Messina."

Detective Dykstra left a few minutes later. Lucy thought the man looked exhausted but happy. He'd just solved a double homicide. A grand slam for a police detective in a small jurisdiction, she guessed.

Of course, even after he left, the knitting group couldn't talk about anything else.

"What does Nadine think of all this?" Dana asked Maggie.

"I don't know, I called her this afternoon to tell her about the ball of alpaca, but didn't get through and she never called back. I'll have to try to tomorrow. Don't worry, I'll keep you all posted," Maggie promised.

When Lucy left the knitting shop, she was surprised to find Matt waiting by her car.

"What are you doing here?"

"Waiting for you," he said simply. "I was at my office late, doing paperwork and stuff, and I saw that you guys were still in there. So I thought I'd just hang out for a few minutes, see if you came out. You said you wanted to talk," he reminded her.

"I do," she agreed. She opened her car door and tossed in her knitting bag. "Let's just walk, okay?"

Dana and Suzanne had also come out of the shop and Lucy noticed their curious but supportive glances. Suzanne smiled from her car window and waved at the couple as she drove by. Lucy waved back, then suddenly felt like running after the SUV. Wait, take me with you!

"How was your meeting?" Matt asked.

"Interesting. I never got to tell you about the weekend. It was unbelievable, really . . . but that's not what I wanted to talk about," she told him.

"Okay," he said evenly. "So . . . what's up?"

Lucy took a deep breath. Calm and centered, she reminded herself. Don't get all crazy and sound like Detective Dykstra with PMS. You need to keep your dignity.

"Good question," she said finally. "What's up with you? I mean, what's up with us?"

He glanced over at her, looking surprised. His cheeks flushed and she could tell he knew what she was talking about.

"What do you mean . . . exactly? Our relationship, you mean?"

Lucy took a breath. "Well, it's like you're so distant lately. You're really in some other place. I can just feel it. We don't see each other anymore during the week. You've always got something important going on . . . your dad's computer. Canine dentistry. Changing the oil in your car . . ." That last one was an exaggeration. He'd never given her that excuse, but she expected to hear it sooner or later.

Matt stopped walking. He looked down at her, his mouth a tight line. He didn't deny it or argue with her, she noticed. He just stared down unhappily.

That was not a good sign. Lucy felt her heart sink, but she pushed on.

"I'm a grown-up, Matt. Just be honest with me. Are you seeing someone else? Do you want to?"

Matt shook his head. He stared down at the ground when he spoke to her, though Lucy tried to meet his eye.

"It's complicated, Lucy. I care for you. A lot. I don't want to upset you or hurt your feelings."

Lucy hated the sound of that. She felt a giant, painful knot bunch up in her stomach. "Okay, what does that mean? Do you need to take a break for a while? I am the first person you dated since you left Claire."

She was going to say "got divorced," but Matt was not really divorced yet. Just separated. Too fresh, her friends said. Tempting, yes. But throw him back. Of course, she hadn't.

"Maybe I'm just your transitional person or something. People say that never works out. You know, that person in between your marriage and—"

"I know what a transitional relationship is, Lucy," he interrupted, sounding a little weary. "You don't have to make excuses for me. I can make my own excuses."

Lucy felt suddenly stupid and self-conscious. He was right. Now she was standing here, breaking up with herself. Good move, Lucy.

Well, at least I said it. Somebody had to. The dreaded code words: "take a break," translated to date-speak, always mean "break up." Take a hike. *Vaya con Dios*, my darling.

They had come to the end of Main Street and walked out to the town dock. The water was inky black with only a few boats left moored in the harbor. Across the inlet she saw lights on the other shoreline twinkling brightly.

"I know I've been distant. I know I've pulled back and made excuses and avoided you lately," he admitted sadly. "But I'm not seeing someone else. Not the way you mean," he clarified.

Lucy stared at him. A noise in her head was buzzing so loudly, she could hardly concentrate on what he was actually saying. He wasn't seeing someone else. Not the way she meant. How many ways were there?

"What is it then? What's going on?"

"I've been going to family counseling with Claire. We've even taken Dara a few times. Claire has been pushing for this for months. Ever since we split up. It's part of the reason she won't agree to a divorce."

"I think you told me that." He *had* told her, but had always sounded so angry and disdainful of the demand, she never though he'd agree to it.

"Claire and I had a final argument one day and I moved out. Of course, things had built up and built up and it all just spilled over. But it did seem sudden at the time. We never really tried to figure it out. We never went to a marriage counselor or anything like that."

He had told her that, too, at some point. She didn't interrupt him, interested in what he had to say.

"There are issues we never resolved. I can see that now. It would be better for me, too. What are the chances of a new relationship with you, or anyone else for that matter, working out, if I don't understand the last one?"

She didn't like the way he tossed in "anyone else," but she just nodded. "I think that's true."

"I resisted at first, but Claire convinced me. This will be good for Dara, too. I can see that we all have some closure issues to work out."

Closure issues . . . or reopening issues? The door in the marriage counselor's office swung both ways. Lucy thought about that, too, but didn't say so.

So her instincts had been right. He was seeing someone. His ex-wife. With a shrink and his daughter present. But Lucy could just imagine it. There was probably dinner after or some coffee at least and going back to Claire's house, tucking Dara in together . . .

She knew the instant she'd opened her mouth it was the wrong thing to say, but she just couldn't help it. Her inner witch took over.

"Does Claire want to get back together with you? Is that what this is about, Matt? Because if it is . . . well, you should have told me. I don't think that's right . . . or fair."

Matt had been standing a bit apart, looking out at the water. He suddenly turned to face her. "I knew you would say that. That's exactly why I didn't tell you."

Lucy felt stung. "But I have a right to know, don't you think?"

"I'm not sure, Lucy. I am sure now that you'd have a bad reaction and get all defensive. And start accusing me of . . . of something. I thought it was better not to say anything."

"Right. And act distant and distracted and like some zombie boyfriend," she reminded him. "That was better. Of course

I'd feel insecure. I didn't know what was going on. I still don't." He didn't answer and she could see he was shutting down. But she was on a roll now, she couldn't stop herself. "Especially all those excuses about not getting together as much as we always did. A canine dentistry certificate? Anybody would get suspicious of that."

He had the grace to look embarrassed. "There really is such a thing. But I already have one." His expression softened and his shoulders relaxed again. "I'm sorry . . . I didn't know what to do. Were you really worried? You know, I . . . you know how much I care for you."

He'd almost said "love you." She could even see his mouth about to form the words, but he stopped himself. He wasn't ready yet. Neither was she. This was not the right time, during their first fight.

Lucy never thought of herself as someone who needed a lot of assurances, but this time she did.

"Maybe I wasn't as sure as you thought. Or as I thought, either," she added. "I guess I can understand why you didn't tell me. Therapy sessions with your wife aren't really any of my business."

"Ex-wife," he corrected her. "Soon to be." That was another sticky wicket.

Lucy didn't even want to go there.

"What I'm trying to say is, I'm not sure what I would have done in your position. Maybe I would have met with Eric a time or two, if it meant so much to him. But after a while, I think I would have told you about it. I do feel bad that you were afraid to tell me. I thought you trusted me more than that."

"It's not that I don't trust you, Lucy. I'd trust you with my life. I tell you everything . . . honestly. The deepest secrets of my soul," he insisted.

She liked to think that. That was the way she felt about him. "Except this one," she reminded him.

Now she felt like she might cry. Darn it. She didn't want to cry. That was so dumb. She swept her fingers under her eyes and blinked a few times.

"This one wasn't so deep . . . just messy. I guess I was afraid you'd get the wrong idea and back away from me. Maybe even decide that I wasn't that committed and you wanted to see other people." He paused and looked at her squarely. "Part of the reason I didn't tell you about the counseling with Claire was because I didn't want to risk losing you."

Lucy felt her heart jump. Well, that was something good. She wouldn't forget he'd said that so easily.

They had come to the end of the dock, which was covered, like a gazebo, with benches underneath. Lucy grabbed one of the columns and stared out at the harbor. They'd sat here on their first date. It had been freezing cold, but they'd sat and sat until finally Matt kissed her. She couldn't forget that, either, could she?

Matt came up behind her and touched her shoulder. "If there's one thing those sessions helped me see, it's how you and I are so in tune with each other. How we connect just . . . automatically. You either have that with someone or you don't. I never had it with Claire," he added. "Not really. Two people can talk about a relationship until they're blue in the face. And you can work on it forever in counseling. But that certain feeling is either there, or it's not. It's very simple, really."

Lucy understood. She'd felt the same about Matt from the first time they'd met. It was simple. Scary simple.

"Well, one thing I've learned from all this is that we have to be more honest with each other." She turned to face him. "Even if we're afraid we might have a fight. I hate confrontation, you know that, but it seems the alternative is even worse. I think our relationship can take a little conflict once in a while, don't you?"

"I do. But you seemed very cool about breaking up, I must say. That line about being a grown-up? Whoa . . ." He shook his head. "I thought you were going to walk right off and leave me in the dust."

Lucy laughed. "Don't worry. I talk tough, but I don't think you'd get rid of me that easily, even if we did have another argument."

"Good to know." He took her hands and smiled into her eyes, then touched her face. "But let's not argue anymore now. To tell you the truth, I'm thinking about just the opposite."

"Me, too. See how in tune we are?"

Matt leaned over and kissed her and Lucy kissed him back. It was a little hard at first, since she was smiling so widely.

But more serious feelings soon set in. It had been a while and she'd missed him.

The next morning, Matt left her house at half past seven. He didn't have to be at his office until nine, but he needed to stop home first to check on Wally. "I ought to leave a few things here. For emergencies," he said, tugging on his socks. "Would that be all right?"

Last night was an emergency? Well . . . sort of, she thought. She watched him, too tired to move her head off the pillow.

"That would be all right. I'll make some space in the closet and maybe a drawer."

"Perfect. I'll talk to you later." He leaned over and kissed her good-bye, and she nearly thought she had to make room in the bed again, never mind the closet.

* * *

Lucy was glad she'd handed in her project the day before. She had a new one to start, but needed to clean up her office and her house a bit. She felt too energized and happy to stay inside and it was a beautiful day. She'd also left her car in front of Maggie's shop last night, since Matt drove them home. So that was another excuse to blow off work and head for town with Tink in tow.

As Lucy walked into the shop, a group of women were filing out. The Perfect Poncho class had just finished, Lucy realized. Good timing.

Maggie was not surprised to see her. Neither was Dana, who sat in the front room, working on her dress. "Hello, Lucy. Good timing. Maggie just finished her class."

Dana rose and walked with Lucy to the back, where Maggie stood at the oak table, clearing up the supplies from the workshop.

"I knew you had to come back sooner or later for your car. So Matt gave you a lift home last night?"

"How did you know that?" Lucy asked, though she could already suspect how.

"I told her, of course. He was waiting for you. That was cute," Dana noted. "Did you have a good talk?"

"We did. I just laid it on the line, like you told me." Lucy nodded. "He's been in counseling sessions with Claire and was afraid to tell me. He was afraid I'd get upset and feel threatened or something."

"But instead, you felt upset and threatened anyway," Maggie finished for her.

"Exactly. We agreed we have to be more honest. Even if we rock the boat a little."

266 / Anne Canadeo

"Good communicating. You guys did all right. For ama-
teurs," Dana approved with a smile.

"There was some good communicating going on," Maggie
murmured. "She looks pretty cheerful today. And relaxed. I
think that's a given."

Lucy felt herself blush. "Oh . . . stop." Then she started
to laugh. She couldn't help it. "So, did you call Nadine?" she
asked quickly, changing the subject. "What does she think
about the Schumachers?"

"I did speak to her," Maggie answered quickly. "She got my
message about the ball of alpaca and was very relieved. She had
her fingers crossed that the police would take the story seriously.
I guess they followed up on it faster than anyone expected. She
was shocked about the Schumachers," Maggie added. "I think
we were all surprised with that one. She's just relieved that
Brian is no longer a suspect. That was her main worry."

"I expect that they're all celebrating by now," Dana said.
"I hope that Brian can make peace with his mother now," she
said wistfully. "They've both been through so much."

"I hope so, too," Lucy said, "but I think Brian will go his
own way after this. He told me he had plans to move on once
he had enough money." Lucy paused. "Hey, remember that
argument I saw Alice and Brian having when we first got to
the inn? I think I understand what they were arguing about
now. Brian wanted to get paid and leave the inn as soon as
the weekend was over and he'd done all the work, setting up
for the investors meeting. But his mother wanted him to stay
at the inn longer. She said they weren't going to pay him until
he did." Lucy took a breath. "It wasn't about some conspiracy
between Alice and Brian to kill Curtis Hill . . . or Max. Funny
how things can be misunderstood out of context."

"That's very true. When you told us the story, we all jumped to the same conclusion, too," Maggie reminded everyone. "Brian will leave the inn now, I'm sure. But Nadine will stay on to run the place with Alice. She said they were already talking about making it a more conventional hotel again. Though they still have a spa and might have some arts and crafts weekends—knitting, quilting, pottery, scrapbooks. That sort of thing."

Dana had started knitting again, but put her work down. "Don't tell me. You sound like you're thinking of going back. Would you really?"

Maggie laughed. "What do you think?" she asked her friends.

"Go ahead, if you want, but leave us out of it," Lucy said, speaking for the rest.

"Come on now," Maggie urged them. "Let's not toss out the Buddha with the spring water. Some of these ideas have real merit and can enrich your work and life and relationships . . . and your knitting. When I was young, we believed that if enough people treated each other in a loving way, there would be a tipping point and the entire world would live in peace and harmony. I still believe that strategy could work, too," Maggie insisted. "And isn't better to view your own life from a positive perspective? To try to see the good in others, to imagine the best and even try to see the pluses that can arise when our lives are turned upside down by changes and misfortune? I don't discount all that positive thinking and positive energy talk, either. Not entirely."

"I understand what you're saying." Dana looked up from her knitting and nodded. "We all know that the brain is constantly emitting electricity and so does the heart. And physicists have proven that expectations can effect and alter physical outcomes, of neutrons and protons bouncing off each other, and that sort of thing. There's definitely more going on in this universe than meets the eye. That's all I have to say."

"That's just my point. Who knows? And who am I to say?" Maggie asked with a shrug. "We all have our own journey and you all know the road I recommend—knitting as the path to serenity and happiness."

"That goes without saying," Lucy knew Maggie wasn't entirely serious. But she seemed to be. "I know there's a joke about llamas and the Dali Llama in there somewhere . . . I just can't figure it out."

"You get back to me on that, Lucy. I'm sure you'll come up with something." Maggie cast her a wry grin. "I do know that I'm definitely going to do some random knitting and mindful knitting workshops here."

"I think that would be fun. I'll help you with the meditation part again," Dana offered.

"Thank you, Dana. And I did love taking a trip with all of you," Maggie added, "even if turned out to be a bit of a disaster."

"It was an adventure," Dana corrected her.

"It sure was," Lucy agreed. "But I suggest that next time we skip the holistic-wellness stuff and just go for a trashy, toxic weekend in Vegas. I think Suzanne would sign on for that one, too."

Maggie considered the idea a moment. "That could be fun," she speculated. "Can you knit in a casino? I think we need to find that out first."

Notes from the Black Sheep Knitting Shop
Bulletin Board

To all my dear friends and fellow knitters—

By now, you've all heard the story of our disastrous and frightening weekend at the Crystal Lake Inn. Thanks for your concern. Just goes to show, there's no such thing as a free massage . . . or something like that.

But as I told my knitting group, I won't toss the Buddha out with the spring water. Both workshops I gave at the spa—Random Knitting and Mindful Knitting—will be available this winter. These techniques are interesting, fun, and a worthwhile addition to your knitting repertoire.

In the meantime, I've put together a list of website links that touch upon these techniques and more. There's an interesting blog (we used to call it an article or essay in the old days, remember?) called "Is Knitting the New Yoga?" at http://knittingcrochet.suite101.com/article. cfm/knitting__as__the__new__yoga. And another explaining similarites between knitting and meditation at http://www.meditationoasis .com/2009/04/09/knitting-as-meditation/.

Also another that explains and explores the amazing therapeutic benefits of knitting. Did you know knitting regularly relieves depression and lowers your blood pressure? Betsan Corkhill, formerly a physiotherapist, has been studying the physical and psychological benefits of knitting for years. Her findings explain why you feel so good when you're knitting and why knitting is so good for you. Check out "Therapeutic Knitting" by Betsan Corkhill at http://www.kniton-thenet.com/issue4/features/therapeuticknitting/.

Dr. Max told us he learned how to knit in a small village in the Himalayas. Perhaps that was just one of his tall tales. But the truth is, high up in the clouds, in the small villages perched on mountain tops, there really are hardworking women who support their families, and lift up the entire economy of the region, simply by knitting. You can visit the home page of a terrific organization that helps these women, and learn how you can help, too, at Women's Knitting project in the Himalayas, http://himalayasarvodaya.org/radha/about.htm.

Last but not least, I'm sharing a link to the pattern I gave out at the spa—the Namaste Yoga Mat Bag. This is a free pattern offered on Knitty.com. Dana has already made one. Very handy and it looks terrific: http://knitty.com/ISSUEwinter05/PATTnamaste.html.

Take a deep, calming breath, my friends . . . and keep knitting.

Maggie

p.s. By the way, this weekend I learned that "namaste" means "the divine in me honors the divine in you." How true.

To Everybody (especially the people who keep bugging me for that crumble recipe)—

Can there ever be too much of a good thing? I'm not sure, but maybe I'm about to find out. Ever since I made this crumble for Matt he needs to have a steady supply. A small price to pay for boyfriend devotion, I guess.

Please note, this dish is truly a crumble for all seasons. I've made it with pears, peaches, blueberries, plums . . . and a mixture of most of the above. This dish could have been served at the Crystal Lake Spa. With all the vitamins and antioxidants from the fruit, and the fiber from the oatmeal, it's practically health food. If you don't count the butter and sugar. Okay, you got me there. But some things are worth a splurge. I don't think you'll regret it.

Lucy

p.s. Special tip, make sure the butter is cold or the crumbs won't form.

Lucy's Very Crummy Fruit Crumble

Heat oven to 350 degrees
9 x 12 x pan or baking dish, about 2 inches deep

4 to 6 cups sliced apples, any variety or mixed (a few
    of my favorites—Macintosh, Empire, Macoon,
    Fuji, Golden Delicious), or any other fruit as
    noted above
2–3 tablespoons fresh lemon juice
1–2 tablespoons grated lemon zest
½ cup plus 2 tablespoons white sugar
¼ cup plus 4 tablespoons brown sugar
½ lb cold unsalted butter
¾ cups plus 1–2 tablespoons flour
½ cup quick cooking oatmeal
cinnamon & nutmeg

Wash, peel, and core apples. Slice into thin wedges.
Toss with lemon juice and zest. Mix in 2 tablespoons
white sugar, 4 tablespoons brown sugar and 1 tablespoon of flour, 1–2 tablespoons cinnamon and 1 teaspoon nutmeg. Add a little more flour if apples are
juicy. Set aside.

Lightly butter the inside of pan. Pour apples in.

To make the crumbs: In a large bowl, cut the butter into small pieces, add ¾ cups flour, ½ cup white sugar, ¼ brown sugar, ½ cup oatmeal, 1 tablespoon cinnamon, ½ teaspoon nutmeg.

Mix with a fork or dampened hands (or in an electric mixer with paddle attachment) until ingredients are blended and crumbs form. Sprinkle over the top of fruit and bake for 20 to 30 minutes, until crumbs are crisp and golden and fruit is bubbly.

Serve warm with whipped cream or ice cream.

Hi everyone,

Yes, we survived our weekend at the Crystal Lake Inn. We did get some nice massages and beauty treatments. The food wasn't bad either—real gourmet health fare. They served some awesome salmon, prepared with an Asian slant. I finally got the recipe and wanted to share it. It's easy to make and healthy to eat. My kind of cooking. I fix this dish for Jack and the boys with snap peas (sauté in a drop of oil and a dash of soy sauce) and brown rice.

Namaste,
Dana

Ginger Salmon from the Crystal Lake Spa

(serves 4)

2 lbs of fresh wild salmon filet, cut from the wide part
of fish (no tail)

2–3 tablespoon fresh ginger, sliced and diced into
small pieces

Juice of ½ fresh squeezed lemon, about 2–3 tablespoons

¼ cup olive oil

¼ cup low sodium soy sauce

2 tablespoon Dijon mustard

2 tablespoons stir fry sauce

Preheat broiler. Prepare a broiling pan with a wire rack.

Cut salmon into 4 strips of equal size, about 2 inches
wide each. (Or ask the clerk at the fish store to do that.
They usually have sharper knives.)

Mix the rest of the ingredients in a wide, shallow bowl
or stainless pan, wide enough to fit the fish pieces without layering. Place fish in mixture fleshy side down and
marinate 10 to 30 minutes.

Place fish slices on rack and broil until golden brown on top. Leave space so they cook on sides. Broil about 5 minutes. Shut broiler and turn on oven to 375 degrees. Let fish bake 3 minutes. Spoon on extra marinade and bake another 3 to 5 minutes, then test for doneness. Serve with a few thin lemon slices on each dish.

A Note to the Reader

This is the point in the story when the curtain is pulled back and instead of a powerful Wizard, out comes a small, rumpled little man.

Well here I am. I usually prefer to let my characters do the talking. That way I'm allowed to hold many different opinions about the same issue simultaneously. But after completing this book I felt obliged to offer a few more thoughts and clarify my own position on new age ideas.

Anyone reading this book would think that the author totally dismisses these theories and philosophies. And some might even take offense at my satiric exaggerations. In truth, I am interested and have always been what you might call spiritually curious.

After all, I'm the kid who did a science project on brain waves, sending positive and negative "messages" to a set of unsuspecting house plants. I actually had the nerve to get up in front of the class and present it, too. I recall that the boy at the next lab table, who had dissected a pig embryo for his project, laughed the hardest . . . and went on to became a neurosurgeon. Fine. I bet I have a better garden than he does.

In real life, I take the position of my characters, particularly Maggie and Dana, who maintain that many of these practices and perspectives can truly enrich your life—such as meditation, yoga, healthy eating, and approaching the world with a positive and even spiritual outlook. But as Maggie also notes, she believes in positive thinking, but also finds that the harder she works the luckier she gets.

I've honestly meant no offense and have created a parody of this miniculture first, because it's easy to find humor here and I enjoy writing social satire.

Second, because what I am skeptical of, and hope to debunk a bit, are the false promises of new age gurus, the unhelpful self-help that blames the victim. Is there really some big Secret that will deliver my heart's desires . . . if I can only manage to hold the "right" thought? The right thoughts mainly seem to me to be to respect the humanity, and even the divinity, in everyone we meet, and to remember that the greatest wisdom is kindness.

Beyond that?

To paraphrase the famous words of Prince Hamlet, there's definitely more going on here than meets the eye, Horatio. Exactly what? I'm not sure anyone has solved that mystery yet.

Namaste ~

Anne Canadeo

Anne Canadeo

You can contact me at: anne@annecanadeo.com

visit: www.annecanadeo.com